DARKNESS FALLS

Seer of Caplana: Book One

A.E. Dawson

Thanks for your support!
♡ Anastasia

To my loving husband, Benjamin, without whom this book would have never been written.

You have encouraged, inspired, and supported me at every turn. Despite everything we've faced together, you've never lost faith in me, and that means everything.

CONTENTS

THE BATTLE FOR CALLE

Tree limbs whipping by her, Angela dodged a low branch and leaped over a fallen log, sprinting through the forest towards the caves at the far side of the plateau. They were just a few miles ahead, and she prayed she would be able to reach them in time.

She didn't know how long it would be before her father noticed that she was missing and came looking for her. When her brother hadn't come home the night before, he'd expressly forbidden her to go out and search, claiming that he was already taking care of it. But after years of training with him, Angela could tell when he was lying. She couldn't know for sure if he was the reason for Calle's disappearance, but she felt certain he had no intentions of searching for him.

They'd been so close for so many years. . . But after her mom had died, that had started to change. Some of her earliest memories were of him teaching her to fight, hunt, and trap so that she could take over his trade when she got old enough. But lately, her sparring sessions with him had turned violent, many times leaving her scarcely able to stumble out of the practice ring. She'd never dared to ask him why he was training her to fight. After all, Caplana was a peaceful town, no one needed guards or soldiers here.

Dodging a low branch, her mind was forced back to the reason she was running. The pounding of the forest floor under her feet brought her mind into focus as she tried to work through what might have happened. When she'd first noticed Calle missing she'd gone to her father, but had been shocked by his strange response to the news. Thinking about it now, he hadn't seemed surprised at all, only frustrated. But frustrated by what?

Finally reaching her destination, she began climbing up the

cliffside, trying to get as high as possible. Maybe if she could get close enough to the top, she might be able to spot Calle in the woods below. It was still early in the morning, so if he had a fire going, she should be able to see the smoke through the trees and at least have an idea of which area of the wood to start looking in.

As she climbed, her feet slid along a slanted ledge. Scraping at the rock with her toes, she tried to find a ledge to support her weight, but the rock was slick from years of rain. Her fingers shook as she tried to hold herself up, one finger after another slipping from their hold. Desperate to find a foothold she swung her legs wide. She just needed a small lip in the stone, anything!

Not able to find purchase with her feet, she let go, praying she'd be able to find a handhold after she slipped off the ledge. As she fell sideways, it looked as if she was headed straight into the cliff face that guarded the caves. Turning, she clawed at the rock for handholds but found nothing right as her feet slid off the edge and into empty air.

❋ ❋ ❋

Sluggishly, Angela opened her eyes and blinked several times to try to clear her vision. All she could see was a blurred, dull light above her. Everything else was pitch black. Steadily, her eyes began to adjust and pick out shapes around her. Rock walls and large stones surrounded her.

Gingerly, Angela tried to sit up but stopped as a shooting pain stabbed through her head. *That's going to be fun.* She thought, rubbing the back of her head. Turning carefully, she looked to either side. She was definitely in a cave, but it wasn't anything like the shallow one she had been trying to reach. This one stretched deep into the rock. A long tunnel leading the opposite direction she wanted to go - out.

"Ughh, could this get any worse?" She groaned as she gingerly rose to her feet. The light she had seen came from the mouth of the cave which she must have fallen through. Though 'mouth' was a generous term. The opening was about as high off the ground as she was tall, which explained the headache, and was only a couple of feet wide. She must have hit her head pretty good when she fell, knocking herself out. But for how long?

Moving over to the opening, she reached up hoping she could climb out the way she'd come in. But the entrance had been worn smooth and she couldn't find any purchase to pull herself up with. Looking around, she tried to find a rock that she might be able to move over to stand on, but soon realized that even if she could get high enough to reach out of the cave opening, the ledge around her little entrance was equally smooth and would offer no handholds for her to climb out with.

Jumping, she tried to get high enough to look down at the ground to see how high up she was, but without luck. Judging by how dark the sky was though, she guessed she'd been out for most of the day. Sighing, she turned back to look at where the cave disappeared into the mountain.

"This isn't going to be fun," Angela muttered as she started walking deeper into the mountain. It was slow going since she couldn't see and so had to keep one hand on the cave wall, the other held up above her head to try and warn her of any low hanging ceilings. As she moved deeper in, she found that the floor slanted downward, causing her to stumble forwards as she tripped over unexpected ledges and rocks.

Reaching a point where she'd have to crawl on her hands and knees to get through, Angela stopped. How could she know if she went through that she wouldn't get stuck halfway in? With no light, she had no way to tell how small the tunnel got. With a shudder she took a step back. She'd come up to the caves often enough, but she'd never actually explored them.

I can't do this. She thought, sitting back against the tunnel's wall. Pulling her knees up to her chest she rested her forehead on them and took several deep breaths. The damp cave air filled her lungs, reminding her of where she was, no matter how hard she tried to imagine otherwise. *What if the stories were true? What if there were creatures living in these tunnels?* But she shrugged the thought away as swiftly as it'd come. As often as she'd come up to the caverns, she'd never heard anything larger than a mouse and had never seen any tracks for anything larger either.

Deciding she was stuck whether she stayed or went on, she lowered herself to her hands and knees and pushed her way into the small opening. Rocks dug into her kneecaps and small ledges bashed her shins as she struggled forward. Hanging rock from the ceiling forced her to continually duck lower as she crawled.

She couldn't tell how long she'd been traveling through the tunnel when she saw a soft light coming from around a bend ahead of her. With renewed energy, and a few extra bumps and bruises to show for it, Angela inched forward, anxious to see if she'd be able to make it out of this exit. But when she rounded the curve, all she saw was more cave walls. The light she'd seen came from a small pool not far from where her tunnel let out. As she squirmed the last few feet and stepped out of the shaft, the sound of rocks skittering at her feet echoed around her as if she'd just entered into a large cavern, but she couldn't make out enough around her to tell for sure.

In exhaustion, Angela made her way over to the pool and sat down to inspect the damage done by her many run-ins with cave walls, rocks, and other obstacles during her journey through the tunnel. Finding no real damage other than shallow cuts and bruises across her arms and legs, Angela bent over the pool and brought several handfuls of water up to her lips before laying back on the stone floor. Her head throbbed from where she'd hit it after her fall and she was weak and shaking. It was easy to tell that she'd missed both lunch and dinner while she'd been in the caves.

Closing her eyes she tried to fight back despair. *Why did I have to climb up a different way this time?! Why couldn't I have just been content going my usual route? How am I going to find Calle stuck in this place? What do I do?*

But, no surprise, no voice came from the walls to tell her the way out. Laughing at herself, she laid her head back and let her mind slow down. She was stuck in a cave. With no way out, and no light to guide her. What was her next move?

Distractedly Angela turned and stared into the faintly glowing water, trying to figure out what to do next. But as she looked into the pool, she realized it wasn't the water that was gleaming, it was the stones! Quickly reaching in she grabbed one, pulling it out and lifting it up to her face. The stone was covered in phosphorescent algae, and even out of the water the light illuminated the space a foot or so around the rock!

Tucking her legs under her, she carefully tried to stand without hurting her head overly much. Holding the stone out front, she made her way to the edge of the cavern, hoping to find another tunnel leading out. But instead of an exit, she came across torches. Every dozen paces or so there were small beacons placed in crevices around the room. *Too bad I don't have my flint and steel on me,* she thought ruthfully as she kept making her way along the edge of the cave.

Reaching up to run her hand over the cavern wall, she stumbled into a large stalagmite on the ground, bashing her knee into the top of it before falling, cursing her luck. Crawling over to where her rock had fallen, Angela grabbed it and crawled back over to the offending stone.

As she drew closer to it she saw that it wasn't a stone at all, but a chest! Lightly touching the surface she found it was smooth and glossy from years of cave residue. Bashing it with a rock from the cavern floor, she was able to pry the lid open.

To her surprise, lying on top of the pile inside the chest was an old leather hunting coat. Underneath it were several hand-made blankets, a couple of old journals, and a rolled-up piece of leather that she assumed contained a letter. Picking up the journals, she turned them over in her hands, briefly flipping through the pages to find small flowing script etched across the sheets, too faded to make out.

Hmmm, I wonder who wrote these? Angela thought absently as she sat the journals back into the chest and looked around. She needed to find a way out of here. She didn't know how much longer Calle could last on his own. If her father was involved in his disappearance, she shuddered to think of where he might be.

She'd been at the Training Center the previous day practicing for the tournaments and so hadn't noticed Calle missing until that evening. She'd always been so certain that she'd take over her father's hunting business when she turned twenty-five and so had never been to the Center before this year. But as her relationship with her dad had digressed, she no longer felt secure that his contracts would be handed down to her. She had no marriage prospects and no other skill sets to draw on, so her only hope was to win an apprenticeship through the games.

With renewed determination, she got up and started working her way around the cave. As she walked, Angela noticed that it held more than just the chest she had tripped over. Using the stone, she was only able to see a foot or two in front of her. But even still, it was easy for her to tell that the cavern she found herself in was large. Easily bigger than her entire living space back home!

To her surprise, she came across a small cot against the opposite wall of the chest. Several shelves were carved into the walls of the cave along with an old wood table & two chairs with an oddly cylindrical rock tucked back in a corner. It looked as if everything had been made inside the cavern. Like someone had lived there long before. There was even an old fire ring near the center of the cave with a cooking pot and stand off to the side. In awe, Angela made her way back to the chest she'd first tripped over. *If I can find Calle, this would be the perfect place for us to hide out until I can get an apprenticeship! We could be free and clear from dad. The games are in a couple of weeks, so hopefully we wouldn't have to stay here long. If I can just find him...*

He could have simply been hiding the night before and was safe at home now, but Angela doubted it. He wouldn't leave without telling her where he was going. And he certainly wouldn't have stayed away all day. He was only fifteen, but he had a good head on his shoulders. It wasn't like him to be gone for so long. Her gut told her that something was wrong and he needed her.

Sorting through the chest, Angela picked up the rolled leather she'd seen earlier. Unfolding it, she held the rock up closer and realized it wasn't a letter like she'd thought, but a map! And it looked like a map to the very cave she was in.

Easily finding the large cavern where she now knelt, Angela followed the drawings to a different exit than the one she'd come in through. *Let's hope this one is easier to climb out of too!* She thought as she worked her way out of the cavern and down the new tunnel. Taking one of the unlit torches with her so she'd be able to use it when she came back, she used the stone to avoid running into as many rocks and boulders as she could during her journey through the tunnels.

Coming to the end of the shaft, pale light from the two moons high in the sky trickled in through a large opening only a couple of feet off the ground. The moons bathed the area around her in light as nighttime crickets and bugs filled the air with their songs. *Cursed stones, it must be close to midnight!*

Tucking the map into her tunic, she sat the torch down by the entrance before jumping off the ledge and back on familiar ground. Easily finding the correct path, she turned and headed towards her dad's property. If Calle still wasn't home, she needed to sneak in and grab some supplies, then get out before her father noticed her. She'd set up camp in the caves tonight and start her search for her brother tomorrow at first light.

Thanks to her bruised shins and piercing headache, it was another hour or so before she saw her house nestled amongst the trees. Her father had built it back when he'd first married her mom. It was the only house located in the forest, all the others being up with the farmers or in town. It was also the only house made with logs rather than clay or stones. It wasn't anything fancy, but it had everything they needed. A good wood stove where they could cook their meals and heat the house when it got cold, with openings in each room to let the cool breezes through the house at night.

Drawing up next to the cottage, she slunk between the shadows towards the front door. But as she passed under her father's window Angela heard something that made her pause. Inching closer, careful to keep herself low enough so as not to be seen, she leaned her ear against the wall.

She could just barely make out her dad's deep voice in the silence, "Angela has to go. I can't trust her, and I can't just send her to Eurcalp like I did Calle. That would never do. . . " His voice trailed off as he moved away from the window.

Pulling back in shock Angela's hands went limp as she connected the dots. At least she knew why her brother had disappeared, it had been because of her dad! And it seemed he had something different planned for her. No matter how hard she tried, she couldn't shake the feeling that it would be something she didn't want to stick around to find out.

Well, now I know that I won't be able to find Calle in the woods. Angela sighed, slinking back towards the front door where she waited until she could hear her dad's snores before she opened it and stepped inside. It was so dark in the house that she found herself wishing for one of the torches from the cave. *I'll be thankful it's at the cave entrance when I come back tonight,* she thought, moving deeper into the house.

Keeping one hand on the wall and testing each step before letting her feet fall, she cautiously made her way to her room. Once inside she shut the door and used the light of the moons through her window to find her large hunting pack and stuffed several sets of clothes into it, along with her boots, an extra knife, flint & steel, and some food, pausing to take several bites before slinging the pack over her shoulder and heading back into the house.

Rushing across the hall to their wood stove she used a stick to scrape the warm coals aside. Underneath the remains of that day's fire, she pulled on one of the bricks until it gave way under her hands, revealing a small metal box. Reaching in, careful not to touch the live coals, she painstakingly lifted the box out of its hiding place. The metal was hot and she hurried to wrap it in her shirt so she could touch it without burning herself. She'd found the chest when she was a young child playing in the ashes. But being unable to open it, she'd almost forgotten it was there until about a year ago when she'd come across a small key in her dad's things.

Reaching into a pouch on her belt, she pulled out the key that she'd found and slipped it into the lock, hearing the satisfying click as the lock disengaged and the lid raised a hair. Lifting it the rest of the way, Angela reached in and smoothly removed the pieces of silver out of the tin one at a time. After safely wrapping each piece in her extra clothing so they wouldn't make any noises in her pack, she closed the chest and heard the soft click as the lock reengaged.

Anxious to leave, Angela reached back into the stove to return the small container to its hiding place. But as she tried to lower it in, the hot metal from the box burned through her shirt and scorched her fingers, causing it to slip from her hand, the metal edge scraping against the stones as it fell back in place. Holding her breath, she heard the creak of the wood as her dad sat up in bed. Cursing quietly, she slung her pack over her shoulders and started making her way towards the front door.

Keeping an eye over her shoulder, she moved swiftly, not as worried about being quiet now that her dad was awake. Rounding the last bend a dark shape moved in front of the open doorway, his form nearly blocking out the moonlight.

"And what have we here?" His deep voice was jarring in the silence of the evening.

Reaching behind her back to pull out her two knives Angela twirled them in her fingers."Let me pass, father. I won't let you stop me this time." Taking her stance, she brought her hands up to her face, blades held low.

Raising an eyebrow, he stared at her for a minute, "I can't let you do that, Angela" he said, nonchalantly reaching behind his back to pull out his own knife which was easily twice the size of her own.

How many times had they dueled together? How many times had they sparred? He'd taught her everything she knew. And she knew he could beat her in a fair fight. So how could she turn things in her favor??

Making a quick decision, she sprinted towards him and kicked her legs out in front, spinning awkwardly to catch herself as they missed his shins. The pack on her back was slowing her down and throwing her off balance. Knowing he'd have seen the kick coming, she hadn't expected to make contact anyway. Her goal was to push him back so he'd have to stumble through the doorway. That would be her one shot. Without hesitating, she rolled to the side, just missing his knife as it sunk into the dirt floor. Twisting her legs under her she let one fly wide, connecting with his jaw. Stumbling back he kept hold of his blade. Realizing too late that his stumble had been staged, she saw him twirl, bringing his knife across at eye level.

Barely managing to duck under the pass, Angela got off a jab to his kidneys while slipping past him through the doorway. Once outside she had more room to maneuver. If she could keep him in the house, maybe she could best him enough to get away. With that intent, she spun back towards the door to find her dad already charging through.

In desperation, she brought her knife up to throw. But as she released, she felt his blade slice through her shoulder, causing her to throw low. Too late she realized he'd beaten her to the turn, anticipating her choice of attack and sending his knife flying across the gap between them to take out her dominant arm. Feeling the heat of fresh blood flowing down her arm she looked down to see his dagger embedded in her shoulder just below the collar bone. Sucking in her breath against the nausea she tried to move her arm, realized just how deep the knife had gone.

Gripping the handle, she tenderly pulled it out of her shoulder, looking up in time to see her father's fist come in contact with her jaw. Her head spinning, she hit the ground and rolled before he could pin her on her back. Turning over just before he was on her, she managed to lift his knife and sink it handle deep into his thigh, pushing him off to the side.

Sucking in air between her clenched teeth she pulled herself to her feet and half ran, half stumbled away, her dad's threats and curses following her through the woods. *I can't make it back to the caves, they're too far.* Pausing, she ripped the bottom of her tunic off and wrapped it around her shoulder to try and slow the bleeding.

Attempting to remember where she was, she followed a familiar deer path to where she kept her bow and arrows hidden, along with another knife and a slingshot. Tucking them through the loops in her pack she began haltingly making her way towards the Training Center. She could get water there, maybe even find some bandages and medicine. Surely, a dagger to the thigh would slow her dad down enough that he wouldn't be following her tonight. If she could just make it.

* * *

Daryn gradually made his way through the garden paths, anxious to fulfill his responsibility to his parents and return home. His mother had spent weeks preparing the garden for the night's festivities, and it was expected that he would make an appearance. Small torches were scattered throughout the space, candles set on every solid surface available. As his was one of the three leading families at Caplana, everyone who wanted to be anyone was in attendance. City officials, middle-class members who'd been able to use their connections to secure an invite, and young ladies of every station who were hoping to find a match. It was, in short, the party to be at. And Daryn was counting down the moments until he could leave.

When he'd been younger, he'd embraced this life with wholehearted abandon. He'd had everything he could have ever wanted. A 'bright future' as his parents liked to refer to it. But that had all changed when his baby sister had almost died at only thirteen years old. It turned out that she'd been starving herself in her attempts to live up to their parent's expectations.

The day he'd stepped through the healer's hut and saw her laying on the bed, he'd stopped caring about the impression he was making on society. He'd ceased attending the parties and events and had instead joined some of his peers in training at the Center. Located outside the city walls, the Training Center was an equal ground for both the highborn and lower class citizens. His peers in the upper class mostly competed in the annual competitions for the fun of it, or to prove their worth to a lady they had their eye on. Very few were ever seen practicing on the grounds though, choosing rather to hire personal trainers and then show up on competition day.

The middle and lower classes were the ones filling the Center during training days. These families sent their second and third-born sons and daughters to compete in the tournaments with the hopes of them winning an apprenticeship. It irked his parents to no end that he spent his days sharing space with people who could offer little to no type of political or economical gain to their family. But that's precisely what he loved about being there.

As he worked his way through the guests in attendance, all Daryn could see was the emptiness their life of privilege had brought them. The pettiness behind the flirtations and coy glances of the women. And the self-serving aims of the business owners who were there simply to try and win favor with an upper-class family.

Finally catching sight of his parents up ahead he hurried forward, anxious to say his hello's and be able to leave the party. Waving, he drew near and kissed his mother's cheeks before turning and shaking hands with his father.

"Glad to see you could take time out of your busy schedule to support your brother," his father commented dryly, nodding to a gentleman passing by.

Ignoring the comment, Daryn turned to his mother instead, "Everything looks beautiful, mom. You really outdid yourself tonight."

"Why thank you, Daryn." She smiled, pausing as she glanced at his father before continuing. "We have something important we plan to announce this evening. Will you please stay long enough to be here for that? We'd like to have the whole family together when we share the news."

Bowing, Daryn plastered on a polite smile, "I would be happy to". Making his excuses he moved back through the garden space, looking for a distraction until they called on him.

He didn't have to wait long before he found himself on a stand in the center of the garden next to his parents, two older brothers, and three sisters. Most of the guests were crowded around, more anxious to hear what his parents had to say than he was.

"First, we'd like to thank you all for coming out tonight," His father began, making a grand gesture around the crowd. "As you all know, we're here celebrating the thirty-fifth birthday of our oldest son, Kadon. He and his brother have been an integral part of the family estate for over ten years now, and we couldn't be prouder. It is because of that, that we'd like to take this opportunity to proclaim, while all of you are here to witness, that he and our second oldest will be taking over the business and name. Come the first of the year, I will be stepping down and allowing them free rein."

The crowd around them fell into excited whispers and applause as his father finished, but Daryn scarcely heard it. They were cutting him out. And now everyone in town would be aware of it. Looking around, he caught his youngest sister's eye and saw her shock mirrored his own. To make such an announcement without having spoken to him first was more than just oversight, it had been intentional.

Feelings of betrayal boiled up inside of him as he watched his father and mother move across the stand to embrace his brothers. Trying to act as if he'd been aware of the news long before the party, he unclenched his hands and went over to congratulate them as well, before slipping from the stage and into the unlit section of the gardens.

Reaching a deserted section, he pulled at his necktie and threw it into the bushes, breathing hard as he tried to get his temper under control. Desperately needing an escape, he slunk through the garden beds and back towards the house to grab his training clothes before ducking out onto the deserted streets of Caplana and making his way towards the Training Center.

* * *

Only half-conscious, Angela stumbled through the thick wooden doors of the Center and fell back against its stone walls as they swung shut behind her. The sudden pressure on her wounded shoulder caused her to cry out and fall to the floor, gasping for air. She knew she needed to keep moving, but she couldn't find the strength to. All she wanted to do was lay on the cool dirt floors and catch her breath.

But instead, she heard hurried footsteps coming her way and watched as a young man about three years older than herself came running towards her from the other side of the Center. Absently, she took in his even stride and well-toned arms. He was strong, she was sure of that. And he was in the training uniform of the wealthy class. *What he was doing at the Center so late at night?* She guessed he stood about a head taller than she did, but it was an idle thought that hardly registered as she frantically tried to think of an explanation for her current condition. In horror she watched as he knelt in front of her, the concern written plainly across his face.

This wasn't good. She couldn't go to the town healer - that's precisely where her father would look for her! Not to mention if her dad found out that this man had seen her, she felt certain that he'd make sure he regretted it. She had to get rid of him. But how? Her arm was hurting so bad that she could hardly breathe. Her head swam and she almost blacked out as she pushed herself to a kneeling position. Almost.

"What happened to you!? You need a healer. And fast. Here, let me help you," He reached over to help her stand, but Angela turned away, forcing herself to her feet and leaning against the wall with her good arm.

"No. . . Healer," She bit out between breaths. "Not safe. Go. Leave now. He'll... He'll hurt you. . . if he knew". She sucked in a breath as another round of nausea hit her. Talking was taking its toll and Angela could feel her head starting to swim. Don't blackout. She repeated to herself as she took a step towards where the Center kept the medical supplies.

"Ok, ok, no healer," He raised his hands to show he wasn't going to do anything, but stepped in front of her so she couldn't walk any further without going around him. "Whoever it is you're scared of, he's not here right now. So let me help."

"Fine," Angela bit out, "I need bandages. Water. Medicine."

"Got it, got it. Don't move!" He yelled as he ran off to grab what she needed. *Don't move. Funny guy.* She thought absently as she slid back down to the floor. It seemed like a much safer alternative to standing. Just in case. It wasn't long before the young man returned, carrying enough bandages to wrap her entire body.

"How many cuts do you think I have?" Angela laughed weakly, immediately regretting the movement.

"Hey, judging by the look of you I have no idea. But better to have too much than not enough, right? Unless you'd prefer I put them back?" He asked, raising an eyebrow at her.

"You win," Angela sighed, straining to take her makeshift bandage off. But her vision went dark as the knot pulled sickeningly through her wound and her hand fell to the floor.

"Here, let me," he said, gingerly reaching over and lifting the tunic from her shoulder, his lips draining of color as he saw the damage. "Oh my. . ." He trailed off as he turned back to the bandages he'd brought and began ripping strips long enough to tie around her arm.

"Need to get somewhere safe." Angela mumbled, "Can't stay here. He'll find me..."

"Where do you need to go," He asked, his eyes trained on her shoulder as he worked on tying off the wrappings he'd just put on.

"Caves," Angela muttered. "Need to get to the caves. Only safe place. He doesn't know. . ." she trailed off, feeling her body lighten as he unbuckled the straps from her pack and hoisted it off her, re-buckling them and placing it on his shoulders after adding the remaining medical supplies to it. Once he was done, he knelt down and carefully lifted her off the floor as well, holding her so that her injured shoulder was facing away from his body and her arm could lay across her stomach.

His strong arms wrapped under her legs and across her back, pressing her snuggly against him. Not having the energy to resist, she let her head fall against his chest, her eyes sliding closed as everything began to fade except the swaying motion of his gait as he carried her out of the building and back into the night.

LIFE ON DEATH'S BLADE

Sighing, Daryn paused as he stepped out in the dark. Thankfully both moons were full, so it was easy to see the path. Glancing down at the girl in his arms he couldn't help the protective feeling that came over him. She was much smaller than him but covered in well-toned muscle. Thinking about it, he was pretty sure he'd noticed her at the training grounds a couple of times. Moving towards the shadows under the trees, he cautiously started making his way up the path that would lead to the caves.

Why she had chosen them as a safe place to hide he had no idea! He didn't know a single person that would go anywhere near the place. It gave him shivers just thinking about them. Didn't she have family, friends maybe, that could protect her? He knew that if he ever saw his baby sister in the kind of shape this girl was in, he'd kill the monster that had done it. Where were her defenders?

Walking down the path, his mind flitted back to his last encounter with his own family. How petty it seemed now. He knew his elder siblings were his parents' favorites. But he'd never imagined they'd go so far as to cut him out! Especially not without first consulting with him.

But suddenly, losing his temper over something so trivial seemed foolish. He hadn't cared for the family business anyway. And if he had been offered the option, he'd have happily given up his share to his brothers. But that's what chafed. He hadn't had a say. They hadn't even taken the time to discuss it with him beforehand, but instead chose to let him find out at a public event.

His arms tightened as he clenched his teeth, his anger seeping to the top.

Get it together man. This isn't the time to think about that. Looking down, he had the fleeting thought of turning around and taking the girl to the healer's hut. Or even back to his house. He might not be the favorite, but his family wouldn't turn away an injured girl. Even if she was from the lower classes... would they?

No. Her terror had seemed real enough back in the Center. And he couldn't doubt that with injuries like hers, whoever she was running from meant business. He briefly wondered if it was an upset lover. Even with only the light of the moons to go off of, he could tell she was beautiful. But again he had to shake himself. Whatever had happened, no matter who had done it, Daryn knew he'd do his best to make sure it didn't happen again.

Seeing her collapsed at the Center had sent his mind back to the day when he'd found Gabriella laying on the floor of their home, too weak to get up. The day they'd almost lost her. His vision blurred as his mind went back to that moment She'd been so helpless, so close to death. He couldn't abandon another girl to that fate. Not if he had the chance to do something about it. *And I'm going to leave it at that,* he thought, returning his focus to the path before him.

Making his way through the farms surrounding Caplana he finally spotted the caves up ahead. It'd taken longer than he'd expected, as he'd had to take several breaks along the way. He'd never actually been around the caverns before and so hadn't realized how large the cliff face was where they were sheltered. Softly lowering the girl to the ground so she was leaning against the rock walls, he took a second to stretch out his arms. *Now what??*

The sound of movement drew his eyes down to find his charge attempting to stand. "Woah there, what do you think you're doing?? Lay back down." He knelt beside her, putting a hand on her good shoulder to keep her from expending any more energy.

"Map," She said softly, pulling a piece of leather out of the front of her tunic. Gingerly Daryn took it and unrolled it, holding it so the moonlight would shine on the writing.

"It's. . . Of the caves. They are labyrinths," she murmured. "We need to get here," she pointed to a large space on the map, then drew her finger down what he assumed represented a tunnel. Turning her head she indicated an opening just a few feet above them to the right. "There's a torch," she said haltingly, her eyes beginning to close again. "Flint and steel in the pack, near the top." She reached over taking his hand and looked like she was about to say something else, but went limp before she was able to finish.

Reaching out to keep her from falling to the side, Daryn took her wrist in his hand and checked her pulse. It was much too slow for his liking. "Oh man. . ." Daryn mumbled out loud before standing up to take the pack off. *Well, let's hope that last bit wasn't too important* he thought as he flipped the top open and found the flint and steel underneath the bandages he'd collected from the Center. Slinging the pack back on he looked over at the cave opening she'd indicated.

Glancing back to make sure she was supported, he jogged over to the entrance and easily jumped inside. Sure enough, there was a torch laying there on the ground just as she'd said. It looked as if it'd never been used. If this was a protected place, why did she leave it? And if she had been here before, why not use the torch to get out? Why choose to stumble through the dark rather than light it? He had too many questions, and the only one who could answer them wasn't in a state to do so.

"Let's get you inside, and then we can take a look at that arm," He said, jogging back over to her and gingerly picked her up, trying not to jostle her shoulder in the process.

Reaching the cave entrance he pushed a stone over with his feet so he could hoist himself and the girl up, setting her on the ledge once he was tall enough. Hoping down again, he moved the rock back to where it had been and jumped up with her. Leaning down, he lit the torch and tucked the flint and steel back into the pack. Slinging it onto his back, he bent down and picked the girl up, grabbing the torch with one hand while holding the map with the other.

Gradually, he started making his way through the winding tunnels towards the large room she had indicated on the drawing. He had to double back several times due to the endless alleyways and dead ends that weren't on the map, but eventually, he stepped into the cavern and breathed a sigh of relief.

Noticing other torches along the wall, Daryn touched his to a couple of them so he could get a better idea of the space. Seeing a half-opened chest with a blanket spilling over the side, he made his way across the area towards it, passing a cot along the way. Setting the girl down by the cot he continued over to the chest and pulled the blanket out. Walking back to the bed, careful to give the pool a wide berth so he wouldn't slip, he spread the blanket out and rolled up one end to use as a pillow for her.

Picking her up he gently laid her down for what he hoped was the last time that night. Despite all his training, his arms were shot. After he was sure she was as comfortable as he could make her, he jogged back over to a couple of the lit torches and brought them next to the cot. Placing them on notches beside the bed, he was able to get a good look at her for the first time.

Reaching over, he tentatively put his hand on her forehead but quickly jerked it back. She was burning up! Racing over to the pack, he grabbed the bandages, rags, and medicine he'd brought from the Center before running back over to her, stopping by the pool on his way to dip a couple of the scraps in the water.

Kneeling next to her he brushed the hair off her face. "I'm sorry, Mesholi. I'm going to do the best I can, but I'm no physician," he whispered before placing one of the cool cloths on her forehead. Moaning, her eyes fluttered open for a brief second. The pain he saw there made him gulp.

Looking her over he noticed many other scrapes and bruises along her arms and legs. Even in the flickering torchlight, he could tell that her jaw was starting to darken and swell up. What had she been through before they'd met? Sighing, he turned back towards her shoulder and began to gradually peel the bandages away, gingerly ripped the sleeve off her shirt so he could take a better look at the damage. What he saw there made him flinch.

The cut was deep and made a jagged line along the inside of her arm from the middle of her bicep up her arm and into her shoulder just below the collar bone. He couldn't see anything in the hole and could only assume that whatever had been there, she'd already removed it.

Spinning back towards the pack, he found some thread and a needle. Holding the pin over the flames to clean it, he drew the string through the eye before leaning over.

"I have to close up this wound or you're going to bleed out. I'm sorry, I've only ever done this to one of my horses, so I can't promise it's going to be pretty." He grimaced. Hating himself as he said it. Shuffling through the supplies he'd brought from the Center he pulled out salve and. . . Yes! Willow bark!

"Here, bite down on this," he whispered, holding it up to her mouth. To his surprise, her lips parted and he was able to slide the bark in. "Now clamp down hard," he instructed, before turning back to her arm. He started by taking one of the wet rags and squeezed water over the wound, trying to wash it off as best he could and dabbing at it as he went. After he was sure the cut was clean he leaned back on his heels and surveyed the area. The bleeding had slowed enough for him to be able to start working.

Taking a deep breath to steal his nerves he closed his eyes, *Just pretend it's a horse.* He repeated to himself a couple of times before opening his eyes, picking up the needle and thread, and starting to sew. Other than a few low moans, she was silent, her whole body tense as he sewed up the gash along her arm. Reaching the point where the wound sunk into her shoulder, he paused.

Should he leave it open so it wouldn't get infected? But seeing the blood that was still spilling from the injury he made up his mind and finished sewing her up. Cutting the thread with his teeth, he bent over to pick up the salve and began spreading it over the wound. He had no idea what was in it but hoped it had a little magic. She was going to need it. Even in the dim light, he could see that her face was pale and her body had begun shaking by the time he was finished with the cream.

Once he was finished, he ripped up some new bandages and wrapped her arm and shoulder, praying that what he had done would be enough. Standing stiffly, he turned back towards the chest and found another blanket, bringing it over and laying it on top of her. Exhausted, he lowered himself onto the floor next to her bed, making sure he was on her good side so as not to risk bumping her shoulder, and rested his head on the cot.

To his surprise, he felt her fingers lightly reach out and touch his hair. Jerking up he looked up to find her eyes still closed, but her lips moved, a weak, "Thank you" slipping out in a barely audible whisper. Reaching over he smiled and took her hand between both of his.

"You're welcome, Mesholi," he murmured before getting up and grabbing the last blanket out of the chest and bringing it back for him to lay on by the girl's cot, using one of the wet rags to dampen out the remaining torches before closing his eyes and succumbing to the exhaustion that was pulling at him.

* * *

"Ugh," Daryn groaned, sitting up and stretching his hands above his head. It felt like he'd been run over by a herd of horses. Looking down at the cave floor where he'd slept, he wasn't all that surprised. Getting up he made his way over to the pool and bent down to get a drink while splashing water on his face, the cold shocking him awake. Hearing a yawn behind him, he turned and headed back towards the cot, picking up the flint and steel on his way.

"Morning!" He said, forcing a smile as he lit up the torch by the bed.

"Morning," she responded groggily, rubbing at her eyes with her good hand.

"How's the arm feeling?"

"It's been better. . ." she grimaced. "I don't think I'm going to be using it any time soon," She sighed as she looked over at her shoulder. "To be honest, I didn't expect to see you here. I thought you would have gone back home last night."

"And leave you here by yourself? Are you kidding me, Mesholi?"

"Why do you keep calling me that?"

"What? Mesholi? Well. . . I don't know your name. And I had to call you something," He trailed off uncomfortably.

"It's Angela," she said with a pained sigh. "Angela Argon".

"Angela Argon... It suits you. I'm Daryn, it's nice to meet you," he smiled, reaching out and shaking her good hand, "Now what do you say we take a look at those bandages?"

"How about some breakfast first?" She offered, looking away. "There's some food in my pack. I managed to get a little in there before. . ." Trailing off, her eyes glazed over, lost in memories.

Rather than pester her, Daryn headed towards the bag to grab the food. After a little digging, he was able to locate some nuts, dried fruit, and cheese, bringing his findings back over and dragging a chair from the table with him.

Sitting down beside the cot Daryn handed her some cheese and fruit. "Do you have any cups or bowls in here that I could use to get you some water?" He asked, biting into some of the fruit.

"I'm not sure." Angela whispered, "I found all of this stuff here. I haven't had the chance to explore it much yet."

Getting up Daryn began walking around the cave with new eyes. *Who had lived here before? And how long ago??* He wondered as he ran his hand over the wood table. On a hunch, he went back over to the chest and spotted a small wooden dish tucked away in the bottom corner under what looked like an old hunting coat.

"Hey, I found something!" He hollered over his shoulder as he picked the bowl up and headed over to the pool to fill it up.

"Any chance you know why that water glows?" He asked, handing her the water.

"It's the algae on the rocks," She said weakly, her eyes drifting closed.

Seeing that she wouldn't be awake for much longer, he quickly changed subjects, "I'm going to head into town today. I need to take a bath and grab a few things. Do you think you'll be okay for a couple of hours?" Glancing over at her he was surprised to see fear in her eyes. "Hey, I'll come back!"

"No, it's not that..." She said cautiously. "I'm worried he'll follow you back here..."

"I know you probably don't want to talk about it, but could you tell me who I should be looking out for?"

"Ben Argon" she whispered as if the name might make the man appear.

Argon... So they're related. That's why she doesn't have any family to go to. Daryn thought, absently rubbing a hand across his forehead.

"I'll be careful to not be followed. And I'll leave some food and water on the chair here for you. Is there anything else you might need?" He asked, softly touching her arm.

"I'll be fine," She said weakly, trying to shove him away. "Please," she said, lifting her eyes to his, "You have a life. Go back to it. You don't need to worry about me. All I need is some rest and I'll be good as new. You shouldn't get mixed up with me."

"I'm not leaving you. Not until I know you're safe and feeling better. Just promise me you'll relax and won't try to do anything stupid while I'm gone." He said in mock sternness. "We'll leave your shoulder alone and let it heal up a bit more before messing with it, so you're off the hook till I get back." Squeezing her hand, he stood up. Looking back down he saw Angela's lips twitch in what could have been a smile before going slack again.

Leaving some food and water on the chair by the cot as he'd promised, Daryn grabbed a torch and the map and headed back to the entrance of the cave. As he came to the last bend and saw the sunlight filtering in, he damped the torch on the floor, stowing it behind a large rock in the hopes that no one would happen upon it while he was gone. Though, considering no one came near the caves he figured that was unlikely.

Briskly strolling over to the entrance he jumped down onto the dirt path. Looking around to make sure no one was nearby, he stretched his arms above his head and yawned. There was a lot to do, but the first thing was first, he needed a bath!

Trotting up to the path, he took the first fork that would lead him to town. Moving through the small city he blessed the fact that today was market day. He should be able to find everything he required with ease. Reaching the upper level of the village, he turned off and headed for his family's home.

Opening the front door he made his way to the stairs leading to his rooms. Calling out to a servant passing by, he instructed her to have a hot bath drawn up for him. While he waited, he went into his room and started pulling out some of his older clothes and training uniforms. Loading them up into a small pack he looked around the room. He didn't have much else that would be useful to him while he was away.

Stepping out into the hall he asked the servant stationed there if any of his family was up yet.

"No sir, the ball last night seems to have worn them out pretty good." The man said with a bow of his head.

"Perfect. Could you let them know that I'm going to stay with a friend for a week or so?" Daryn asked as he began walking towards the bathing rooms.

"Of course, sir. Is there anything else I can do for you?"

"No, that will be all. Thank you, Claude." he said as he turned the corner to where his bath waited. After thoroughly enjoying what he imagined would be his last warm soak for a while Daryn dressed in his oldest set of clothes and headed down towards his family's market station.

The streets of Caplana were packed with people jostling for the freshest, newest items and it took Daryn a good hour just to get to his family's stall. Waving at their store manager, he walked over and shook the man's hand before handing him the list of supplies he'd made up.

"Do you think you could find this for me?"

"It shouldn't be a problem, sir." He said, looking up from the parchment. "Going on a trip?"

"Yea, some buddies and I are going camping for a couple of weeks." Daryn rolled his eyes, trying to look put out just like any high-class gentleman would be at the thought of spending a week in the woods.

"I understand sir. Give me till about high sun and I should have everything ready for you." The manager turned around and motioned one of the younger apprentices over, pointing to the list.

"Thank you!" Daryn hollered, heading out of the small building and into the market throng. *Now to find out something about this Ben Argon.* He thought to himself as he made his way down to the lower markets. Stopping now and then to look at the stalls, he made his way towards the butcher's hut. If he didn't know anything, the baker would for sure.

Stepping through the door, Daryn browsed the sausages and cured hams as he waited for the man to finish up with a customer before walking over to him.

Eyeing him head to toe, the man stiffened, clearly not used to seeing upper-class colors in his store, even if they were a little tattered. Daryn's mind raced as he tried to come up with an excuse for his presence in the shop.

Sticking his hand out he grinned, "Just got hired on for one of the upper-class houses, but I can't seem to find anything worth buying up in that upper market mess!" He scoffed, relieved to see the man relax and return his grin.

"Eh, it's a mess up there al' right!" He agreed, rubbing the stubble on his chin. "Whatcha looking for?"

Giving him a list of some cured meats, Daryn was glad he had thought to bring his purse with him. As the man moved behind the counter to gather up the items he needed, Daryn causally leaned against the ledge, "Any chance you know a man by the name of Ben Argon?"

"Sure do!" The butcher boomed, "Half the contents of this shop come from him. He's a good man. Shame what's happened to him though."

"What do you mean?" Daryn asked, looking around and trying to sound uninterested.

"It's a sad business, that." The man said, piling the meats up on the counter. "Wife passed away a couple years ago, leaving him to take care of that little girl and boy all on his own. He don't got no other family in town to take them on. Why he hasn't arranged a marriage for his daughter, I can't imagine. She's a pretty little thing with that long hair and big ol 'brown eyes! He wouldn't have any trouble finding someone who'd want her. But then, what business is it of mine." He shrugged his large shoulders.

Thanking him for his help, Daryn handed over the payment for the meat before heading back out onto the streets. The man could have only been talking about Angela. *It was her dad who'd gone after her!* He thought in horror. Even in the lower levels, beating a family member was considered deplorable. And what he'd done to her went well beyond a simple flogging.

Lost in thought Daryn made his way back up to the upper markets to grab the rest of his items from his family's stall. When he got there he was pleased to see that their manager had been able to find everything on his list, plus a couple of things he'd forgotten to put down.

"You never disappoint, Archabold" He praised as he started loading his new supplies into the hunting pack the man had found for him. The shop manager beamed before turning back to see to his other customers.

Hoisting the bag onto his back, Daryn was pleasantly surprised at how well it fit. The weight rested on his hips instead of his shoulders, which made it feel much lighter. Waving to Archabold, he ducked out of the stall and started making his way through the crowds and towards the path that would take him back to the caves.

ANGELA'S HISTORY REVEALED

The sun's rays were a deep orange by the time Daryn reached the caves. He'd taken several cross paths on his way back to ensure no one had followed him, which had added at least an hour to his trip. But to his relief, he hadn't seen anyone during his journey and was able to breathe a little easier as the cliffs came into view. Veering off the path and into the trees, he used an axe to gather up several limbs about as big around as his forearms.

Carrying the branches over into a pile, he loaded them onto one of his shoulders and walked the last stretch to the caves. Throwing his logs into the entrance he hoisted himself up behind them, quickly dragging them back to where he'd left the torch.

Lighting up the torch and loading the branches back onto his shoulders, it wasn't long before the tale-tell soft glow of the pond colored the walls of the tunnel. Picking up his pace, he trotted into the cavern, dropping the timbers to the floor before heading over to Angela's cot.

Kneeling beside her bed and gently moved some of her hair aside, his hands came back moist from sweat. Pressing the back of his hand against her forehead, he cursed himself for leaving her alone for so long. Her body shook beneath the blanket, her head moving from side to side as her moans filled the cavern. Grabbing some rags, he hurried to the pool before bringing them back and placing them against her forehead.

"Mom..." She moaned, eyes darting from side to side under her eyelids. "Mom, no..."

"Shh" Daryn hushed, stroking the cool cloth over her face, "It's me. It's just me. It's going to be alright. You're going to be okay,"

The passage of time was impossible to track in the cave, but his legs were sore and cramped by the time her breathing began to slow and she slipped into a more natural sleep. Leaning back on his heels, Daryn let out a breath, rubbing at his eyes. "You need a doctor, girl. I don't know what I'm doing here." Moving towards the pool, he paused as he heard movement behind him.

Turning, he saw Angela looking at him with wide eyes, "Daryn?"

"It's me," He gave her a small smile as he moved to sit beside her cot. Lowering himself to the ground, he reached over and grasped one of her hands in his. "I'm here."

"I thought you were just a dream . . ." She trailed off, looking down at where his hands held hers.

Following her gaze, he gave her hand a squeeze before letting go, "Nope, I'm real. Though I'm sorry it took me so long to come back".

"I was scared," She murmured, looking away. "I thought I was going to die alone."

"Hey, don't go there, okay? You're not dying in this cave. I won't let that happen. Even if I have to get help."

"No healers," She looked up at him in panic. "You bring a healer in here and I'm as good as dead."

After searching her gaze for a moment, Daryn nodded, "Okay, no healers. But you had me pretty scared. I'm worried your shoulder's infected".

Weakly, Angela just nodded in agreement as her eyes drooped shut once more.

"I got something for you," Daryn said, turning back to his pack and pulling a large loaf out from the top. Breaking off a piece, he handed it over to her, "It's not much, but it's still warm".

Opening her eyes, she gently grasped the bread and brought it up to her lips, "I haven't had fresh bread in years" she moaned, looking down at the piece he'd given her. "My mom used to make it, but that was a long time ago. Now we just get it on the odd times dad goes into the markets".

"Well, if it's going to be your last meal it might as well be a good one," Daryn winked at her.

"Ha! Fair point," Angela said, resting back into the blankets on her cot, "I've got to ask, what are the logs for?"

Glancing over at them, Daryn grinned, "There's no way I'm sleeping on that cave floor one more night! So I'm going to try to copy the design of your cot and build myself a bed."

"Have you ever built anything before," Angela asked doubtfully, eyeing the logs.

Laughing, he shook his head, "Nope, but something tells me you have," Standing up and brushed off his hands on his pants, "Ready to help me build this bed then? I am your pupil, just tell me what to do." He said before walking over to the branches and bringing them closer.

Looking over at them dubiously, she hesitated, "Well, first you'll want to cut four thicker pieces to use as corner posts. They'll need to be a little taller than the ones on this bed since you're heavier than I am."

After several hours and plenty of frustration on both sides, the bed was complete. Walking over to his pack, Daryn pulled out two of the thicker blankets he'd brought and laid them over the bed, testing it out before sighing with pleasure. Looking over at Angela, he saw that she'd drifted back to sleep as he'd finished working. Watching her rest, it was hard to believe they'd grown up just a few miles apart. How different her life must have been from the one he was used to! All the girls he'd met had been like his sisters. Their lives consisted of parties and the latest fashion. He doubted whether he'd ever known a girl who would have been able to survive what Angela had been through.

Getting up so as not to make any noise, he snuck back to the woods and gathered up as much firewood as he could carry to use for a fire. He'd noticed an old pot and a holster for it in the cave and hoped he'd be able to use it to make a stew for their evening meal.

Getting back to the cavern, Daryn was grateful to see the flame

take without too much trouble and before long he had vegetables and meat cooking over the fire. Sitting down, he watched
the flames lick around the bowl, lost in his thoughts. As the
stew finished cooking, he glanced over at Angela and cleared his
throat self consciously when he found her watching him.

"Morning," He grinned, trying to cover his surprise.

Giving him a half-smile she began using one arm to push herself up.

"Hey, hold up there!" Daryn yelled, rushing over to her cot and
helping her raise the rest of the way up. "What do you think
you're doing?"

"If that food tastes half as good as it smells, I want to be sitting
up to eat it. Not laying down like an invalid." She retorted, looking over at the pot by the fire longingly.

"Fair enough, but next time, let me help you?" Missing the
glare she directed at his back, he walked back over to the kettle.
Dipping her bowl in and grabbing another one out of his pack
Daryn headed back over to the cots and handed Angela her stew.
Lifting the dish to her lips she sighed, the warm broth driving
back the damp cold that lingered in the cave. "Maybe I'm just
famished, but you make good soup," She said softly, smiling at
him.

"Eh, you're just starved," He joked, raising his dish to his
mouth. To his surprise, it tasted pretty good! "I went to the markets today and had Archabold load me up with enough food to
last us a couple of weeks if need be."

"Who's Archabold?"

"He's my family's head merchant," Daryn responded absently,
trying to figure out what it was about the soup that had made it
taste so good.

"It must be a pretty big shock for you, being out here and not
back in the upper ring."

"It's not as bad as you'd think. In case it wasn't obvious, I don't
fit in the higher circles too well." He gestured, motioning to his
unclipped hair, broad chest, and old boots. Taking on a prim
posture, he raised his voice an octave, "A true gentleman would

never waste his time mingling with commoners at the Center. We must be above such things." He chuckled as he relaxed and turned back to his soup.

"I guess you have a point there. You aren't like any high-born I've ever met." Angela conceded.

"Thank you!" Daryn gave a half bow, pulling a grin from her.

Finishing their stew in companionable silence, Daryn took their bowls over to the table before pausing. "Do you think you're strong enough for us to look at your arm and see how it's doing?"

Angela's expression fell, but she nodded her head.

Walking over to the other side of her bed where he'd stored the medical supplies, Daryn knelt next to her and hesitated. Even though he had worked on her arm the night before, being this close when she was awake and not in a state of danger seemed oddly... personal. Meeting her eyes, she gave him a small nod.

"It's okay Daryn, I can't take the bandages off myself without pulling on the stitches."

"You're right," he sighed, taking a deep breath and turning back to her arm, slowly untying the knots and unwrapping it. The clothes were soaked a deep red and the wound dark and swollen, covered in half-dried pus and scabs around the stitches. Retrieving a wet rag, he brought it over and touched it to her arm. She sucked in a quick breath as the rag met her skin, bunching the blankets up in her hands as her body went rigid.

"I'm sorry" Daryn grimaced, trying to clean the scabs and puss away as gently as he could. But it wasn't until he'd finished re-applying the salve and wrapped her arm in fresh bandages that her body relaxed. Her face was pale and her body had resumed shaking as he'd finished. Sometime during the ordeal, she'd passed out again. Rubbing a hand over his eyes, he let out a heavy breath.

"I'm sorry, girl," He whispered, putting his forehead against her hands as a tear slid down his cheek. Pulling himself to his feet, he looked down at her one more time.

Roughly grabbing a torch, Daryn headed down a side passage of the cavern. He didn't know where it led, but he didn't care. All he knew was that he needed to get away. Coming to a dead end he banged his fist into the wall and sunk to the ground, laying his arms across his knees. *I can't do this. Healing is a foreign art to me. What do I think I'm playing at out here? Hero?*

But no matter how hard he tried, he couldn't force himself to leave. It didn't matter what areas he was lacking, Angela needed someone, and he couldn't think of anyone else that he'd trust enough to stay with her. Besides, the quiet and solitude of life outside the city suited him. *Maybe it's selfish of me, but I won't leave. Not till she asks me to.*

Pushing himself to his feet he headed back into the cavern where he sat down by the embers of the fire and started whittling on a small stick. Letting his mind wander, he enjoyed the quiet for a while before turning to his cot for the night.

* * *

The next week fell into an easy routine for them. In the morning, Daryn would head out and collect the firewood they'd need for the day and spend some time exploring to make sure no one was following him before returning to the cave. He and Angela would share breakfast, after which she'd rest as he explored the caves or worked on carving spoons and other small items for their makeshift camp.

In the evenings he'd make up a stew and they'd change out her bandages before bed. For most of the week Angela flitted in and out of fever dreams, and he started to wonder if she would ever recover. It took over a week of constant care before her color started returning and she was able to stay awake for longer periods of time.

It was nearly a week after that point that Daryn came back from collecting wood to find her sitting up in bed, her hair wet from presumably taking a bath in the pool, and a fresh set of clothes on in place of the outfit she'd worn all week.

"Well, you look refreshed!" He said, setting the wood down by the fire ring.

"And exhausted," She said, laughing. "But to be clean again was well worth it!"

"I bet!" Grabbing their breakfast, he headed back to the cots, "Here you go".

"Thanks," She said, leaning back against the headboard of the bed as she bit into the loaf.

It felt like an eternity since she'd been able to do anything but lay in that small cot. How she had ached to get up and move about as Daryn did! Hastily finishing off the bread and cheese he'd given her, she wiped her hand on her pants and pulled her knees up to her chest, a small smile playing at her lips.

"Angela?" Daryn muttered, looking off to the side uncomfortably "What happened to you?"

Closing her eyes, she fought against the memories of the night she'd met Daryn. But glancing over at him, she didn't feel like she had the right to deny him his request. Afterall, where would she be without his help?

"I'll tell you... but I'd like to start at the beginning so you understand the full story."

"I don't have anywhere I need to be." He chuckled, folding his arms behind his head and leaning back against the cave wall.

"Okay. . ." She paused, looking down at her hands, "Well, if I'd met you five years ago I would have told you I had the perfect family. My mom was. . . She was everything good about life. She was like the summer sun on a dewy morning. Her goodness went beyond anything I'd ever known. She was born from one of the three high families, though she never told us which. But when she'd fallen in love with my father, her family had disowned her. She wasn't bitter about it though. Always soft spoken and gentle, she was able to find the bright side in anything." Angela's eyes trailed across the cavern ceiling, watching the firelight flicker over its surface.

"My brother and I grew up listening to her stories of times long gone and dreaming of what life might have been like back then.

She'd tell us tales of seers and warriors. Stories of creatures who were long forgotten, like dragons and nymphs. And the stories she'd tell would make you believe that you could do anything. Be anything." Picking up a bread crumb she rolled it between her fingers.

"She was my best friend. . . But about three years ago she fell ill. I did everything I could, but I couldn't save her. It's been two years since she passed." Angela swallowed, unbidden feelings of remorse and guilt rising up in her throat.

"That just left my dad, me, and my brother. Dad's a trapper and a hunter. The best there is. And from the time I could walk, he's been taking me out hunting with him. He's taught me how to take care of myself, training me to fight, to trap, to strategize. . . He and I have been two peas in a pod for as long as I can remember. We'd trained for hours every day, trying to best each other at archery or one-on-one combat. My brother, Calle, preferred to work with herbs and medicine rather than to hunt. He takes after my mother. And so I was sure that I'd take over my dad's trapping orders once I got old enough," Angela sighed, memories flooding through her.

"After my mom died that all changed though... He'd go on hunting trips alone and be gone for weeks at a time, while I stayed home and cared for Calle. We thought that he was just grieving and that it would pass, but it didn't. This year it got worse. He was around more, but our training sessions became increasingly violent. He didn't hold back his punches anymore. His strikes in combat were intended to injure. It was like he blamed me for mom's death. I couldn't see my father in him anymore. He was a different man... And I was scared," her face turned hard as she pushed down the pain that tried to come up. *It wasn't my fault mom died. . . Was it?*

Reaching over from his cot, Daryn briefly rested his hand on her arm.

Taking a deep breath, she continued, "A couple months ago I started training at the Center. I knew I couldn't depend on dad's hunting business being passed down to me anymore, so I needed to find a new trade. I hoped that by performing well in the games this year that I might have someone offer me an apprenticeship. I trained hard, hoping that if I did well enough that maybe I could get away. Maybe I could win a good enough position to take Calle and I out of dad's reach for good. Though with the games taking place any day now, I don't suppose I'll be competing this year," Pausing, she fiddled with her blankets, the realization that she had no future sinking in for the first time.

"Dad doesn't have any family on the plateau, at least not that I know of, so we don't have anyone we can go to for help. And I can't leave Calle and go off on my own. Dad has always trained me to think logically. To not let emotions get in the way of what needed to be done. To protect myself... But I can't bring myself to leave Calle with him, even though that's what I should do. Dad's never hurt him, but..." Shaking her head, Angela sighed.

"I've cried myself to sleep more times than I can count the past few years. At times, it feels like I've lost so much. Too much. First mom, now my father. In his place is a monster that I don't even recognize." Squeezing her eyes shut, she tried to keep the tears from falling. But finding their way through anyway, they snuck down her cheeks and dripped to the blankets below.

"He used to want a daughter who could take on the world, you know? When he'd teach me to fight he'd tell me, 'There are few things up here that you have to struggle to get or keep, but no matter how many years pass and how many people come into power, man will always have to fight for himself.' Did he know that one day I'd need to protect myself from him? If so, why teach me at all?" Her eyes scanned the room as if she might be able to find the answers in the cave walls.

"I don't know if the man I have come to know this year is who my father's always been, and he just put on an act for mom, or if he truly changed with her passing." Painfully, Angela pulled her mind away from the memories to what had happened the night before she'd run away.

"The night before I met you, I came home late from training at the Center to find Calle missing. I searched everywhere, but couldn't find any sign of him. Even though dad and I weren't on good terms, I thought maybe he would help me. He loves Calle after all."

"Running into his room, I hurried to tell him about Calle's disappearance. I had been too panicked at the time to notice his expressions, but thinking back on it now, he didn't seem all that surprised..." Pausing, Angela eyed Daryn, trying to read what he was thinking.

"Anyway," She continued. "Dad wouldn't let me search for him, saying that he'd take care of it, and sent me back to my room. But I didn't believe him. If he'd been worried about finding Calle, he would have left that night. He would have asked for my help. The next morning I managed to sneak out of the house and raced to the caves, hoping to find a cleft high enough up to catch sight of Calle. Maybe he was just hiding and I could spot him from there. But as I was climbing, I slipped and fell into a cavern which led me here." She swept her hand around, covering the expanse of the cave area that they were sitting in.

"It was the perfect set up. I could hole up here as I looked for Calle. Maybe I could win in the games and then he and I could leave dad's. Be free of him and make a fresh start in the city. So I headed back out to collect my supplies from the house. The goal was to grab what I needed and get out of there without getting caught."

"That was the night that you saw me. I had slunk past dad's window to get into the house when I heard him saying he needed to get rid of me. That he couldn't send me to Eurcalp where he had Calle..."

"If dad was the one who'd gotten rid of Calle, I needed to get out of there. And Eurcalp? I've never heard of such a place... I feel pretty certain that whatever dad had planned for me, it wouldn't be good. So I waited until he was asleep and then I snuck into my room to grab my pack and supplies. But he heard me and met me at the doorway as I was trying to leave."

"I tried to fight my way through, but he's got years of experience on me and anticipated every move I made. After he threw his knife," Angela gestured at the makeshift bandages wrapped around her arm. "He charged me, thinking he'd won. That's when I was able to get a blade deep in his leg. He wasn't capable of chasing me after that, and I was able to get away. The caves were too far, so I grabbed my hunting gear and headed for the Center. The rest you know," laying her head back on the bed, she let her eyes drift about the cave.

Emotions flickered across Daryn's face as he processed her story. It was one of the things she appreciated about him. His face always gave him away. Where her father's expressions were schooled and controlled, Daryn's were open and honest.

"I'm sorry, Angela." He whispered after a long pause. "He's wrong, you know. It wasn't your fault your mom died and it wasn't right for him to take it out on you. I wish I had been there..." His hands clenched into fists around his blankets, looking for all the world like he was going to find the man and duel him right then and there.

Reaching over she put her hand on his arm, waiting for his hands to relax before letting go, "Hey, it's okay. You didn't cause any of this," Looking up, she smiled softly. *What man would get so riled up over a stranger's story?*

"I think I need to rest." She said softly, trying to change the subject. She was tired of talking about her life. She'd had enough time to mull it over as she'd waited for her arm to heal and was quite frankly getting sick of it. No matter how much time she spent on it, she couldn't make any sense out of what had happened. *Why had her dad changed so drastically? Why send her brother away? Why try to keep her from looking for him?* Resting into the blankets, she turned over so her back was to Daryn and closed her eyes.

THE BIRTH OF
A LEGEND

"Crraacckkkk!" The sound reverberated across the cave and Daryn's head snapped up as if pulled by a string. Spilling his cot over as he jumped up, he spun around to try to find where the noise was coming from. Angela and Daryn were both wide awake by the time it happened again, the high pitched noise bouncing off the walls of the cave and echoing all around them.

His heart beating almost as loud as the disturbance, Daryn raced around the cavern, lighting torches as he went. Soon, the cavern was ablaze in light, but there was no intruder to be found. Only a large rock in the corner, it's outer edge scattered in pieces around it. With the exterior crust removed, all that remained was an inky black stone. Daryn's eyes were wide as he turned back to where Angela sat on her cot before rushing over to where the rock lay.

"It's an egg!" Angela whispered in awe, coming to crouch behind him.

As they watched, a crack formed around the edge of the egg. Then a nose poked through, followed by a mouth and two eyes. Once the head breached the confinement of the shell, Daryn jumped back in surprise. He was at a loss as to what it could be. It was unlike any bird he'd ever seen. But as he leaned back in to get a better look, the egg teetered and rolled over, covering the newborn. Pushing its nose under the casing, it slithered out from under it and stood regally before Angela and Daryn, taking in the room around it.

"A dragon," She whispered in awe.

"What on earth is a dragon doing here?" He asked, turning to look at her in surprise.

But she just shook her head, her eyes trained on the youngling before them. The baby's head was shaped more like a large horse than a bird, except that it had razor canines that hung over his lips; the armored plates across its face getting darker and thicker as they branched away from the dragon's nose. It had catlike, intelligent eyes, which were striking against its solid black scales.

Not only was its body plated, but the young dragon's ears were shielded and spiked as well, just as its face was. It had very small spines that started a little bit above its eyes. As the ridges progressed down its neck they became wider, but still stayed the same height until they reached its hip bones. Here they began to get smaller as they made their way down its tail. The spikes seemed to be the same inky black as its hide.

The scales covering it didn't look like separate plates at all, but rather looked as if they were one, solid sheet. He would have thought it had a coat of fur, except for how the firelight from the torches skittered over the scale's surface. When the dragon moved, it looked as if a wave had washed over each muscle. Which in this little dragon's case, there weren't very many "waves" at all.

It had a long, regal neck, which it was currently craning around to get a better look at everything. It had a powerful look in its eyes, but its body looked like a newborn foal's; not quite developed. The dragon's tail was about the length of its body.

When the youngling stood up at his full height, its head came to about Daryn's elbow and as he started to walk over towards it, it unfurled its wings, which had previously been pinned to its sides. Daryn hadn't even known that they were there, and judging by Angela's shocked expression, neither had she. The dragon's wingspan was about as long as Daryn was tall, looking disproportionate to the rest of the poor thing's body, which it found out when it tried to take a step towards them.

As the dragon lifted its paw, it nearly toppled over onto its side. It was as if it had drunk one too many tankards of ale as it wobbled around the room. Daryn and Angela looked from the dragon to one another, grins tugging on the edge of their faces. A small squeal brought their heads around in time to see it trip over its wingtip and stumble across the floor only to slide into a stalagmite.

Collapsing into fits of laughter the two slid down to the ground where they stood. It had been so long since either of them had laughed that they found they couldn't stop. Holding her side, Angela sucked air into her lungs, trying to gain control once more. But just as she was able to speak again, the dragon drew itself up, his eyes slitted as he looked down at her with a look so like her father's when she'd done something foolish that her mirth returned and she doubled over once more, gasping for air.

Drawing back, it cocked its head in surprise before tentatively making his way towards her. Feeling cool scales pressed against her forehead, Angela stumbled back, bringing her hands up to either side of her head. Doubling over she clasped her head to her knees, a low moan escaping as she rocked back and forth. Scrambling over to her, Daryn slipped a hand under her chin and lifted, but allowed her head to fall back down when he couldn't see any physical damage. Wrapping his arm around her protectively, he placed himself between her and the dragon, glancing down to see her lift her eyes to meet his.

"What happened??" Daryn asked. "One second you were fine, the next..."

But she just shook her head, her eyebrows drawing down into a scowl. "I can't explain it... It was like something snapped inside me when that thing touched me." She spat out, slinging her hand towards the dragon before rising to her feet and making her way over to her cot.

Looking between Angela and the newborn, Daryn scowled. *Surely it was just stress from the long day. An animal can't harm your mind. . . can it?* Curiosity getting the better of him, he walked over to where the baby dragon laid and knelt in front of it. The beast was perfectly still, its eyes closed and its breath coming in long, slow drags. Reaching his hand out to touch one of the spines, Daryn pulled back as its eyes snapped open, the head whipping around and touching his forehead before he was able to get away. A burning shock seared behind his eyes and through his head, a blaze that obliterated all thought. Gasping, Daryn tried to scramble back, his sight going dark as the pain destroyed all awareness.

Wrestling for control of it, he brought his fists up to the side of his head when, without warning, the pain was gone. Vanishing as quickly as it'd come and leaving only a dull ache in its place. Lifting his head to stare at the little devil to make sure it wasn't coming anywhere near him, Daryn pressed his hands onto the cool floor, preparing to stand. That's when the second round hit him.

This pain was different from the previous one. This one was heavier; like there was a darkness inside him that hadn't been there before, gradually growing as if it meant to consume him. Daryn expected that, just as the headache had subsided after a few minutes, so would the weight in his chest. But it didn't.

In a panic he focused inward, trying to push it back, to force it down, but to no avail. He forgot who his parents were, forgot why he was in the cave. All he knew was the darkness. In desperation he tried to find something, anything, that he could hold on to - any fact or solid event that could show him a way out from the gloom. His terror must have been clear, because the next thing he knew, Angela had both her hands on either side of his face and was saying something that he couldn't seem to make out or understand. He watched her mouth move, but his mind couldn't connect the sounds with their meanings. In a daze, his eyes drifted up to hers and their intensity gave him something to hold on to.

Those eyes sparked something inside of him. And they seemed to push the darkness back a step. Confused, he looked deeper. He noticed every fleck of gold around the pupil, every dilation, the flick of her eyelashes obscuring them when she blinked . . .

and then the weight within him began to take shape. No longer was it just an indistinguishable enemy. Now he could tell, it was emotions. It was feelings. It was memories. Hurts, pains, losses. It was Angela. He could feel it. And at that moment, that name made more sense to him than his own did.

He could feel her deep sorrow as her father turned on her in their sparing practices. Tears slid down his cheeks as he distinguished the heart of it. The agony that her mother's death had brought. He hadn't been able to relate before, because he had never been that close with his parents, but now he could feel the anguish that burned inside of her at every sunrise when her mother wasn't there. The pain of so much as braiding her hair in the same way her mother used to do. This darkness lived in Angela and now somehow was a part of Daryn as well.

Continuing to hold her gaze, he tried to push back the feelings that were attempting to steal his sanity. Going through each piece, each pain, he reconciled it, and recognized it for what it was before pushing it down. He didn't know how long it took, but as he was able to force the last of it down to a controllable level he gasped, sucking in a deep breath as he tried to slow his racing heart.

Memories and feelings raced through his mind as he broke eye contact and hung his head. His shoulders shook as sobs wracked his body. He couldn't remember the last time he had cried so wretchedly, but he couldn't stop. Now that the danger was past, he couldn't distract himself from everything he had just learned and felt. Slipping her arm around him, Angela let him lean against her, but it only served to make him feel worse. Who was she to be comforting him?

"I told you not to touch it," she whispered. "What did it do to you?"

But Daryn only shook his head, unable to find the words to answer her.

She couldn't tell how long they had sat there, but by the time Daryn looked over at her, she could no longer feel her legs. His eyes were so mournful, she was hesitant to repeat her question.

"Angela, I'm so sorry." The tips of his hair were damp from tears and his eyes were heavy, sunken in like he had aged ten years in the past couple of hours. Looking down at his hands, he reached over and took hold of one of Angela's with both of his. His grip was so gentle it was as if he thought he might break her. Confused, Angela looked from their hands up to his face.

"I want to tell you what happened, but I'm worried you won't take it well. Will you promise to at least hear me out before you leave, and once you do, to come back?"

"I swear, I won't leave at all. Just tell me what is going on. I don't understand."

Closing his eyes, Daryn tried to explain what had happened to him, and he watched her face shift from confusion to anger, and then finally to fear. What was worse, he could feel the emotions rolling off of her. Like small waves, they lapped at his consciousness. And with each new wave, he sought to reassure her. But without knowing why she felt the way she did, every word he said seemed to only make matters worse. By the time he was done talking, she looked as if she was about to bolt.

"Angela, I'm sorry. I didn't choose this. I didn't ask for it. Please, talk to me. Tell me what you're thinking"

"Why should I bother? You already know everything," Angela's eyes darted around the cave looking for an escape, but her gaze ended back at Daryn's sad eyes no matter how hard she tried. Reaching over he took her other hand in his.

"Your thoughts are all your own. I might know how you feel, but I don't know why you feel that way. You still have to talk to me." Her eyes flash at that and he quickly backpedaled. "No, I'm sorry, you don't have to. But for me to understand, you will need to speak to me... I'm not doing any good at this. Talking seems to just be making things worse. I'll just sit here until you are ready to talk. And no, I am not letting go of your hands. You're going to deal with this right in front of me, just as you gave me your word that you would."

And so patiently Daryn waited as Angela went from one emotion to another. Pulling at his hands to no avail, she closed her eyes, feeling trapped. This man, whom she hardly knew, now knew everything. She couldn't hide it, and she couldn't run from it. *I wonder if distance affects his perception of my emotions?* But no matter how hard she tried, she couldn't get mad at him. It wasn't his fault. He hadn't asked for it. The image of him sobbing played over in her mind. What man had ever cried for her like that?

Daryn's eyes were closed, his head hanging dejectedly against his chest. Watching him, Angela saw a side of things that she hadn't considered before. He couldn't get away from her either. He couldn't get rid of the memories and the pains anymore than she could. He was just as trapped as she and had had just as little say in the matter. Glaring at the sleeping dragon Angela began to gather herself up, gently trying to pull her hands free. Meeting Daryn's gaze, she forced a small smile.

"We're good." She reassured, but his hands only squeezed hers tighter. Sighing, she sat back down. "I need some time to myself, but we will work this out. Somehow, we'll find a solution. One that we both can live with."

Letting go of her hands, he watched Angela walk over to her cot and lay down. Her movements slow, belying the strain the evenings events had taken on her. Getting to his feet, he made his way over to the sleeping dragon. As he bent down the youngling opened its eyes, their violet glow piercing into him. How on earth did it do that? They stayed that way until Daryn was finally forced to look away. The beast didn't seem perturbed by the events of the evening at all. If it were possible, it almost seemed amused.

Scowling at the little thing he ground his teeth as it blinked and closed its eyes once more. Standing up, Daryn stepped quietly over to his pack so as not to disturb Angela. Pulling out a clean shirt he wandered off into a side passage, running his hand along the cave wall until he came to a dead end and clenched his hands into fists, slamming them into the stone. *This is so much more than I bargained for. . . How did it do that??*

Angrily stripping out of his old shirt, he slipped the new one over his head. It was one thing to help a girl out for a week or two - another thing altogether to be somehow connected to her! Stalking back through the cavern he let Angela know he was going for a walk before grabbing a torch and heading towards the exit.

The cool evening breeze kissed his face as he jumped down into the moonlight. Taking a deep breath, he closed his eyes and let it out, a weight leaving his chest as he did so. The mixed feelings that he now associated with Angela seemed to have lightened. *Maybe if I get far enough away from her, I won't feel her at all. I can just pretend this was all a terrible dream and go back home.* And with that thought, he started walking towards town, feeling lighter with each step.

❋ ❋ ❋

When Angela woke she immediately knew something was off. Her stomach told her it was past the time they normally ate, but the cave was pitch black except for the pool's dim glow. *Where is Daryn??* Angela cautiously got up and made her way to her pack where she pulled out flint and steel and lit up a torch. The cavern was empty save for the baby dragon curled up in the corner.

He left. The thought sunk into her like a weight. He'd never been gone this long before, except when he'd gone to the market that first day. And it was too late for the markets to still be open, even if it was the right day for them. Walking over to his pack she pulled out rations for their meal and moved to the fire ring to start working on dinner. But if he had left, wouldn't he take his bag with him? *No,* Angela thought *as a high born, he'd probably have no use for it back in the city.* The flint and steel dug into her fingers as she scraped them together, sending sparks flying into the cave. Time and again she tried, but the kindling remained stoically cold. Throwing down the rock, she glared at where the fire ought to have been.

I wanted to be alone, she told herself, pacing the cavern. *He was never meant to stay permanently. Eventually, he'd have to return to his life in the city.* With her well enough to get around now, it only made sense for him to go. *But he didn't say goodbye.* Angela tucked her legs under her and picked up the flint once more, fiercely scraping it against the steel. It dug into her hand as she tried to get the fire to light, and soon she felt blood drip down her fingers and onto the kindling. Growling in frustration, she threw the flint across the cave and moved off into one of the tunnels.

Why do I care? I should be happy for the solitude. I've always preferred being on my own. Sighing, she slumped down against the cave wall. *I should have never grown comfortable with him. Should have never gotten attached.* She couldn't put her finger on it, but it had just felt... right having him around. She had trusted him with her life and he'd come through for her. He had comforted her when she'd cried, cared for her when she couldn't and had always made sure she had everything she needed.

"Angela??" The call echoed through the cave from further down the tunnel. Jumping to her feet she ran back the way she'd come to find Daryn looking around the cavern in concern.

"You came back!" She exclaimed, throwing her arms around his neck before realizing what she was doing and taking a step back, dropping her hands to her sides.

Chuckling, he pulled her back into him, rested his head on the top of hers, "I couldn't just leave you," He whispered. Returning the embrace, she clenched his shirt between her fists as she desperately fought back tears.

Squeezing her shoulders he stepped back, smiling down at her, "How about some dinner?" he asked as he turned and headed towards the fire ring.

Watching his back as he walked away, Angela was struck by how she had acted. Her life had felt... wrong without him in it. And that worried her. After all, he wouldn't be following her off the plateau. *I need to keep my distance. I'm getting too attached and I'm just going to get hurt because of it.* She thought to herself as she headed over to join Daryn.

Looking up from where he knelt by the fire ring, his eyes were heavy, "Is there anything I can do for you?"

Turning away from his gaze, she looked at the ground, "Could you help me get to the cave exit? I'm not sure I'm strong enough to make it there and back on my own yet, but I miss seeing the sky. It's been so long..." She trailed off, knowing how pitiful she must sound.

"Sure! Let me get the stew going, and we can head out there while we wait for it to cook. Hang on..."

"It's no use. I was trying, but the kindling must be wet or something. I couldn't get it to start," Angela said, glaring down at the cut she'd gained on her finger as he started scraping the flint and steel together. But before she had finished her sentence, a spark took to the shavings and began spreading through the strips of bark, the flaim licking hungrily at the wood.

Not saying a word, he added larger logs to the fire and set the stew pot above it. After the fixings for dinner were in the bowl and warming up, he extended his hand and helped Angela to her feet.

"Do you want me to carry you, or do you want to try and walk?" He asked once she was standing. Her eyes hardened and she glared, turning towards the cave exit, "I'll walk."

Chuckling, Daryn followed her out of the cavern, grabbing a torch and the map as he went. "You'd think I'd have the passages memorized by now," he said, looking down at the parchment. "But it just never seems to stick in my head".

"Do you ever wonder if maybe these tunnels have a bit of magic to them?" She asked, running her hands along the walls as they made their way down the tunnel. "Like a labyrinth, meant to keep people from finding something.

"I hadn't really thought of it before, but after seeing a dragon I'm open to believing just about anything at this point." Daryn said, looking around the tunnels, "How did you find this place anyway?"

"The passageway that I fell into led me straight to the cavern.

No side shoots or anything. It's almost like the cave wanted me to find it. To find the egg," Angela chuckled. "I know that doesn't make any sense. Maybe the fever dreams have gone to my head."

But Daryn just shrugged, lost in his own thoughts. A faint glow painted the floor of the cavern from around the bend ahead of them and Daryn sat the torch down, careful not to dampen it before following Angela the rest of the way to the entrance.

The moons were up, though not quite as bright as they'd been the night she'd first come to the cave. A fresh breeze brushed her face, its fingers carrying familiar scents from the woods. The sounds of the forest encompassed them and she closed her eyes with a sigh. How she had missed this! Sitting down on the ledge she leaned her head against the cave wall, breathing deeply.

Lowering himself down beside her, Daryn watched her. He felt like he was seeing the real Angela for the first time. He could feel the peace, joy, and confidence washing over to him through their bond. He'd gotten so used to the darkness, it was strange to realize that the connection could bring something beautiful too.

Looking over, she had a thoughtful expression on her face, "This evening when you were gone for so long, were you thinking about leaving?"

Looking down at his hands, he hesitated, "Yes," he said softly, "I was".

"Why didn't you?"

"Well. . ." he said, reflecting back on his walk towards the city. "I originally went out just to get some fresh air and clear my head. But I realized that the further I went, the weaker our connection was. By the time I made it to the edge of town, I couldn't feel you at all." Rubbing a hand over his eyes, he shrugged. "It was tempting to just go back to the life I had. The hot baths, the pampering, the meals prepared for me."

"But the more I thought about it, the less appealing that life sounded. I've learned more by being with you for two weeks than I have in twenty-seven years in the city. I've found a sense of peace, of purpose, out here that I never had back there." Daryn watched as fireflies danced through the grass below their cave, trying to find his next words.

"I made a promise to myself shortly after I met you; that I wouldn't leave you until you asked me to. I've never broken my word before in my life, and I have no intention of starting now." Looking over at Angela, he saw that she had her eyes trained on the sky.

"I know what you mean about finding peace out here," she whispered after a pause. "That's how I felt when dad started teaching me to hunt. The woods... they've always felt like home to me. Life out here made more sense than living in town. To be surrounded by a world that has existed for centuries before we came along, and will continue on in much the same way hundreds of years after we leave. There's a feeling of rightness in that. That even if we make mistakes or get something wrong, the world will keep moving." She leaned her head over onto his shoulder. "Thanks for coming back".

Smiling down, he knew that he'd go through anything to have more moments like this with her. They sat like that for a long time, watching the stars in silence until Angela pulled her head off his arm and stretched.

"Well, what do you say we go check on that soup? I'm famished," she said, starting to stand up.

Stiffly rising to his feet, Daryn offered her his hand and looped it through his arm, "Here, lean on me."

"Thanks," she said, leaning into him. "It probably wasn't the best idea to walk out here, but it was worth it."

Making their way back to the cave, they found the dragon with its head completely submerged in their pot of stew.

"Hey, get out of there!" Daryn yelled, throwing up his hand to try and scare it away.

Raising its head from the pot, Daryn heard a voice in his head, "That was really quite delicious. Thank you for the excellent meal."

Looking over at Angela to see if she'd caught it too, he saw her shock mirrored his own.

"You. . . You can talk??" Daryn stuttered, turning back to the dragon, who nodded its head in a type of bow.

"I am Sacari. It is very nice to meet both of you," it said in a voice that sounded much older than it should have, judging by the dragon's age.

"I think I need another walk," Daryn said, running his hand through his hair.

"I'll second that," Angela whispered. If it was possible, she looked even more stunned than he did. "I also think we're going to need to get some more meat. Sacari just ate four helpings of stew."

"I do apologize, was that not for me? I assumed when you put it on and left that you had intended it as my dinner. Very thoughtful of you by the way. Though next time, please, none of those root things." Looking down at the pot in disgust, he turned back to the edge of the cavern where he'd taken to sleeping.

"Grab the cured sausage and cheese and meet me in the tunnel," Angela whispered, heading back the way they'd come.

Nodding, Daryn went over to their pack and grabbed enough for them before following Angela out. They walked in silence until they got far enough away from the cavern to not have to worry about being overheard.

"It can talk!" They exclaimed at the same time, sliding down against the cave wall. Pulling out his knife Daryn started cutting strips of cheese and meat for them to eat, handing a handful over to Angela.

Eating in silence, they were lost in their thoughts. It was Angela who broke the quiet first, putting down her dinner and staring at the rock wall in front of her, "In all the stories my mom told, the dragons were beasts. More like horses or bears. They were smart, sure. But they couldn't talk!"

Daryn shook his head, "I don't even know where to start. What do we do with a talking dragon..."

"Or what does it do with us?" Angela finished.

Finishing off his meal before responding, Daryn glanced over at her "Well, for now, we need the cave. And it doesn't seem like it intends on leaving any time soon. So I think we need to find a way to stay on its good side and get you back up to health as quickly as we can."

"I think the first step to that would be going hunting tomorrow. We're going to need a lot more meat if we're feeding that guy as well as ourselves. We'll have to take it slow, but the exercise would be good for me. The only problem is, my arm isn't healed up enough to be much good so we'll need to mostly rely on snares."

"I'm assuming you know how to set traps?" Daryn asked.

"You don't??"

"It's not really something taught in the high circles" He shrugged.

"Well, tomorrow will be your lucky day then," Angela grinned. "You'll learn how to set a snare. And if we're successful, maybe you'll even get to watch me skin a rabbit."

"Then I guess we'd better get to bed. You're going to need your strength for that!"

Taking his offered hand she allowed him to pull her to her feet and followed him back towards the cavern. What was it about this man that made it so easy to get along with him?

SURVIVING THE OLD WOOD

Waking early the next morning, they gathered up the supplies they'd need for their hunt and headed off into different areas to get dressed. Daryn had chosen one of his old practice uniforms for the day. Loose leggings were tucked into his well-worn boots. A tight shirt cut off at the sleeves went overtop, giving his arms full freedom of movement as they hunted that day. Running a hand through his hair and yawning, the damp cave air filled his lungs causing him to grimace and cough. The oppressive weight of the walls were an ever present reminder of just how far from home he was. Heading back into the cavern, he began stuffing his used clothes into his pack, making a mental note to have the servants give them a double wash when he got back.

Meanwhile, Angela was in a separate tunnel changing into one of her hunting outfits. Pulling up her thick brown leggings and tying her knee-high leather moccasins she paused, feeling the comfort of the familiar attire work its way into her soul, soothing her taut nerves. Slipping a loose-fitting green top over her head, she slid her arms through the sleeves which hung in a relaxed cut around her biceps and ended above her elbow. The style allowed her to move freely, while also protecting her shoulders from any stray branches and bugs.

To avoid getting tangled in the excess fabric of a shirt that was now several sizes too large, she wrapped a thick piece of leather around her waist a few times. Tying a pouch to the belt, she tucked her flint and steel into it. A second bag would hold the thread she'd need for snares. Slipping her arm through a cross strap, she let it fall across the front of her chest, tucking two hunting knives through the loops that had been sewn to it. She contemplated putting a second strap on, but doubted whether she'd need four knives for such a simple hunt. Her slingshot was then tucked behind her into the leather waistband. Deftly braiding her hair down either side she tied it off with two small strips and headed back into the cavern.

As she stepped into the flickering light of the torches, Daryn let out a low whistle, "Remind me to never get on your bad side!" He joked as he stood up and walked over. "How are you feeling?"

"Honestly? A little nervous. I've never hunted with an audience before. But I'm anxious to get outside and feel the sun on my face again,"

"Well, let's head out then! I'm excited to learn something new today".

Following Angela out of the cavern and into the tunnel, Daryn studied her. She moved with a lethal grace, her shoulders square and her eyes scanning the area before her. Every step she took was effortlessly silent, not so much as a pebble being pushed out of place as she made her way down the tunnel. He couldn't fathom how she had reconciled herself with what her father had done, but there was no sign of the raw, broken pain he'd seen when she'd shared her story with him but days before.

"So, what's the plan out here?" he asked as they jumped from the cave and stepped into the shelter of the trees surrounding the caves.

"Well, first we need to get a decent distance from the cliffs. Game doesn't come around this area. Then we'll start setting some traps and see what I can manage to catch."

"Oh, whatever you catch, huh? I see how it is," Folding his arms over his chest, he glared at her. "You never know, the student might surpass the master today."

"Do you know how long it took me before I was finally able to get something in my traps? An entire winter! No offense, but I don't think you'll be catching much, no matter how good of a teacher I am" Angela scoffed, before lowering her voice. "Ok, look at this".

Kneeling, she pointed out a line that ran through the bushes ahead of them, "See how the leaves are slightly indented here? And how the branches seem to have grown over themselves in an arch? That's a small game trail. You'll want your snare to be set just a little way into the path." Studying it a minute longer she stood back up. "But it looks like this could be an old one. I'd rather get a little further in before we start setting snares".

After walking ways in silence she paused and suggested they spread out a bit. Showing him how to tie a trap she had him repeat the motion a couple of times before nodding and handing him some twine.

"If you see a good trail, set a snare and then come find me. Half the battle of trapping is remembering where you put your traps. I'll try and help you out in that department. Now, have you ever used a slingshot before?"

"Not since I was a kid! It's been a long time since I've even seen one."

Laughing, Angela handed him the one she'd tucked behind her back, "Well, today's your lucky day! I'm not a very good shot with my left hand, and I don't think my right is healed up enough to be of any use. If I scare up a rabbit, your job is to shoot it. Try and stay a little ways away from me so you have time to aim at it. Sound like a plan?"

Nodding, Daryn tried to hide his doubts. He'd be lucky if he was able to hit the broadside of a tree, much less a moving rabbit. Getting a feel for the sling, he glanced up, seeing nothing but the blur of Angela's hunting top passing through the trees ahead of him. After following her for a while without spotting any game, he paused, stooping down to run his hands over the rough leaves as the rich smell of the forest floor reached his senses. A breeze flitted through the branches, tousling the leaves at his feet and obscuring any paths that might have been there. Sighing, he stood back up and glanced around him, searching for movement. Picking up his pace, he strode out in the direction he'd last seen Angela heading and before long spotted her kneeling by a tree, motionlessly watching a young deer grazing on the underbrush several paces ahead of her.

Scanning the forest, he noticed someone else as well. An older man, maybe in his late 40's with silver starting to etch its way through his dark hair. The sleek, agile way the man moved was nearly a mirror image of Angela's. Not making a sound, the man smoothly knocked an arrow to his bow and took aim.

"Angela!" Daryn yelled as the bow string twanged with the released shaft. Rolling from where she knelt, the bolt whizzed past her cheek, showering her with flecks of wood as it tore through the bark where her head had been moments before.

Aiming for the man's bow to keep him from taking a second shot, Daryn swung his slingshot, the stone hitting the man in the side of his head and dropping him to his knees. Tossing the slingshot aside, Daryn bent to grab a branch by his feet, rushing at the man while he was still stunned. Raising his head to meet Daryn's eyes, the man brought his arms up just as Daryn swung the limb across the back of the man's head. Not stopping in his charge, he dodged the hunter's falling body and sprinted for where Angela still knelt, her hand pressed against a scratch on her cheek as she stared at the man laying on the ground.

Grabbing her arm, Daryn yanked her to her feet, "Come on, we've got to go! I don't know how long he'll stay down."

"He shot at me. . . He was going to kill me." Angela whispered, her eyes still trained on the man lying behind Daryn. Pulling her eyes from the scene she met Daryn's, her emotions crackling across their bond before something in her broke. Twisting out of his grasp, she sprinted off through the woods, lithely bounding over fallen limbs and dodging tree branches.

The way she moved reminded him of the deer she'd been watching, her skin and clothes blending in with the forest around her. Taking one last look at the man on the ground to insure he wasn't getting up, he took off after her. His legs were longer than hers, but he was unable to match her grace as he found himself stumbling over rocks and suffering abuse from branches and leaves he wasn't able to avoid. Pushing himself faster, he worked to keep sight of her as she weaved through the trees, never slowing.

* * *

Running as far as her body would take her, Angela was eventually forced to her knees, desperately sucking air into her lungs. It wasn't long before Daryn's heavy breathing joined hers as he came and crouched down a little ways away. Without the run to distract her, she was no longer able to keep her mind from what had happened and her gasps for air turned to sobs. Drawing her knees up to her chest, she buried her face between them, wrapping her arms around herself to create a barrier. A soft touch on her back startled her into lifting her gaze, finding Daryn sitting on his heels beside her.

Shrugging his hand off, she laid her forehead back on her forearms. "Leave me be, Daryn,".

The soothing scent of broken pine needles drifted up to her as he changed positions, his hand returning to her back as he softly drew circles on her shirt with his fingers. The motion helped her slow her breathing as she worked to calm her racing thoughts. Once her cries had quieted, she heard him shift, his hands moving from her back to grasp both her arms, his thumbs stroking over her skin in a silent question. Lifting her head to meet his gaze, tears continued to slide soundlessly down her face and across the cut on her cheek, small pins digging reality back into her with every painful streak.

Wanting only to draw into herself, she let her head fall back to her knees, clenching her eyes closed against the pain that threatened to consume her. Daryn lowered his forehead to rest on hers, wordlessly sharing in her grief as he waited for her sobs to slow.

"Ange, will you look at me?" Daryn asked, his voice gentle and soothing.

"I can't," Angela choked, fighting a new wave of sorrow as it tore through her. "That was my dad, Daryn. That was my dad who tried to..."

Letting go of her arms, he moved so he was sitting beside her as he wrapped his arm around her shoulders and pulled her against him, "It's going to be okay. I'm here".

He couldn't tell how long they stayed like that as he let Angela work through what had happened. Once her sobs slowed down to hiccups every few seconds, Daryn looked down at the girl he knew better than he knew himself.

As he felt her emotions calm, she lifted her head from his now wet shoulder, keeping her eyes trained on the ground in front of her, "Thanks, I needed that. I never thought dad would actually try to kill me. Hurt me, yea. Hunt me, sure. But never take a headshot from behind... Why? How can he hate his own daughter so much?" Angela swallowed, gazing out into the wood without seeing.

"I don't know, Ange. I don't understand it either. Maybe one day you'll be able to ask him yourself. And then I'll get to drag a knife through his arm and see how he likes it." Daryn glared up at the trees, relishing the thought, before pushing it aside and standing up. Reaching out, he held his hand down, helping her to her feet.

"Angela, your shoulder!" Daryn choked out in shock as he let go of her hand.

Looking down, she saw where blood had soaked through her sleeve and onto her shirt. Cursing, she pulled her sleeve up. The bandages were drenched. "I must have broken open the scabs sprinting here," She groaned. "And this is my only hunting shirt!"

"Ok, no more running for you," Daryn said, untucking his pant legs from his boots and ripped a large strip off, tying it around Angela's arm. "We need to get back to the caves and get that washed off and new bandages on it. No wonder you didn't want to go to the doctor when I first saw you - they must hate you over there!"

Elbowing him in the ribs, she looked around, "I'm not 100%

sure where we are, let me try and get my bearings." Walking on ahead, Angela lost herself to her thoughts and after a glance to the side, she was pretty sure Daryn was feeling the same. The shock she'd felt as the arrow had grazed past her cheek kept running through her mind, trying to find a place to rest but without success. She couldn't make it fit. Why would her dad take a head shot at her from behind?

Sure, after mom died he had changed, but surely not that much! Despite everything that had happened, Angela had never feared for her life. . . What could be motivating him? And why now?? Nothing made sense and she was too tired to sort it all out. It had been a long day, and it was only a few hours after noon.

Scanning the forest, she noticed how different it seemed from the one they had been hunting in. Instead of being surrounded by oaks and maples as she'd expected, all around them were towering pines, moss and ferns clinging to their bases like small children. Craning back her head, she tried to see the tops of the bows, but without luck. They were so close together that it was impossible to get a clear view. There certainly aren't any places for small game to hide around here. . . . If there even is any. And forget about tracking with only pine needles on the forest floor! This is going to be a nightmare.

"Hey Daryn. . ." Angela trailed off, turning circles as she tried to get her bearings, a weight settling deep in her stomach.

"What is it?" Daryn asked, his lips forming a thin line as he met her gaze.

"What do you know about the Old Wood?"

"Not much, just that it's the oldest part of the forest on the plateau. No one dares go in it - they say that all the fiercest creatures that had previously inhabited this place were driven there, and since then no one who has gone into it has returned. Why?"

"Well. . . . I think we might need to prove those stories false because I'm pretty sure that's exactly where we are," Scanning the forest for any movement.

"Do you enjoy near-death experiences, Angela? Seriously, I'm beginning to wonder."

"Oh come on, it's not like I meant to come here! I might have explored the caves, but the Old Wood isn't like those ghost stories told by kids. Even my father would never enter the Wood - and he's the bravest hunter I know... Hey, at least we don't have to worry about him following us in here!" Hope rose up in her chest for a brief moment before being snuffed out. It wouldn't matter whether her dad followed them or not if something else found them first.

"Ok, so we're in the one place no one wants to be. What's our plan?"

"I think our first priority should still be to find water. The land is pretty steep around here. A stream should be at the base of one of these hills. We won't make it far without water - and that's our best chance of catching some game to eat." Angela finished, starting forward once more.

Moving at a brisk pace, they both kept their eyes open, listening for any movement besides their own. Despite all the stories she'd heard, she couldn't help but notice the beauty of the wood. Sunlight weaved its way through the pine bows down to the forest floor where the ferns eagerly reached out to catch it. Jagged rock outcroppings made small ledges on the slopes of the hills where the rain had washed the dirt away to expose the massive rocks beneath. It was unlike anything she'd ever seen before.

"No water here, let's follow the ridgelines and keep looking," Daryn said as they reached the ridgeline before moving on. Happy to let him take the lead, Angela fell back, taking in the strange land around them. What kind of creatures must live here? But something about the Wood that made it hard to be afraid. High above she could hear bird song, its unfamiliar melodies hauntingly beautiful. Whispers of life teased at her senses, pulling her in.

"Hey, I see something!" Daryn whispered, his voice breaking the spell. In a daze, she made her way over to where he stood, pointing down the hill to a curving line of thin brush snaking its way between the rocks. A natural rock ledge jutting out from the hillside opposite them.

"Daryn, I think you might have found the perfect campsite for tonight!" Angela exclaimed, slapping him on the back as she jogged down the slope towards the brook.

"Wait, we're staying the night out here?! I thought we were just getting water..." Daryn trailed off as he looked around. The gentle whispers of the stream as it danced over the small pebbles in its way twisted through the air around him. Reaching the base of the hill, sunlight reflected off the water's surface as it peeked out between the brush and shrubs surrounding it.

"Look!" Angela said, motioning him over and pointing to the ground. "It's a small game trail. I'd say rabbit for sure if we were back in familiar territory, but I can't be certain out here. Let's get something to drink a little further downstream and then I'll start setting some traps."

Bending down over the stream, Angela breathed a sigh of pleasure as the earthy taste of the cool water relieved her aching throat. Lifting her face from the brook, she faltered. Daryn's whole face was inches deep in the water, greedily slurping while splashing handfuls of it onto his face and arms.

"What?? It took everything I had trying to keep up with you when you took off. I'd go for a swim if it was deep enough for that!"

Sputtering, she looked away, struggling for control. "Well when you're done enjoying yourself, would you mind getting a spot cleared for us up there under that rock overhang? Just try and get the branches moved out and make sure there aren't any snakes hiding out waiting for us. I'll be back soon. I'm going to go along the stream and set some traps."

Giving her a thumbs up, Daryn went back to gulping mouthfuls of water, oblivious to the world around him. Chuckling, she wiped her hands off on her pants and looked around. Making her way back upstream, she began setting up snares.

"Hey, look what I found!" Angela called as she worked her way up the hill towards Daryn.

Squinting, he tried to make out what she was holding up, "Umm.... A rock??"

"No, silly, it's flint! I spotted it down by the stream a couple of bends up. We can make a fire tonight! I lost mine while we were running and I was worried we'd have to go to sleep cold." Angela grinned as she took in his work on their campsite. "Looks pretty good. Where'd you find the rocks for the fire ring?"

"On up the ridge. This place is covered with them - not like back home! No wonder the early settlers left this spot alone, I'd hate to try and grow anything out here. You'd break your back trying to get rid of all the stones so you could plow!" he looked down the hill towards the stream. "It sure is beautiful though".

"It sure is... Almost too much so." Angela murmured, shaking a chill from her spine before raising her voice so Daryn could hear her, "How about we see what we can find by way of deadwood to burn in that fire circle of yours? And maybe by the time we get back, my traps will have caught something".

"Sure, let's do it!" More than happy to explore a little more, he leapt to his feet. It was hard to explain, but it was almost as if he could hear small snatches of song in the sounds of the forest. But every time he focused in on it, the melody slipped away.

As they walked Angela pointed out the types of wood that they'd want for a cooking fire. Some was best for heat, others were long-lasting, and some added flavor to the food you cooked over it. Unfortunately, pine, as Daryn soon found out, was not the kind of timber you wanted to cook with. According to Angela, it popped sparks everywhere, making it difficult to tend to the meat you were trying to cook above it. He planned to test her out on that theory once they got back. Part of him was convinced she just liked making things more tedious than they needed to be.

But before long they both had armfuls of small sticks and twigs for the fire. The only downed trees they'd been able to find were pines, so after they dropped off their kindling Daryn headed back up the hill to collect some larger logs to put on the fire after they'd finished cooking. In the meantime, Angela went off in the opposite direction to see if her snares had caught anything.

An hour later they were huddled up around a small fire, two skinned rabbits twirling on a stick above the flames with two more sitting off to the side. Leaning back against the rock outcropping behind them, Daryn twirled a twig absentmindedly as he watched Angela. From the moment they had met, he'd been going on instinct. Reacting to the situation in front of him. Now that they had time to slow down, he couldn't help but wonder what tomorrow might bring. Or the day after that. She obviously didn't need him anymore. Would he just go back to life on his parent's estate?

Every path that took him away from her felt wrong, but so did assuming that he'd stay with this strange girl. What were her plans? He hadn't thought to ask. She wouldn't be going back home to live with her dad. So then. . . what? And what right did he have to even be wondering? She hadn't invited him along. In fact, she'd been pretty adamant that she didn't want him around when they'd first met. Did she still feel that way?

Lost in his thoughts, he jumped as he felt Angela's fingers clench around his arm, her nails digging into him. Nodding her head towards the stream, she pointed to where Daryn could just make out the brush moving in the dim evening light. Swaying and rustling with movement the bushes shook as something large made its way through them. Holding his breath, Daryn watched as the creature made a path directly below them. Grabbed a rock, he held it ready as he waited for a clear throw, his heart almost louder than the animal's movements. Trying to calm himself, he waited as the creature's trail paused below them, and then turned, towards their campsite!

Without thinking, Daryn threw his rock as hard as he could to where he thought the head of the creature should have been and heard a loud hssssss as the stone thudded through the brush and onto the dirt beneath. Before either could react, a shape flew at them from the bushes. The next thing Daryn knew, he was on his back looking up at a dragon's slitted violet eyes, Angela's muffled laughter echoing off the rocks behind him.

Clearing his throat, he looked off to the side as he tried to push the dragon off, "Sorry about that."

"Careful what you aim at next time, boy." Sacari hissed before leaping to the ground and stalking over to where Angela had laid out their extra rabbits.

"Careful who you sneak up on next time".

"Excuse me??"

"You heard me. You could have let us know it was you. You have no idea what kind of day we've had. My nerves are on edge enough as it is without you creeping up on us." Daryn glared at the dragon.

To his surprise, the beast looked over at him thoughtfully for a time before nodding, "You have a fair point, young sir. Next time I shall try to be more considerate of my travel companions."

"How did you find us anyway?" Angela asked.

"Are you kidding? You two made a trail a mile wide!" The dragon snorted. "It did take a little bit of work to get around that trapper outside the caves though. . . Looked like he had a pretty good-sized bump on his head and a temper to match. I'm assuming that was one of you two?" He looked over and eyed Angela, then Daryn.

"That would have been me," Daryn growled, thinking back on the moment he'd saved Angela.

Gulping down the last of his rabbit, Sacari curled up around the edge of the fire, and hummed with pleasure, heat radiating off his scales.

Clearing her throat, Angela fiddled with a stick, twisting it between her fingers, "Ummm Sacari?"

"Yes?" he answered lazily.

"What happened to all the dragons? My mother used to tell me stories of what they were like, but even she didn't know what had passed to drive them away."

"You mean you all don't know the histories?" Sacari asked incredulously, raising his head. "You don't know of the great war?

The fall of the old races? The dragon's last sacrifice? How could this be? After all, you are. . . ." Trailing off as he noticed their blank faces.

"Well then, I guess you'd better get comfortable. I'll share as much as I know about that time." he sighed, curling tighter around the fire. Angela handed one of the cooked rabbits to Daryn, taking the other for herself before they both leaned back against the rock ledge, watching the dragon which lay before them.

"Long ago. . . long enough for the stories to have been lost to memory, there was a great land. It was bountiful - covered in forests, rolling grassland, rivers, and springs. Beasts blanketed the fields and the people lived at peace with the old races. There were three nations, the Arachians, the Blackoffs, and the Shurkans. The Shurkans were a plains people. Nomads that followed the herds across the grasslands. The Blackoffs worked in the mountains mining ores and precious metals. And the Arachians lived in the forests. They were mighty hunters and warriors. Wonder and magic were everywhere."

"The Old Races admired the way the people from the three nations toiled and labored and wished to make their lives a little easier. So they came together in what became known as the Great Blessing, pooling their magic to bestow gifts upon people from the three nations. After that time, people began discovering that some of them would be born with special abilities such as far-sight, added strength or agility, or healing. At first, the humans were grateful for the powers the tree spirits, nymphs, and others had given them. The three kingdoms lived in harmony, and so the world was at peace and the land prospered."

"But it couldn't last. Those with heightened abilities were placed in positions of power, while those without remained in the lower classes. They started breeding those with particular powers to try and create new skills. And as those with the gifts from the old races grew in their pride and viciousness, the ungifted rose up in rebellion and a mighty battle ensued. Thousands died and the two armies were nearly wiped out. The destruction stretched for miles, decimating forests and sweeping aside mountains. Where once magnificent woods stood, there was only scorched earth remaining. That is when the dragons stepped in. They brokered a peace treaty between the two factions and from that time on, one dragon accompanied each ruler of the three nations to ensure that the peace would be kept and justice upheld."

"For you see, every dragon, male or female, lays what is known as an Incarnate Stone. Once a dragon dies, all their memories pass on to their stone and they are reborn. So our memories are endless, though our lives are not. This made us the perfect guardians of peace in the land, thus protecting it from war and strife."

"What would happen if a dragon died before laying a stone?" Angela asked.

"If a dragon were to die before laying their stone, that dragon would truly have passed, with no hope of being reborn," Sacari said sadly, returning to his story. "Now, as to where the dragons went? The three dragons who volunteered to stay with the humans took up their places with the three nations, while the rest of the dragons flew across the sea to a new home, to live out their days free from the pettiness of human squabbles."

"And for a time there was peace. Each dragon watching over their nation, protecting it from men and women who would try to enslave their fellow man. But in our pride, we hadn't set anything in place to protect against our own race. Which ultimately led to my death." Looking down at the flames, a low growl rolled off Sacari.

"The dragon over the Arachian nation, I will not speak his name, grew tired of the human's shortsighted bickering. So he convinced the brother of the rightful ruler of Arachia that he deserved to sit on the throne and a coup took place without the other lands knowing. It didn't stop there, though. The dragon then convinced his new king, who was un-gifted, that those with special abilities in the other kingdoms were oppressing their citizens. That great injustice was being done in the other regions and the only thing that would set it right would be to establish the Arachian's as rulers over all the lands. To keep the peace, of course."

"It really was a brilliant plan. Through using his nation's army, the dragon was able to decimate the once-mighty Blackoff nation to a paltry handful of stragglers left as slaves for the Arachians. Any of the gifted that remained after the battle fled to the Shurkans for shelter."

"The Shurkans' dragon was a gentle creature. It knew it could not defeat the Arachian's dragon and their army so it devised a plan. Those with abilities from the old races and the Shurkan's leader came before the dragon and begged to have their their abilities taken away so they could flee and not be discovered. No dragon can give or remove the gift from someone, but there was a way to shield their gifts so they would no longer be able to sense it."

"The people then fled for what they called Heaven's Rock, a mountainous pillar that rose high above the clouds. The Shurkans had always revered it as sacred ground and believed it would protect them from the Arachian's rule. The dragon sent its Incarnate Stone with the band of travelers but remained behind to fight. It knew it could not win, but it didn't matter. Its one desire was to destroy the Arachian's dragon for what he had done. To give the nations a chance to rebuild before he could be reborn. The Shurkan's dragon died in its attempt, unsure if it had succeeded." Laying his head on his forefeet, a tear fell to the ground.

"The stone in the cave was the stone the travelers brought with them, wasn't it?" Angela asked, laying her hand on the dragon's side.

"It was" Sacari sighed. "And my destiny is to fix the mistakes of the past. To restore peace and balance to this world... Somehow."

"So what you did to us back in the cave, that hot poker to the brain? Was that..." Daryn trailed off, as he put the pieces together.

"Yes, you are both gifted. I merely removed the barrier that had been keeping your abilities suppressed. You are descendents of those who fled the Arachians." Sacari confirmed. "And it was not by accident that the two of you found each other and my stone."

"Back when gifted covered the land, there was a rare phenomenon called the 'Bonding'. It was something the Old Races hadn't predicted. After all, our magic is as wild as we are, twisting and turning in directions we could never predict. The bonding took place when two with special abilites met and their energies merged. The individuals involved could understand one another in ways no one else could comprehend. Those with an especially strong bond were able to compound their gifts when close to one another. It was remarkably rare to find your bond mate, and those who did became powerful leaders and warriors in their respective nations. By removing the barrier on your gifts, that bond became possible once more." Sacari finished, pointedly looking between Angela and Daryn.

Daryn looked down at the dirt clotting his boots. *Is this what Angela and I have??* He could feel her turmoil washing into him through their bond even as he thought it.

"What if they didn't want to be bonded?" Angela asked, staring down at her hands.

"It is possible to reject a bond. Of course. It doesn't go away, but you can separate yourselves to the point that you don't feel it anymore." Sacari said, a soft smile danced in his eyes.

"But I think you might have misunderstood me. The bond didn't just happen between a male and a female. Sometimes it would be between two men or two women. It's nothing like mating. It was more like a partnership. Think of your bonded as your greatest champion. Someone who always has your back, who understands you at a level others could only dream of. It's the perfect pairing. To find your bond mate was considered the highest honor." Turning to look at Angela, he paused, "Do you feel anything of the bond from Daryn?" Angela shook her head. "But Daryn, you can feel Angela, correct?" He questioned and

Daryn nodded.

"The bond can only form after the gifted in question trusted the other enough to share their histories. By sharing their personal accounts, it created a level of trust and understanding that allowed the bond to form. If it was there at all. So you see? Two gifted who were destined to be bonded could stand side by side and never know it if they didn't form a relationship first. It's one of the reasons it was so rare."

"So until Daryn shares his story, I won't feel the bond?" Angela asked, glancing over to where Daryn sat, his eyes trained on his boots, brows drawn low.

"That's correct." Looking back and forth between the two, Sacari lithely rose and walked around Angela to grab the last rabbit, taking it back to the corner of their shelter before swallowing it in one bite and lying down to sleep, "Now if you will excuse me, I'd like to get some rest".

The moons had risen high in the sky before the quiet between Angela and Daryn was broken. What had once been companionable silence now felt stifling. Bonded. It felt so. . . Final. Daryn shook his head. He didn't know what to think. And judging by the myriad of emotions still rolling off her, he guessed she didn't either. Walking over closer to her, he sat down, mere inches away as they faced the fire.

"I have a thought," he whispered. "Now, just hear me out. But what if we forget about the whole bonded thing for now? Let's pretend, for the sake of discussion, that it doesn't exist. What would be your next move?"

For a while, he wasn't sure if she'd answer. But after a long pause, Angela looked up at him, the firelight dancing in her eyes. "I would leave the plateau and find my brother. I overheard my dad before he and I fought. He said he sent him to Eurcalp. There isn't a place by that name on the mountain, so it must be somewhere down below. If he tried to kill me, I hate to think what's happening to Calle. I have to find him. My only option is to run and hope my father assumes I died in this forest and doesn't follow me down."

"You'd go after your brother alone?" Daryn asked in surprise.

"Of course. He's family. My father might have forgotten what that means, but I haven't. It's a blood bond." She finished, squaring her shoulders before looking down at the flames, twirling a stick between her fingers.

Returning his gaze to the fire, he tried to sort through the options before him. He could let her run and return to his old life, or... "Your dad saw me when I attacked him in the forest. He might not know who I am, but given my family's station, I bet he can find out pretty quick. If he hasn't already. It's not safe for me in Caplana any longer," he swallowed, tendrils of smoke filling his senses with the promise of change.

"I'm sorry Daryn," Angela whispered, briefly putting her hand on his arm before returning it to her lap. "I wish you'd never have gotten mixed up with me."

Daryn watched the embers dance across the dying timber, life springing from the death of the wood. "I don't. If I had to do it all over again, I'd still make sure I was at the Center when you came in. And I'd still run over to help you. I'm not going to lie and say I don't miss my warm baths," he chuckled.

"But this life, the things I'm learning and experiencing... I feel like I'm finally living for the first time. I know when we first met you told me to go back to my home and leave you alone. Do you still want me to go? Or would you let me come with you and help you find your brother?" Daryn looked over at her, tensely waiting for her answer.

"If you are sure that this is what you want, I will let you come with me," Angela said slowly, keeping her eyes trained on the fire.

"It's settled then. Bond or no bond, our paths would have been the same. We haven't been forced into anything," he smiled "I just wish. . ."

But before he could finish his sentence a deep growl echoed around their campsite, causing their heads to snap up, coming to face to face with a pair of glowing orange eyes. The firelight danced in their golden spheres, making them appear as if they were shifting. First one set, then two, then three... there were more than Daryn could count! Without thought, he rolled forward into a crouch, grabbed for a thick branch protruding from the fire and holding it off to the side menacingly. He might not win, but he'd be sure to make it hurt.

Just as it looked like the leader of the pack was about to lunge, Daryn felt a powerful rush of wind behind him, a screech filling the night sky. Glancing over his shoulder he saw Sacari standing up on his hind legs, wings outstretched behind Daryn and Angela, a threatening curve to his lips revealing a long row of sharp canines. Swiftly turning back towards the threat at hand Daryn's eyes widened as he watched the beasts lower to the ground before sinking back into the night. Pausing, the leader looked up at Daryn, winking before returning to the night with the rest of the pack.

"What were those things?!" Angela hissed, never taking her eyes off where the beasts had stood.

Sacari shook his head, following the pack's movement. "They are what your kind calls wolvrons. A fearsome predator for sure, though I'm surprised to find any remaining here. They are covered in thick fur, making it difficult to injure them. As pack animals, they move as one single unit when they hunt. That along with their heightened intelligence makes them extremely dangerous, even to my kind. A full-grown wolvron is about the size of one of your horses."

"Then why did they leave without a fight?" Daryn asked, shaking out his arms to try and relieve himself of the adrenaline still coursing through them.

"Thankfully, they have longer memories than you humans do," Sacari responded. "Before your kind came to this place, dragons ruled the wilds of this land. And after the humans came, part of our jobs as peacekeepers was to protect the old races. Wolvrons, while they appear to be beasts, are still one of the old races that came together to bless the humans so many lifetimes ago."

"The dragons prevented any mass huntings, which allowed many of the creatures that now hide out in this forest to exist for as long as they have. My kind is greatly respected for the part we played. Now that the Wood knows you are under my protection, we shouldn't have to worry about any threats to our safety here." With that being said, he walked back to where he had lain and rested his head on his forefeet, closing his eyes.

"Nothing like a near-death experience to put you to sleep, huh?" Daryn muttered, leaning back on his hands.

"You know, I had been wondering why we hadn't been attacked by anything since we'd been here. The tales my dad would tell. . . It'd make a grown man quiver. At least now I know it wasn't all just stories. . . Strangely enough, I almost feel safer now." She laughed.

"Safer?? Did that fever fry your brain?"

"Think about it. If this forest was as tame as it's seemed, my father, and anyone else for that matter, could simply follow us in here and hunt us down. Now, at least I know that anyone else who comes through here will be met with all the horror stories I heard as a child. River nymphs that drown you. Wood spirits that lure men off the cliffs. Wolvrons. Damions. And who knows what else! I'd like to see my dad get through all of that!" She said, tossing a twig into the fire.

"Well, at least we'll be safe tonight. Tomorrow we can figure out what we need to get for our journey off the plateau." Daryn yawned and rolled onto his side and tucked his arm under his head as a pillow, "Night, Ange," he whispered.

"Good night Daryn," Angela murmured, still staring into the flames.

A WOOD LORD REBORN

Rolling over onto her back, Angela yawned. It had been a long time after the others had fallen asleep before she'd finally been able to lay down and follow suit. So much was changing. *I'm going to be leaving the plateau soon.* The thought ran through her mind like a shock, driving sleep from before it.

Getting up and stretching, Angela climbed up their hill to try and get a better feel for the area. The sun was just starting to peep through the trees as she reached the top, casting shadows across the pine-covered hillsides. Breathing deeply, she let the crisp morning air fill her chest and lungs. The forest was just beginning to stir, birds sending up their greeting to the new day as she walked back down to their campsite and saw Daryn sitting up, rubbing the sleep from his eyes.

"Morning!" She grinned as she strolled in.

"Morning," He grumbled, the night thick on his voice. "Why is it that I always end up sleeping in the most uncomfortable places when I'm with you? I feel like I've got knots all up my back!"

"I don't know what you're talking about. Other than a sore arm, I'm feeling pretty good."

Grunting in reply he got up and walked down to the stream for a drink. As he made his way back up to camp, his eyes were drawn low. "How are we going to go about getting our supplies? I'm assuming that grumpy trapper Sacari was referring to last night was your dad. And based on what you've told me, I'm not sure I want to go head to head with him in a fair fight just yet. And that's if we can even find our way out of here."

"I was thinking about that last night. Hopefully, he was just outside the caves yesterday because he followed our tracks back there, not because he'd figured out that that's where we were staying. I think maybe today we should try and get out of this wood and see about sneaking in to get our stuff from the cave. Who knows, maybe he won't be in the woods at all. Then we can come back here and set up a little more permanent camp while we wait for my arm to heal a bit more." Angela paused, rubbing on her bandages.

"I'm worried that if we have to climb down the side of the plateau at any point that I won't make it in the shape my shoulder is in now. Having another week to recover would make a big difference. Besides, this is the only place that we don't have to worry about him finding us. So if we can make it back here with supplies, we should be safe." Angela said, stretching out her right arm and grimacing.

"Ok," Daryn said, nodding. "And during that time while we're hiding out here I can try to find an opportunity to sneak back into the city and get the other things we're going to need... And say goodbye to my sister."

"You have a sister??" Angela asked, looking up in surprise.

"Yea, I've got three of them actually. But the older two aren't around much. Gabriella though. . . she's only fourteen. I'd like to explain to her why I'm leaving."

Looking down, Angela fiddled with her bootstraps. *I never pictured Daryn with a family, much less one he likes. And I'm going to be taking him away from all of that.*

"Daryn, are you sure you want to come with me?" She asked. "You don't need to feel obligated, you've helped me more than anyone would have expected. You can go home guilt-free and with my gratitude."

"You're forgetting something, Ange. Your dad saw me," Daryn shook his head. "I can't go back, even if I wanted to. I'd be living with a target on my back. I'm not going to do that." He glanced over at her with a scowl. "My family is safe, your brother is not. What kind of man would I be to go back to mine and let you risk your life trying to save yours?"

"Well, when you put it like that," she shrugged. "I won't mention it again I suppose."

"You ready to find our way out of here then?" Daryn asked, standing up and holding his hand out to her. Taking it Angela stood up, wiping off her pants.

"Do you think we should tell Sacari where we're going? I feel kind of bad that we keep leaving him behind," She asked, looking over at the dragon who was still asleep in the corner.

"Nah. He seemed to find us pretty easily last time. And I don't think he'd be much help in getting our supplies. Better to let him rest. He is a newborn after all." Daryn said, moving off towards the top of their hill.

"Ok then," Angela shrugged, following him up with one last parting look back. Jogging to catch up to Daryn, she grabbed his arm to stop him and pointed to the trees. "See how the moss grows a lot higher up one side of the pines? And how the ferns seem to prefer the same side?" she asked and Daryn nodded. "That's the north side of the tree. Since the Old Wood is the northernmost part of the plateau, I'm voting we head due south and see where that gets us."

"Sounds good to me," Shrugging, Daryn turning slightly so they'd be heading in the right direction.

It took them a lot longer traveling this way as they had to walk up and down every valley and hill. It was rare that they'd come across a ridge top that ran due south, and neither of them wanted to risk veering off course to find one. But as the sun reached its zenith, the forest started to change. Smaller trees replaced large pines, the bird song sounding familiar once more. It wasn't long before Angela was able to see small animals moving through the undergrowth around them.

"I think we made it out!" She smiled, breathing a little easier. "Now to figure out where we are. . ." Continuing their path in the same southerly direction to put as much distance between them and the Old Wood as possible, they came upon an area that Angela recognized.

"Ok, I think I know this spot," She said, looking around. "And if

I'm right, we're only a couple of miles from my house. We need to head that way," She pointed off to the west, "and give my home a wide berth. I'd say from here on out we need to be vigilant for my dad and stay as quiet as we can."

Nodding, Daryn followed her in the direction she'd indicated. What would they do if they ran into Ben out here? Every whisper, every sound set him on edge. Their progress was slow as they attempted to be as silent as possible. Now and then, dry leaves rustling over one another would scare them and they'd duck behind a tree only to discover it'd been a deer or a squirrel. *I don't know how much longer I can take this!* Daryn thought, standing up after a doe had passed by. Angela's face was pale and her eyes skittish, never staying in one place for long. The stress was taking its toll on her as well. Maybe this was a mistake. But what choice did they have? They had to get supplies.

As the caves came into sight, Angela grabbed his arm and pulled him down behind a large cedar. He hadn't heard anything and looked over at her questioningly. But the look of terror on her face told him everything he needed to know. Their breathing coming in short bursts, they waited.

A twig snapped just on the other side of their tree and Daryn flinched, wishing for all the world he had a way to see what was on the other side. Leaves skittered over each other as whoever was out there started making their way towards them. Gradually, Daryn and Angela worked their way around the tree, trying to be as quiet as possible. But as Daryn stepped back, a leaf crunched under his boot. Pausing, they both held their breath, waiting to see if it had been heard. The footsteps across from them ceased and Angela reached up for her knives. A crash sounded at their feet as a rabbit sprung out from under the tree's low hanging branches, fleeing in the opposite direction.

"Cursed girl, where is she?" The hunter growled under his breath. After what seemed an eternity, his footsteps moved on until they faded from range. Waiting until she was sure he had left, Angela peeked around the branches before nodding to Daryn, letting him know it was clear. As noiselessly as they could, they dashed from their hiding spot over to the cave entrance. Remaining quiet, they made their way back to where they had left the torch and lit it up before making their way back towards the cavern.

Reaching it, Angela touched her light to another beacon, as Daryn let out a sigh.

"That was too close." She whispered, moving over to her cot.

"Tell me about it!" Daryn said, taking several deep breaths to try and slow his racing heart.

Pulling up her sleeve Angela started unwrapping the bandages, "Could you grab some rags out of my pack and get them wet?" She asked, grimacing as she tried to pull the wrappings off her cut. The blood had dried, clinging to the dressings and tearing as she attempted to tug the dirty clothes aside.

"Yea, hang on!" Daryn called, soaking some cloths from her bag before coming back and kneeling next to her. Instructing her to lay back against the wall of the cave, he soaked the bandages along where the wounds were before gingerly peeling them back. Her muscles tensed as the rags pulled at her gash, the scabs unwilling to release the cotton they'd bonded with.

"Geeze girl, you really did a number on this!" He exclaimed once he was able to get a clear look at the damage. "You busted all your scabs open and even tore some of the stitches. How did you not notice this while you were running?"

"I was worried about other things at the time," She ground out, looking up at the ceiling of the cave as Daryn started wiping the cuts free of dried blood before applying salve and rewrapping them.

Finishing up, Daryn reached up and gently pushed aside a strand of hair that had fallen across her face, "How about you get some rest? I think it's pretty safe in here. Without the map, there's no way your dad could find this cavern, even if he knew which cave entrance to use... Do you have any items you think we'll need from town? This might be my best chance to get them since we know your dad's looking in the woods for us, not in the city."

Angela rattled off a list of things they'd need before slumping down on the cot "There might be more that I'm forgetting, but that should get us started".

"Ok, you rest. I'll see what I can find," Giving her hand a quick squeeze, Daryn stood up and scanned the cave. Moving over to his pack he grabbed a set of his regular clothes and went down a tunnel to change. If he was going into town, he didn't want to be in his training uniform. And there'd be less chance of Ben recognizing him if they happened to cross paths.

Grabbing a torch, he said goodbye to Angela before heading out. As he neared the end of the shaft he dampened the light before he could see the sun from the entrance and felt the rest of the way out by hand, wanting to be certain his light wasn't seen from outside the cave in case Ben was still out there. Kneeling behind a large stone near the entrance, he held his breath, listening for any movement. Hearing nothing but the normal bird song and the angry squirrel chatter he was used to, he jumped down and jogged over to where the road started.

Slowing his pace once he reached it so he wouldn't look suspicious he tried to act relaxed as he made his way into town, covertly looking to either side as he went, his senses on high alert.

Getting to Caplana without incident, he stepped through the gates and let out a deep breath, forcing the tension from his shoulders. Even if he had been followed, he was a member of the upper class here. He was untouchable. Turning down the main thoroughfare through the city, he worked his way through the paths towards his home. Arriving at the gates, he veered off to the side and headed to the stables instead of going in. Stepping under the shadow of the barn he took a deep breath, hay and manure filling his lungs as he let his eyes adjust. Finding his gelding waiting for him, he grinned.

"Hey there Charger, I've missed you!" Daryn exclaimed, jogging over to the stall and wrapping his arms around the big chestnut's neck. Charger returned the greeting by snorting into his hair companionably. "I know, I know, I've been gone too long. But don't you worry," Daryn whispered conspiratorially, leaning in close to the horse's ears, "You and I are going on an adventure together." He said, ruffling the gelding's mane. Charger nickered, pawing at the ground as he sensed Daryn's excitement.

Stepping back out of the stall Daryn motioned one of the stable hands over.

"Could you send Gabriella out to the stables? And let her know it's rather urgent?"

"Sure thing, sir!" The servant answered, taking off at a sprint towards the main house. Not spending the time to watch, Daryn turned and headed over to the tack room before getting Charger ready to ride. How would Gabriella take the news? Will she feel like I'm abandoning her? He wondered, tightening the girth under Charger's saddle.

"Danny!" Turning around he was just in time to catch Gabriella as she flung herself into him.

"Gabby! Oh, I've missed you!" He said, hugging her tight and burying his face in her curls.

"I knew it was you, I just knew it!" She said, giggling as he tickled her before setting her down. "But why do you have Charger saddled up? Are you leaving again so soon?"

"Come here," He wrapped an arm around her shoulder and led her over to a bench just outside Charger's stall.

"Is it because of mom and dad? Because they cut you out of the business?"

"No sweetie, that's not it. You know I never cared for the family estate anyway. Our brothers are better suited to run it than I am."

"Then what is it?" Her blonde curls bounced around her face as she looked up, giving her an almost angelic look. Her green eyes shimmered with a hint of tears and Daryn almost lost his nerve.

Looking down at his hands, he told her about how he'd met a girl the night of the ball. How she'd been badly hurt and needed someone to help her until she recovered.

"So that's what you've been doing!" She exclaimed. "I knew you didn't have any buddies that'd want to go camping. I knew it!"

"Yea, you were right" He laughed, tousling her hair.

"And is she all better now?" She asked.

"She's getting there. But you see, her dad sent her brother away. Far away, off the plateau. He's only a year older than you..."

"And so you're going to help her, huh?" Gabriella asked, putting her hand on his as he nodded. "Good!"

"You're not upset??" He asked in surprise, looking up at her.

"If I were missing, I'd want someone like you to come to find me. You can't let her go off the plateau by herself!" Gabriella shook her head, a bit of mischief coming into her eyes.

"Hey, I know that look!" Daryn said, putting a hand on her shoulder, "Stop it. You can't come with me."

"No silly, I don't want to come with you! And sleep on the ground for weeks on end? No, thank you! I like my warm baths and hot meals. No, I was just thinking about what we could tell mom and dad... What if we said you'd found a business opportunity? That you'd be away for a little while and didn't want to jinx it by telling anyone until you'd be able to prove it was a success. They'd be thrilled! And it'd explain why you'd be pulling money from your inheritance and taking your horse."

"You know, that's not a half-bad idea," Daryn said, laughing. "I almost feel sorry for the man you end up marrying. He's going to have a time trying to keep up with that brain of yours!"

"You wish you had ideas as good as mine!" She giggled, shoving him. "Now get out of here before anyone else sees you. You're a terrible liar, they'd know you were up to something the moment they saw you."

"Oh, and you're an excellent one?" He said, quirking an eyebrow at her.

"A skill I've been perfecting over the years," She smirked before trying to shove him off the seat. "Now get going. I'll write the letter for you and give it to mom and dad".

"Okay, okay," he said, rising to his feet "But come here. I need another hug before I go."

Standing up on the bench so she'd be eye level with him, Gabriella wrapped her arms around his neck. "Just promise me you'll come back." She whispered.

"I give you my word, Gabs. I love you so much," He choked out, squeezing her tight before stepping back. Turning towards the stables, he took Charger's reins and led him out of the barn. Pausing, he turned around to see Gabriella standing in the middle of the aisle, her pink dress bunched in her hands as she watched him go. With a final wave, he turned and headed out onto the path, wiping tears from his eyes as he turned towards his family's shops.

The streets were nearly empty, making the journey to the markets a much easier feat than the last time he'd visited them. Leaving Charger outside, he stepped through the door and waved Archabold over.

Smiling, the broad man shook his hand. "Young Daryn! How was your adventure? I see you're still alive and in one piece."

Daryn chuckled, shaking the man's hand in return, "It's not quite over yet! I found a business opportunity while we were out that I'm going to pursue." He paused, raising his hands to stop any questions. "I'm not going to jinx it by telling anyone what it is until I come back, but I will need some travel supplies."

"Well, now you've got me curious!" The man boomed, slapping him on the back. "What do you need? It'll be a little trickier since it's not market day, but I'll see what strings I can pull to get you on your way. I'm assuming you're wanting to leave here pretty quick?" He asked, eyeing Charger outside the door.

"As soon as I can," He said, rattling off his needs to Archabold.

"That's quite the list my boy. And it sounds like for quite the journey," The old man said, looking at Daryn under bushy eyebrows. "Now I'm not one to pry, but are'n you sure you want to be gone this long?"

Looking down at his boots, Daryn scuffed them against the store's wood floors. Gabriella was right, he was a terrible liar. He had known Archabold since he was a small child and had always liked the man. He'd been more of a father to him than his own had, always letting him tag along whenever he'd managed to slip away from the house. Raising his head to look the shop-keeper in the eyes, he sighed, "Someone needs my help Arch-abold. A young woman that's been hurt."

"Now that sounds more like you, my boy," The man nodded approvingly, scratching at the stubble darkening his face. "You wait here and I'll get what you'll be needing".

Wandering through the shop absently, Daryn didn't have long to explore before Archabold returned with a cart full of sup-plies. "It might have been better that it wasn't market day!" He huffed. "I was able to send out my employees to the different merchants and get what you'll be needing without having to fight the crowds." He started laying everything out on a long table as he finished.

"I was found the blankets, tarps, and foodstuffs with ease. The saddlebags were a little harder to come by. People don't travel much these days. But I found an old set that should work. I went ahead and got you several sets of travel clothes, even though they weren't on your list. I was even able to find some for your lady friend. Had to guess at the size, but," he shrugged, "You didn't give me much to go on there."

Surveying all that the man had gathered, Daryn grinned. "Thank you so much, this will be perfect."

"You've always been my favorite Daryn. Got a good head on your shoulders, you do," he said, nodding his head and patting Daryn on the back. "Now let's get you loaded up and on your way! We're wasting daylight," he said gruffly. Chuckling, Daryn turned to grab the saddlebags.

"Go ahead and bring Charger on in here first. We'd hate to have your family walk by and ask what you're doing," the shopkeeper said, bustling about the table as he started rolling up clothes and bedding so they'd fit in the bags better.

Stepping out to get his horse, Daryn pulled him inside as he spotted a man ducking behind another stall. *Has Ben found me already?* Daryn thought, his heart hammering.

Working together, they were able to get the saddlebags on Charger and packed, the blankets and tarps rolled up and tied behind his saddle.

"And here," Archabold said, holding out a large leather pouch. "I pulled a decent amount from your account. That should be enough silver to help you out with more supplies once you run out."

Taking it gratefully Daryn hid it inside one of the saddlebags. "Thanks again Archabold." He said, turning around to give the old man a hug. "Can I ask one more favor?"

"What do ya need?"

"Do you know a man by the name of Ben Argon?"

"Of course! Best hunter around!" Archabold boomed.

"I need to get out of town without him seeing me." Daryn said, "And I'm pretty sure he's watching the shop. Could you distract him so I can get out without being caught?"

Eyeing Daryn for a long time, the shopkeeper finally nodded. "I trust ye aren't doing nothing you aren't supposed to young man?"

Shaking his head emphatically, Daryn tried to reassure him, "The girl I'm helping - she was injured by him. He's hunting her."

"Well, in that case!" Archabold boomed, turning towards the door of the shop and straightening his vest with a huff. "You take the back door out of here son. I'll keep him stalled for ya. Even if it means I have to get a little creative." He winked over at Daryn before heading out the door.

Throwing up a prayer of thanks, he watched Archabold head straight towards the shack where he'd seen Ben and lead him out onto the street. He wasn't tall, probably just a couple of inches shorter than Daryn. But his movements were lithe and fluid, his eyes hard as he constantly took in his surroundings. A scar across his cheek gave him a fierce appearance and Daryn renewed his wish to never have to come across the man in a fight. Leading Charger out the back of the shop, he made his way down the side alleys and towards the gates.

Once outside the city, Daryn pulled himself into the saddle and headed to the cliffs at a fast trot. It felt so good to ride again! Surely Ben wouldn't be able to catch up to him at this pace, even if he had gotten away from Archabold. Reaching the caves, he reigned in Charger and tied his line to a nearby tree before running over to the cave. Feeling his way back to where he'd left the torch, he hurriedly lit it and jogged down the tunnel towards the cavern.

"Angela!" He called as he got closer, "You up? We need to move!" Coming around the bend he found her kneeling over their packs, buckling them closed.

"I think I got everything we need," She said, her eyes hard as she scanned the cave. "The only things I didn't grab were the blankets and cooking pot. I wasn't sure how we'd carry those."

Running over to his bag Daryn threw it over his shoulders before grabbing the two items Angela had missed. Not commenting, she slung her pack over her good shoulder and followed Daryn down the tunnel. Turning back one last time as they left she sent up a prayer of thanks for the blessing the cave had been before trotting to catch up with Daryn.

Waiting for her eyes to adjust as they reached the opening, she had to do a double-take once the scene around them became clear. "You brought a horse?!"

"I told you I would!" He grinned and patted the animal's flank. "Charger, meet Angela. We're going to be traveling companions for a while." Leading his horse over to her, he let him sniff Angela's hand before taking her pack off her shoulder and looping it over Charger's saddle.

"I suppose I could get used to that," Angela said, rubbing her arm where the pack had been resting.

"Good," Daryn smiled mischievously, reaching over and grabbing her by the waist, swinging her up into the air and onto Charger's back before she could protest.

"Woah, hold up!" Angela whispered fiercely, clinging to the front of the saddle for support, "I don't know how to ride a horse, Daryn!"

"Well, today's the perfect day to learn." Daryn teased before his face fell. "Look, you're dad was in the city while I was gathering supplies. I got someone to distract him, but I don't know how long they'll be able to keep him from coming after us. And we can't afford for you to reopen your arm in a mad dash again." He put his hands against where hers still clenched the edge of the saddle. "It'll be ok. I'll be right here and we'll take it slow. I'm sure you'll get the hang of it in no time." Handing her the reins he headed out at a fast walk, Charger following close behind.

The first couple of minutes, Angela felt like she was going to end up in a heap on the ground, slow walk or not. But the longer they hiked, the easier it became to get a feel for the sway of the horse's gait. Once she figured out she could support herself with her legs, rather than trying to hang on with her arms, she was able to sit up straight and look around them.

"I think I've got it!" She said proudly, looking down at Daryn in time to see an arrow cut through the side of his sleeve.

Glancing behind them, Daryn ducked as another bolt whizzed past his head. Grabbing the saddle, he swung himself up behind Angela, bending low and wrapping his arms around her. Pulling the reins from her hands he dug his heels into the horse's sides. "Ha!" With a snort, the massive beast bent his head and took off at a dead sprint through the trees towards the Old Wood.

Angela bowed over Charger, clinging to the saddle with all her strength. They were moving so fast tears were pulled from her eyes, obscuring her vision. Leaning her head against the horse's neck, she clung to him like a tick, praying that she'd be able to make it until the blasted thing slowed down again. His hooves beat into the ground, snorting as it dodged trees and fallen logs in his path. Like strong cords, Daryn's arms encircled her, keeping her from falling off the sides. She could feel his body all around her, protecting her from the arrows and the whipping branches around them.

"Are you sure we lost him?" She whispered as they slowed down, trying to turn around to see over Daryn's shoulder.

"We've been in the Old Wood for a while now. I took us over a couple hills and ravines, so even if he followed us in, I don't think he'll be able to get a sight on us." He said, hopping down from Charger's back and reaching up to help her down as well.

Letting him lift her from the saddle, she was grateful to feel solid ground beneath her feet once more before her legs lost their strength, landing her in an undignified heap at Daryn's feet.

"Sorry about that!" he laughed, helping her stand up. "It can take a little bit to get your riding legs, especially after a run like that!"

"I think I'd much rather keep my feet on the ground if it's all the same to you," Angela said shakily, looking over at Charger. "But thank you for getting us to safety boy," She said, rubbing his neck.

They walked for a while in silence, both of them enjoying the peace the wood afforded them. After they had traveled a couple of miles, Daryn slowed his pace and looked around, holding a finger to his lips. Pulling her knives from their loops, she looked around them wearily.

Catching movement to their right, she turned and saw a man step out of the pine next to them. Not out from behind the tree, but out of the tree itself! He was several feet higher than she was, his body tall and narrow like the pine he'd just come from. His skin was patterned in the same coloring as the bark and any clothing that he wore blended so seamlessly that it was impossible to make out. His ears were long, reminding her of a cat's. Hair dark as the earth beneath their feet came down to about the middle of his back in a long braid. In short, Angela had never seen a creature like him in all her life.

Casting her eyes around, she discovered that they were surrounded. All of them appeared to be men, but she couldn't see any weapons on them. Preparing for a fight anyway, she stepped back, her gaze sweeping the new arrivals, trying to find any sort of weakness she might be able to use. Although they'd just emerged from the trees, they seemed to be as tangible and solid and Daryn and herself. And she felt sure that a hit from them would hurt just as much as one from anyone else. If not more.

The man directly in front of Daryn stepped forward, his movements like water, smooth and graceful. *So much for their height throwing them off balance* Angela thought ruthfully, eyeing the man.

Raising his hands from his sides, he said something that sounded like wind-tossed leaves, looking at Daryn, who nodded his consent to whatever the man had said. Moving cautiously, the man knelt, reaching one hand up and touching Daryn's forehead before excitedly turning to the men around him.

"Daryn, what's going on?" Angela whispered, leaning close to him without taking her eyes off the strangers around them.

"You can't understand them?" He asked in surprise, glancing down at her. She shook her head impatiently, glaring around them. But before Daryn could explain, the man that had originally spoken came over and bowed before him, the other men in his party following suit.

Standing up, he spoke for a little while before Daryn responded, "A man is hunting us," He pointed back the way they had come, "He's very dangerous. Could you ensure we haven't been followed?" Nodding, the man motioned to three of his men and sent them in the direction Daryn had indicated. Sending the other men off in opposite directions, the leader turned and motioned for Daryn and Angela to follow him.

"Daryn, explain. Now," Angela growled, moving to walk beside him.

"They're pine sprites. And apparently, I am a 'Woodland Folk'. We'll have to talk to Sacari and see what all that means. I wasn't able to get a lot of information from them, but they seem very happy we are here and are taking us to a campsite we can use. They are going to set up guards to ensure we remain safe while there. Be that from your father, or anything else." Nodding his head towards the man leading them he continued, "I'm pretty sure that's the leader, though they don't have titles so it's hard to tell."

"But you think we can trust them?" Angela asked, eyeing the man.

"I think so. He said something about their brothers depending on us? I'm not sure what that meant, but it seems like they have been waiting a long time for a woodland folk to come. Once we get back to camp I'll try and translate more of the conversations for you."

Angela nodded, keeping her knives out as her eyes scanned the area around them, making sure they'd be able to find their way back if need be. After walking a couple of miles at an easy pace they came to a place where the steep hills they were used to started flattening out, becoming rolling dunes. The tree sprite paused at the ridge of one of these and pointed down.

Below them stretched a meadow covered in grasses that had grown so tall they had laid back down on top of themselves, giving the illusion of waves across the ground. There were still the towering pines, but they were far apart, and scattered between them were several smaller types of trees. Apple, cherry, and many other trees that Angela didn't recognize. Running down the middle of it all was a large stream that looked almost deep enough to swim in. It was, quite simply, the most beautiful place she had ever seen.

Making her way to where Daryn and the pine sprite were conversing, she waited for Daryn to translate.

"He says that we are welcome to stay here as long as we would like. This area is sacred to them, and we won't be bothered by any other creatures while we are in the meadow. He's already sent men to show Sacari the way here. Their only request is that we don't cut down any trees or branches. We can use dead limbs on the ground for our fires though."

Nodding, she turned to the sprite and bowed low in the same manner she'd seen him address Daryn earlier, thanking him for his kindness and consideration. After Daryn translated, the sprite smiled and inclined his head in return before turning and fading into the forest behind them.

"I can't believe this. . ." Angela murmured in awe as they made their way through the meadow, taking in the area around her. "I've never seen anything that could compare. If it wasn't for Calle, I'd be tempted to never leave".

"That's what worries me. I think we should be careful until we talk to Sacari. We still don't know anything about this race. For all we know, they were lying about all of it just to get us here. I'd like to think not, but. . ." Daryn shrugged, "Better safe than sorry".

"I agree. Let's find a good spot to set up camp and see what you were able to get from the city while we wait for Sacari to join us."

Leading Charger down to the stream for a drink, they found a small bridge growing across the water wide enough for them all to cross. Once on the other side, it didn't take long to find a flat clearing where they could set up camp. Taking the saddlebags, packs, halter, and saddle off his horse Daryn patted him and let him wander off to find a good place to graze as he and Angela sorted through their supplies.

Taking everything out of their packs they laid it out on the ground, trying to get an idea of what they had to work with. As Angela pulled out the contents of her bag, she carefully unwrapped her clothes and placed the silver she'd been able to obtain on top of one of her shirts so as not to lose any in the grass.

"Where did you get that?!" Daryn asked in surprise when he saw her growing pile.

"Dad," Angela said, continuing to unpack.

"Is it possible he's hunting you because he wants his money back?"

"I wish," She muttered. "No, he didn't even know I'd taken it when we first fought. He was just trying to keep me from leaving. Granted, I'm sure he knows by now and isn't too pleased."

Shaking his head, Daryn turned back to his own supplies. Once everything was out on the grass he sat back on his heels and surveyed what they had.

"Hey, where did you get these?" Angela asked, reaching over to where he'd laid the clothes Archabold had found for her.

"Archabold," He smiled. "Do you think they will fit?"

"They're perfect. . ." She said, running her hands over them. "I've never had a new set of clothes before. Mom would make ours before she passed, and I've just been mending the ones I had ever since. These will be wonderful."

"Well, I'm glad Archabold thought to grab some then! We wouldn't want you to run out of clothes after all," He said, tossing her a wink. Angela's eyes narrowed as she threw a nearby rock at him.

Laughing, he raised his hands in surrender, "Is there anything you see missing?"

"I don't think so. . ." She said, turning back to the supplies. "We've got plenty of blankets, hides, bedding, food, hunting equipment, silver, extra clothes, cooking pot, fire starters, a couple of bars of soap, twine, and a lot of rope. But we have no idea what we're heading into once we get down below," Angela shrugged, "So I really don't know. Your guess would probably be as good as mine." Looking around she added, "But would you mind if we grab a bite to eat? I'm exhausted and starving."

"Of course!" Daryn said, reaching over for some cheese and sausage. Handing some to Angela, the earthy scent of the aged cheese tugged at him, reminding him that they'd missed breakfast that morning. After they'd eaten their fill, Angela unrolled one of the blankets under one of the flowering trees and laid back. After sitting for a minute, Daryn stood up and stretched, deciding to explore the meadow a little bit while she rested.

DARYN'S TRAINING BEGINS

Moving through the glade Daryn found himself continually looking over his shoulder, unable to shake the feeling that someone, or something, was there watching him. After many fruitless attempts at catching whoever he was sharing the meadow with, he lowered himself to the ground. Running his fingers through the grass, he closed his eyes and breathed in the crisp scent of pine and apple blossoms.

The now-familiar tingle crept up his spine and he cracked an eye, doing his best not to move as he watched faces begin peeking out from the trunks of trees. Some were dainty and petite, others round and jovial. As he opened his other eye to get a better look, an apple sprite jumped from her tree and danced over to him, planting a kiss on his cheek before spinning away giggling as laughter skittered across the meadow from the other tree sprites who were watching. I guess not all sprites are tall and solemn like the pines, Daryn thought as he smiled before standing up once more.

Tucking his arm across his chest he made a bow to the trees around him, which elicited more laughter, before turning back towards the meadow and continuing his exploration. All around him were hidden patches of beauty and serenity. Some flowers tucked beneath the base of a tree here, a unique rock outcropping there, a handcrafted stone bridge spanning the stream in another spot. He had never seen any place in his life so intentionally cared for, without any obvious sign of its caretaker. If he didn't know better, he would have thought it had all happened on its own. And he couldn't help but wonder that if tree sprites made their land look like this, why had they ever been chased away?

* * *

Back at camp Angela stretched and sat up, gazing around her for a few moments before pulling herself to her feet and heading towards the edge of the meadow. They'd need wood for a fire, and she hadn't noticed a single fallen twig anywhere in the field as they'd walked through. Hopefully, she'd have more luck in the woods surrounding it. As she crossed, she tried to take in the beauty around her. It was the first time in a while when she didn't have to worry about being ambushed or hunted. She was safe, and she wanted to soak it in. Pausing she listened as the bird's songs ebbed and flowed around her, bees and other pollinators flitting through the song as they flew between trees in search of their next meal.

Reaching the edge of the plain she ducked under the hanging branches of an old pine tree to find herself back in the Old Wood. The birdsong changed, taking the peaceful serenity with it. The Wood was beautiful, but in a wilder sense than the meadow was. Trying to shake the chill that crept up her arms she started scouring the ground for fallen limbs, making a pile of firewood by the large pine tree.

As she worked, the tingle she'd felt as she first stepped into the Wood only increased until she could no longer shrug it off. Something else was out there. The birdsong had all but stopped and the Wood was silent except for her footsteps. Crouching down, she scanned the area around her. She didn't have any of her hunting gear or knives on her and she kicked herself for being so careless as to leave them behind in camp.

Keeping her senses up, she bent down to pick up another branch as she saw a black shape slip through the trees up ahead. Relaxing, Angela sat the sticks down and stood back up, waiting for Sacari to get closer. Moving effortlessly through the shadows left by the tall pines, he was nearly undetectable. If she hadn't known what to look for, she never would have noticed him, even after he drew near.

"Good evening, Angela," Sacari said, dipping his head in greeting. "I hear you and Daryn have made some new acquaintances."

"Yes, the pine sprites. I was hoping to talk to you about that. What do you know of them? They are calling Daryn a 'woodland folk' and offering us protection."

"I had wondered when he might realize his gift. I must admit, I'd hoped it would be in time to secure us a little more comfortable accommodations while we stayed here."

"So you think they can be trusted?" Angela asked, looking around her self consciously.

"In this instance, yes. Ordinarily, no. Sprites, no matter what tree they come from, are notorious tricksters. Luring humans in, just to kill them. They resent the human's treatment of their forests and blame the human wars for the desolation of much of their homelands. Sprites live much longer than humans you see - as long as their trees. And their memories are even longer still. But, with Daryn being a woodland folk, I believe we will be safe with them."

"What does that mean? What is a 'woodland folk'?"

"Since I believe Daryn will probably have a very similar quandary, I'd rather wait till we were all together before giving you my answer."

"Fair enough. But if you knew what Daryn was, why didn't you tell him? And do you know what I am?"

"I do," Sacari said, ignoring her first question and beginning to move past her towards the meadow.

"Then could you tell me?" Angela asked, stepping into his path and forcing him to pull up short.

Drawing back his head, Sacari regarded her for a time. She was a difficult one for him to read. Especially for a human. Normally their intentions were so plain. But with Angela. . . He couldn't perceive a thing. Tilting his head to the side he finally nodded before tucking his hind legs under him and laying down on the forest floor facing her. She in turn gracefully lowered herself cross-legged to the ground, not making a sound. Cocking his head, Sacari puzzled for a moment before beginning.

"When I first touched you to remove the barrier, I could feel the type of talent you contained. But as I've watched you these past couple of days you've surprised me at more than one turn. You see, people with your particular abilities were usually at the top of their societies. They generally held positions of power. But they were all but useless in a fight. Preferring to avoid conflict unless they had others around to do their fighting for them. They were spindly things, not very useful when it came to any type of manual labor. Now, all that hardly describes you, my dear."

Angela stayed quiet, patiently waiting for Sacari to continue.

Sighing, he pushed on, "You have an ability called 'far sight'. It was very rare and very coveted in my previous life. I believe it would be even more so now. Those with far sight were often referred to as 'far-seers' or simply 'seers'."

"As in, they could see the future?" Angela asked carefully.

"No, not precisely. Each seer's abilities were somewhat different, but they could all reach out with their minds to see things the eyes couldn't. For example, say one was traveling at night. A seer would be able to stretch out and see an ambush before their party drew near and alert their companions. In a battle, they could see the enemy troop layouts and warn the general of their numbers and strategies."

Angela looked down at the ground by her feet, trying to make sense of what Sacari was saying. She'd always been able to feel game before she came upon it while hunting, could that be because of her gift?

"The downside is that, while in use, your body will be vulnerable to those around you. Your mind will be away, and thus unaware of what is happening around your body. It can be very dangerous, and it is one of the reasons seers were so rare. Many did not live long enough to have children. They spent so much time training their mind and relying on it to protect them, that the body was neglected. They were terrible fighters and yet extreme threats, making them the first target in any battle. Often, they'd come back to their bodies in time to see the sword falling towards their head, not able to do anything about it," Sacari trailed off, looking intently at Angela.

Raising her head, she met his stare with one of her own, allowing some steel to creep into her voice, "Can you teach me to use far-sight?"

"I can... If you are sure that you would like to learn it."

"I am," Angela said, rising to her feet. "As you mentioned, I am not like the other seers. I have spent years training my body and senses to fight. If my mind can be a weapon, or even just give me a leg up, then I think it's about time I started training with it as well".

"Fair enough. Shall we find Daryn and fill him in on what his new title means?" Sacari asked, also rising to his feet and making his way towards the meadow.

Watching his sleek form move through the trees she hesitated. What if learning how to use this sight made her a target in the land below? What if she used it at the wrong time and ended up dead because of it? Bending under the branches of the last pine she the sun's rays brushed her face as her feet fell on the soft meadow grasses. Closing her eyes, she took a deep breath and held it for a moment before letting it out. Things were changing so quickly, she feared she would make a mistake. Trust the wrong allies or stay too long in this plain and lose her brother. Or worse, not spend enough time and die before ever reaching him.

Opening her eyes she looked down towards their campsite to find Daryn looking at her from across the field, casually bent over a newly started fire. *Cursed stones, how did I end up with a man who can read me like an open book?* Giving him a small smile, she proceeded down the hill to where he sat with Sacari.

"Everything okay, Ange?" He asked as she drew near.

"Yeah, it's nothing," Angela tried to shrug off his concern, pointing back up the slope the way she'd come. "I've got a nice pile of firewood up there by the pine, would you mind helping me get it down here? Should be enough to keep us warm tonight."

"Sure thing," he said, wiping his hands on his pants before standing up to follow her, nodding to Sacari as he passed. He could still feel the undertones of doubt and worry coming through their bond as they walked towards the woods, but didn't want to push her. *What had happened between her and Sacari before they'd come to camp?*

"So, do you think Sacari will be able to fill us in on what my gift means?" He asked, trying to ease her into a conversation.

"It sounds like he will." She said, not taking her eyes from the bordering trees ahead. "If I'm being honest, I don't know who to trust out here. Dragons, tree sprites. . . these are creatures out of myth and legend. And I'm worried that they all have their own plans for us. Plans that have nothing to do with my brother." Sighing, she glanced up at the sky, "I don't want to be a pawn in whatever game they are playing".

Sneaking a look at her, he couldn't see a hint of what she was feeling on her face. But it was wafting through their bond with full force. Anger. Confusion. Fear. Doubt. But what could he say to reassure her? After all, he'd had the same concerns. And though she hadn't said it, he couldn't help wondering if maybe she also didn't fully trust him.

"I'm as lost as you here. These creatures, my new title. . . it's uncharted territory for both of us. But there's at least one thing you can know for sure - I have no hidden agenda. I didn't know who you were until I met you at the Center. And as we saw earlier today, your dad is hunting me as much as he is you. . ." he shrugged. "We are dealing with forces neither of us knew existed a mere few days ago, and I don't entirely trust that they aren't trying to use us for their own ends. But my path is with you. Wherever that takes us and whatever that means".

"I know you intended this journey to look a little different, back before your fight with your father and your unfortunate run-in with myself," He grinned, striving to ease the tension. Getting no response he paused, placing his hand on her shoulder before his face turned serious once more, "But you need a friend. You need someone who will have your back. Choose Sacari, choose the sprites, choose whomever you think best. But I'm offering myself up as an option as well."

Turning to look at him, she searched his face and he felt her come to a decision and relax. Ducking away from his gaze, she continued back up the hillside. "Well, in that case, I accept your offer. And I have a favor to ask."

"What's the favor?" Daryn asked, not trusting the grin that was pulling at her features.

"Let me train you to fight." She said, ducking under the pine branches and disappearing into the woods beyond.

"To fight?!"

"Um-hum, to fight. You've got the build for it. You're quick, you've got good balance, you're strong as a boar, you've got a good reach... And I need someone who can have my back." At this, Angela knelt beside the pile of wood she'd gathered and paused.

"Sacari told me about my gift," She murmured, picking at the bark on one of the logs, "And it would leave me vulnerable any time I'd need to use it. Sounds like it used to be very rare. Partly because those who had it would normally die before ever finding a mate or having children."

"That explains the feelings I was sensing through the bond while you were away," Daryn reasoned, kneeling next to her and starting to gather up the wood in his arms.

"I know it's a lot to ask, and I don't want you to feel pressured to accept. I wouldn't want someone watching my back that felt forced into it. Take a few days to think it over. But know that you would be my first choice." She said, rising to her feet and holding a couple of logs in her good arm.

"I don't need a few days," Daryn said gently, lifting the branches from her and adding them to his pile. "I will be your Guard if that's what you want. My hesitation is more in my lack of ability, rather than my lack of willingness. Surely you could find someone better qualified along our road. Or even back in town. Another hunter perhaps?"

"No," she shook her head adamantly. "There might be others more skilled, but no one that I'd be able to trust the way I can you. Anyone else might be just as likely to stab me in my back as the enemy they were supposed to be protecting me from. And besides, it'll be fun." She said with a gleam in her eyes that told him it was going to be anything but fun for him.

"Only if you call getting beat up by a one-armed girl 'fun'," he mumbled under his breath as they turned back towards camp.

Chuckling, Angela looked over her shoulder at him, "Having someone to train with will help me heal faster. Besides, it'll be months before you're ready for one-on-one combat. First, we've got to turn all that brawn into useful muscle."

"I'd be careful, Ange. That 'useless' muscle is currently carrying all the wood back to camp. And has carried you on more than one occasion if memory serves me." He said, drawing up next to her and giving her a pointed look.

Blushing, Angela hid her face as they drew near their tents, blessing Sacari's presence in that it would force a change of subject. Working together, they got the extra wood on the fire, along with a pot of stew. The tantalizing smell of the bowl's contents danced around them as the sun began its descent behind the trees.

"So I hear you'd like to learn a little more about your new-found title, young Wood Lord?"

"Wood Lord? I thought I was a woodland folk?" Daryn asked in confusion, looking up from a stick he was whittling to see Sacari watching him.

"Woodland folk is the name the Old Races gave to your kind many ages ago. The humans, however, referred to the bearers of the gift as 'Wood Lords'. It makes little difference to me which we use."

"Why didn't you tell me about who I was before? If you know what Angela's talent is, you had to have known mine as well."

"You are. . . different from Angela. Her ability is passed down by blood. Yours is not. No one, not even the tree sprites, knows how a wood lord is chosen. Some say it's destiny. Some that it chooses children with certain character traits. While others will argue that those who have the title are typically blessed with the characteristics common to the bearers of it. All of that to say, since it is not passed down by blood, I had no way of knowing for sure what you were. I had guessed, of course, but I didn't want to get your hopes up if I was wrong."

"Ok. . . So what am I??"

"In short, you are the connection with the old races. Some say that when humans first came to this land, they made a pact with the old races, offering one man up to be their bridge between the two cultures. That man was the first of the wood lords. Ever since then, there has only ever been one at a time. And sometimes hundreds of years would pass before the next one was born. None were living when I was last alive, at least not that I'm aware of."

"Men, or women, with the gift could understand many, if not all, of the other race's tongues, as you have proven. Over time, they would take on many traits that the Old themselves cherish. That of speed, agility, strength. Some would have heightened senses of smell or hearing. Some were master hunters. Others were great warriors. Some could even learn to wield the old magics that the tree sprites and water nymphs possess. But one thing was the same for all of them - they preferred the quiet lives to that of power or prestige. While they were vicious when provoked, they were not considered threats due to their peaceful natures."

Daryn looked down at his hands for a time, "It explains why I was always so different from my brothers. And why I've found so much peace since leaving the city." He paused, thinking back, "That night when the wolvrons attacked our camp, I could have sworn one winked at me. . ."

"It wouldn't surprise me." Sacari growled, "They are like many of the Old Races, they love to tease. Only, their teasing is frequently much less pleasant than some of their other kin in these woods. That they dared to come into our camp at all. . ." Sacari shook his head, muscles tense as he gazed out into the dark meadow, his eyes sharp and threatening.

Angela listened to the exchange in silence. If she were honest with herself, his gift really was the perfect match with hers. But it also meant that he'd be that much harder to beat if he ever turned on her. Mentally shaking herself, she gritted her teeth. He had been nothing but loyal, there was no reason to think she'd ever have to defend herself against him.

Daryn's hand brushed against her arm, causing her to jump. Snapping her head up, she found him holding out a bowl of stew, his attention already back on what Sacari was saying. Smiling softly she took it and began eating, letting Daryn's and Sacari's conversation ebb and flow around her. She'd always wanted to see more of the world than their little plateau. That was certainly coming true, and she hadn't even left yet.

❊ ❊ ❊

Dawn came gradually to the meadow. As the sun worked to get above the tall pines, the mist from the stream spread across the fields, waking the insects that lived there. Birds began singing over their breakfasts and an excited surge traveled up Angela's spine. Training started today.

Rousing herself, she swung her legs over the side of her bedding and hopped up to get the fire going again. Fetching water from the stream, she filled their cooking pot and waited for the water to begin boiling before pouring some of their oats in for porridge. How she'd missed waking up to the sun, rather than a dark cave!

Leaning back on her hands she watched the meadow stirring and smiled. It was going to be nice being greeted by this every morning as they waited for her arm to heal up a little more. Hearing rustling behind her, Angela turned to see Daryn climbing out of his bedding. His hair was tossed from sleep and his clothes wrinkled and matted. Walking over to the fire he sat down beside her, looking more asleep than awake.

"Morning" he yawned, rubbing at his eyes.

"Morning sunshine" Angela laughed brightly, handing him a bowl of porridge.

"Thanks".

Chuckling, she dished up a bowl for herself. If she were honest, his morning moodiness was rather endearing. Finishing off her breakfast, she walked over to the stream and rinsed it out, returning to find Daryn working on his second helping.

"You ready to start training today?" She asked, stowing her dish back in her pack before sitting next to the morning fire.

"Ready, yes. Excited, no. I don't think you understand. I just started practicing at the Center a year or so ago." He shrugged his shoulders in defeat. "I haven't learned anything that would be remotely useful out here".

"You'll do great, you'll see. I've got a good feeling about you."

"Well, that will be a first." He mumbled, walking over to the stream to clean his bowl before coming back to the fire. "So what will we be starting with? Knives?"

"Ha! You'd be more likely to stab yourself than me. No, we'll start with archery. It's a skill you'll be able to practice as I work on my gift with Sacari. And I've got a couple of ideas of things we can try after that."

"Doesn't sound too terrible. Let me go grab my bow".

Once they had their weapons, they headed off towards the edge of the meadow. After reaching the wood and walking a short way in, Angela pointed out a dead stump she'd seen the night before while gathering kindling.

"Could you ask the tree sprites if it's ok for us to use this as target practice?"

"Ummm sure. . ." He said, turning around to try and find a tree sprite in the area. Not finding any, he cupped his hands to his mouth and yelled, "Can we use this stump for archery training?" After listening for a while and hearing nothing he shrugged, "I suppose it's all right then".

"Ok, I guess they can't say we didn't ask. We'll start at thirty paces and then begin working our way back as you get the hang of things," Angela said, walking over to the stump and pacing out the beginning distance. "Now, take your aim".

Striding over to where Angela had marked he raised his bow, looking down the arrow towards the target. Moving to stand beside him, she put her hands on his hips and moved them a little, forcing him to shift his feet so that his body was directly perpendicular to the mark. "That will make you a smaller point to someone returning fire. Make sure your opposing hip is always facing towards the target. Now raise your elbow. . . Yes, that's good. Now release!"

The bow twanged and the arrow flew high, barely grazing the top of the tree. Sighing, Daryn jogged after it, retrieving it from the ground 50 paces beyond the intended stump. Coming back, Daryn shifted his feet so his side was facing the tree and knocked an arrow, raising his bow once more. Taking a deep breath, he held it for a minute and released, letting his shaft fly. This time the shaft went wide and disappeared into a nearby bush.

"Aren't you going to give me any pointers here?" Daryn asked, frustratedly gesturing in the direction the arrow had flown.

"Nope. It takes time to get the feel for your bow. For the stance to feel natural. I'm going to go set some traps while you keep working on it. I'll check back in once I'm done and see how it's going."

Grumbling, Daryn retrieved his arrow and took his position again. Looking around, he saw that Angela was already gone. Lifting his bow he sighted down the shaft and released it. Time and time again he did the same thing with the same results. The arrow never hit the target.

"Gah!" He yelled, throwing down the bow in anger as he stomped off after his missing arrow. "This is a waste of time,".

Returning once again to the tree he took a deep breath and reached down to pick up his bow. Knocking the arrow, he raised it once more. His arms were getting sore from the repeated motion and he was tired of failing. Closing his eyes, he tried to calm himself. Frustration pushed at his consciousness, his muscles tensing and his breathing coming in deep drafts. Unable to take the build-up of pressure, his eyes snapped open and he released, the arrow flying true. It was a perfect hit, dead center of the tree.

Retrieving it, he stepped back and aimed once more. Taking a deep breath, he stopped trying to hold his anger in check and instead let it come to the surface and flow out of him. Moving his bow slightly he felt it come into position, almost as if it were fitting into a mold and released. Once again sending the arrow into the center of the tree.

"Yes!" He yelled as he jumped up, pumping his fist in the air. Slow clapping behind him caused him to whirl in time to watch Angela step out from behind a pine.

Her face was pensive as she came up beside him, "Now let's see if you can do it with an audience".

Walking to the stump, he removed the arrow and returned to his position. Trying to ignore Angela's presence, he knocked his arrow and raised the bow once more. Taking several breaths to loosen up, he sighted down the arrow. But just as he was about to release, a breeze tickled the hair around his ear. Distracted, his arrow went wide and missed the trunk.

Giggling, Angela moved away before he accidentally hit her with his bow as he swung around.

"Hey, not fair!" He said, rubbing at his ear. "You should have warned me!"

"Yea, like the wind is going to warn you before it comes up." Angela scoffed. "You're too focused. Too keyed in. You didn't even hear me come up next to you. That'll get you killed. You've got to see the target as just a piece of the landscape around you. Don't block out your surroundings. Take them all in. Try it again."

Taking up his stance, Daryn raised his bow. Not bothering to check his emotions, he took in the area around him as Angela had suggested. He could hear her moving around behind him, saw a bird flit through the trees to his left, and felt as a soft breeze stirred the branches above him. Finding the now-familiar knot in the air that meant his arrow was true, he released. Just as a small pebble hit him in the back of the head. But it was too late, the arrow had gone hit its mark.

Grinning, Daryn spun around to see Angela staring at the stump. "Again," she said briskly.

Retrieving the bolt, Daryn returned to his normal position. This time, she had him step back several paces before raising his bow. As Daryn released, a small stick whacked him between the shoulder blades. Still, the arrow found its mark.

Again and again, they practiced and every time the bolt ended up dead center of the stump.

"How?" Angela wondered aloud. "It took me two summers to be able to hit a target while being distracted".

Daryn shrugged, unable to keep the grin from his face. "It must be because I'm a wood lord. Maybe archery is my calling".

"Maybe. . ." Angela whispered, staring at the arrow in the tree. "Ok, from now on I want you to come out here when I'm working with Sacari and practice with the bow. See how far back you can go before you start missing and begin there. You need to build up muscle memory. You need to be knocking your arrow and releasing almost at the same time. The longer you take, the more likely your target will move out of range. Got it?" Daryn nodded.

"Good, now let's see if your gift helps you with tracking." She grinned as she turned deeper into the woods. "You can leave your bow by the stump. We'll come back and grab it when we're done," She called over her shoulder.

"What are we tracking?" Daryn asked, turning away from her to set his bow down.

"Me," She grinned before taking off through the woods, disappearing from sight.

"If you break open another one of your stitches I am not fixing you up!" Daryn hollered after her, hearing her laughter filter back towards him through the trees before he sprinted after her.

The sun was cresting the sky above him and he was drenched

in sweat by the time he came to a stop. He couldn't even be sure if he was in the right area of the woods. There wasn't a single trace of her anywhere. In frustration, he slammed his fist into a tree. "I give up!" He yelled.

"You don't have to holler," She grimaced, stepping out from behind the pine he'd just punched. Without thought, Daryn swung his other hand around in surprise, aiming for her head before he realized who it was. Easily jumping back from the blow she grinned, "Want to play again?".

"How did you. . . I don't understand." Daryn said, looking around in confusion. But she just kept laughing.

"How about you follow me back to camp and we'll get a bite to eat. Watch how I move and see if you can do the same. You were as loud as an elk stomping through here. It's all too easy to stay out of your way when you're that noisy.

"You've played this before," Daryn accused, glaring at her.

"My dad and I used to play," She said softly, slipping through the trees.

Trying his best to emulate her movements, Daryn followed her back to camp, pausing along the way to pick up his bow. Grabbing a bite to eat, Angela headed off to work with Sacari. Making the excuse that Charger needed to be tended, Daryn went off in the opposite direction, grateful for the break.

Reaching his horse, he turned back to see Angela sitting cross-legged on the ground in front of the dragon, arms resting on her knees, her eyes closed. *What on earth could they be working on?* But after watching them for several minutes without seeing any movement, he turned his focus back to Charger and began putting him through his lunges.

A SEER IN THE MAKING

Feeling Daryn's attention turn away from her, Angela breathed out a sigh and allowed her shoulders to relax.

"Normally, training for a seer begins shortly after they become five," Sacari said, pulling her concentration back towards him. "Before they've managed to form any unpleasant habits with their gift. Unfortunately, we've missed that window by a long shot. So we're going to come at this a little differently."

"First, try and relax. Pretend you are out hunting. Feel the landscape around you. Close your eyes and use your senses to pick up on any movement that would give your target away. Let's see how far you can push yourself," Sacari directed.

Doing as he asked, Angela concentrated first on listening to the area around them before moving through the other three senses available to her. She couldn't tell if she'd been like that for five seconds or five hours when something changed. As she strained to hear a noise in the grass at her feet, her mind lit up with a dozen pinpricks of dim light.

There in her mind's eye was a small colony of ants. She couldn't see the landscape around them but could tell where they were. Every time their small feet came in contact with the ground, or a blade of grass, that object would flame up. There were no colors in the traditional sense, but rather objects seemed to be colored by thoughts. Intentions. She could tell that some of the ants were gathering food, while others were caring for the young. Curious, Angela tried to reach out and see if she could get a read on Sacari and what he was thinking. But as her mind moved on from the ant colony, there was a shooting pain in her skull and everything went dark.

Blinking up into the sun she saw Sacari looking down at her. "Very good! It only took you a whole of 5 minutes of using your sight to knock yourself out. That's got to be a new record." He said dryly, returning to his place in the grass across from her.

"I could see them! I could see the ants! I could feel them. It was amazing!" She said, attempting to push herself up into a seated position once more.

"And then let me guess, you wanted more?" Sacari asked, raising an eyebrow at her. "Please tell me you didn't try and get a gauge on Daryn over there,".

"No," Angela said stubbornly, omitting the fact that she was striving to get a read on him instead.

"Your mind is much like any other muscle in your body. It has to be strengthened with consistent, daily exercise. Push it further than it's able and it will give out on you. We will want to avoid blacking out in the future, it'll leave you weak and hazy for several hours afterward."

Angela nodded, already beginning to feel a little groggy.

"Come on, you were at that for the majority of the afternoon. It is nearly dark, and I believe Daryn has a large pot of stew ready for us over at the campsite." Sacari said, getting to his feet and sniffing at the air.

"I was out that long?!" Angela asked in surprise, trying to stand up.

"No my dear, you were only out for a few minutes. You were practicing for several hours before that, though. Honestly, it took you longer than I expected."

"Several hours. . ." Angela mumbled to herself, numbly following Sacari back to camp.

"Hey, Ange!" Daryn said as they stepped into the firelight. His voice sounded light-hearted, but she could see the concern on his face.

"You don't have to look at me like that, Daryn. I'm perfectly fine. Just tried to do too much." She said dispassionately as she accepted her bowl from him and sat down by the fire.

"She'll be a little out of it for the next couple of hours," Sacari said softly. "The effects of overextending herself with her particular talent are similar to drinking one too many mugs of ale."

"I'm right here Sacari," Angela grumbled, keeping her eyes on her bowl as she tried to finish her stew as swiftly as possible.

"And it would appear that she isn't a very happy drunk," he finished. "Now if you'll excuse me, I'm going to go find my own dinner. Roots are not a proper meal for a dragon, no matter how skillfully they are disguised." And with that, he disappeared into the shadows around their camp.

An awkward silence descended over the two remaining companions, broken only by the popping of the fire and the occasional owl overhead. Angela finished her stew and rinsed her bowl out before heading to her bed and laying down. After a while she heard Daryn moving around camp, putting up their supplies and dampening the coals. Hearing him crawl into his own bed across from hers she rolled over.

"Daryn?" Angela whispered.

"Yea"

"Why haven't you completed the bond?"

Sitting up on one elbow Daryn looked over at where Angela lay. All he could see was a dark silhouette of her staring up at the stars. He'd thought about completing the bond. Heavens knew he wanted to! But. . . The longer they spent together, the more his feelings for her began to worry him. It wouldn't be fair to let her in until he was sure how he felt and why.

"It's personal," He said, laying back down and rolling over so his back was to her.

"Oh, it's personal? Excuse me, I didn't mean to get into your business," Angela scoffed. "Come on Daryn, you know everything about me. I can have no secrets from you. And yet you lay there saying you won't offer me the same courtesy because it's personal?"

"Yea, it is," Daryn said, sitting up and scowling at her. "If you had known what telling your story to me would do, would you have told it? My guess is no. You would have thought about all the parts of yourself you wouldn't want me to know about

106

and you would have stopped before you even started. The only reason I have your bond is that we didn't know such a thing existed until after you'd already shared and sealed the deal."

"And as far as no secrets? If you have no secrets, what's your gift? Huh? What's put you in this lovely mood this evening?" Angela was silent. "That's right. You're a hypocrite Ange. Asking for those around you to be open and honest while you're anything but." Daryn grabbed his bedding and stomped out of camp.

Angry with herself and with Daryn, she jerked the blanket over her and rolled back over, trying her best to fall asleep. But it was a long time before sleep would come to her.

* * *

Stretching her hands above her head Angela yawned and looked over at Daryn. But both he and his bedroll were missing. In horror, the events of the night before began to sink in. It hadn't been a dream! *Oh no, what did I do?!* She thought as she scrambled out of bed and looked around the meadow. Daryn was nowhere to be seen, and neither was Charger.

Racing across the field towards the tree where they had practiced yesterday she ducked under the pines and ran into the woods. Reaching the stump she paused, finding no sign of him.

"Daryn!" She called out, nearing panic. But all she heard were echoes of her call coming back to her through the forest. "No..." She whispered, sliding down against the tree. *Did I drive him away? If he had attacked me like that I certainly would have left. I had no right. Stupid! How could I have been so stupid?!* Angela dropped her head into her hands, too angry to cry.

After a while, she rose to her feet and started back to the meadow, her head hung in defeat. Hearing hooves behind her, she whipped around to find Charger tearing through the trees towards her, Daryn on his back. Pulling to a stop, Charger snorted and pawed the ground as Daryn jumped off and ran over to her.

"Are you ok? Are you hurt?" He asked, looking her over for any sign of injury before noticing her stunned expression. "I felt your panic. I thought you'd been attacked".

"I thought you'd left," She whispered, looking down at his boots. "I thought I'd driven you away."

"Hey," He said, taking a deep breath and putting a finger under her chin, tenderly raising her head to look at him. "I told you, I'm not going anywhere."

"I know," Angela shrugged, pulling her head away.

"No, you don't," Daryn sighed. Taking a step back, he reached around his neck and pulled out a silver chain. Lifting it over his head he held it up in front of him. At the end of the necklace was a large ring. It looked to be solid gold and so thick that Angela doubted anyone would be able to wear it on their finger. Fine designs and engravings wove their way around it, ending in an archaic symbol in the center. It was one of the most beautiful things she'd ever seen.

Daryn cupped the ring in his hand, looking down at it longingly. "This is my family emblem. Every male in my line gets one. They've been passed down since before we came to the plateau. For me to be allowed through my family doors, I have to hold this ring. Without it, I am a 'forgotten'. Someone worse than dead. I wouldn't even be remembered." Hesitantly, Daryn handed the loop to Angela.

Taking it, she studied the ornate detail. "It's beautiful Daryn," She said, handing it back to him.

But he shook his head, grabbing hold of the chain and slipping it over Angela's head. "I cannot return home without this ring," He repeated, his gaze boring into hers. "So as long as you feel its weight around your neck, you'll know that I will not, can not leave you."

In horror, Angela reached up to take the necklace off, but he gripped her wrists, stopping her. "Daryn, you can't do this! You can't give me your family's band! Please. I have a hard time with trust, yes. But you don't need to do this."

Forcing Angela's hands down, Daryn looked at his ring hanging around her neck, emotions rolling through him. He'd always thought he'd give the band to his future wife. But they couldn't afford to have her panic any time he wasn't around after they'd fought. Riding back to her the way he had this morning hadn't been safe. He could have been injured. Charger could have been injured. But when he'd thought Angela was in trouble, none of that had mattered. He needed her to know that he wasn't going anywhere.

"No, take it," he said with finality, letting go of her hands and allowing his to fall to his sides. "For me. Please".

Touching the ring with her fingers Angela looked at him, feelings of surprise and gratitude washing across their bond. Along with something else. Something deeper. But it was pushed away before he was able to figure out what it was. Nodding her head, Angela took the emblem and tucked it under her shirt allowing it to rest against her chest. Twisting away, Daryn tried not to think about where his family emblem was now laying.

Coming up beside him she touched his arm, "Thank you, Daryn. I'll keep it safe, I promise. And after we find my brother, I'll return it to you."

Giving her a small smile he nodded before turning back towards the meadow, Angela alongside him and Charger following behind.

"So what are we going to work on today?" He asked, trying to change the subject and get back to familiar territory. "I practiced my archery this morning. I can hit the mark from about ninety paces, but then another tree gets in the way, so I can't go back any further."

"That's amazing! I know men who've worked at it their whole lives and still aren't that good." Pausing, Angela thought for a minute, "I wish I had a moving target you could work on or a way for you to practice on Charger while he's running. . . But I think that'll have to wait till we get out of the Wood... So we'll move on. I'd still like you to keep practicing in the mornings, though. Your gift might make it easier for you to hit the target, but you still need that muscle memory and strength to back you up. And there's no shortcut for that. Just lots and lots of practice."

Rolling his shoulders, Daryn could already feel the soreness setting in from just two days of training. "That's ok. I kind of like it. It's peaceful."

"Good, because we're going to start one-on-one combat today," She said with a grin. "And that will be anything but peaceful if I have anything to say about it."

"I thought you'd said it was going to be months before we worked on that?!" Daryn started in surprise. He had no desire to go up against Angela, especially since her shoulder still wasn't healed.

"Well, I thought it'd take you a lot longer to hit the target with archery. And I'm curious to see if your newfound title helps you out in hand-to-hand combat as well."

Reaching their campsite, Daryn took his bedroll off Charger's back and laid it back out in its old spot before removing his riding gear and letting his horse wander off. Seeing Angela a little way up from their camp, he trudged over to meet her.

"Well, you don't have to look like you're walking to the guillotine!" She smirked as she started stretching.

"I might as well be. I hit you and I'm in trouble. I don't hit you and I imagine I'll also be in trouble. I can't win at this."

"Well, not with an attitude like that. How about this? Today, we'll just take stock of where you're at. What you do know. I'll make sure you don't land any punches, and you won't get in trouble for not hitting me. Sound fair?"

"I'm not sure if I should be relieved or insulted," Daryn grumbled, stretching out his arms.

"I don't know a single man in our village that could best me, other than my father. I've seen you guys practice at the Training Center and I wouldn't break a sweat with any of you. I've been trained since I could walk, the rest of you didn't start till you reached manhood. If that. So don't take it personally. Besides, a high born like yourself? I doubt you've ever been in a tousle your entire life!"

Grinding his teeth Daryn could feel his anger rising to the surface. In the back of his mind, he knew she was baiting him. But the idea of landing a hit on her was sounding more and more appealing by the second.

Bouncing on the balls of her feet Angela grinned, "Come on big boy, show me what you've got".

Without warning, Daryn sprung out of his stretch and charged her. Aiming to take her to the ground, his arms reached out to grab her around the waist, but he scarcely felt the fabric of her shirt brush his fingertips as she bent and spun out of his reach. Turning on his heel in mid charge, he swung his elbow out to try and connect with her nose. This time, missing entirely as she ducked again.

"You move slower than my grandmother!" Angela taunted, skipping away, both her hands clasped behind her back.

Growling, Daryn started circling her. Abruptly changing course, he charged again, this time pulling up short and spinning to the side in the same direction she'd avoided him the last time he'd gone at her. Swinging his arm around, he clipped her shoulder as she dropped into a roll to avoid his hit.

Coming back up to her feet, her eyes narrowed as she watched him, both her arms at her sides now. Grinning, he began circling again.

"Come on little rabbit, you going to run all day?"

Faster than his eyes could track, she dove under his reach and landed two hits to his kidneys before spinning behind him, kicking the back of his knees and sending him stumbling.

"Don't get cocky." She growled, bouncing back and letting him get his feet under him.

Daryn grinned as he worked to get his balance back. Maybe this was going to be fun after all. Picking up a stone beside his feet before standing up, he whirled around and flung it at her knee caps, while at the same time sprinting towards where he thought she'd go to avoid the throw. Sure enough, she spun to evade the rock, right into his path. But instead of trying to backpedal or turn away as he expected, she ducked his fist and sent an uppercut to his jaw. Luckily, Daryn had been in enough fights at the Training Center to see the move coming and lifted his head so that the blow just grazed his chin while bringing his other fist around and planting a punch to her side.

Grabbing his arm, she twisted under it and brought it around behind his back. Instead of fighting the grip, Daryn spun with her and took the wrist she was holding up towards her jaw. Realizing she wasn't strong enough to stop the blow, she released him and backed away laughing.

"So you've been in a couple of fights after all, huh? Did some thug insult your mother?" She taunted, ducking under one of his punches and kicking out at his knee caps in response.

After a good half hour of sparring, Daryn had managed to land a few hits of his own and they were both breathing heavily. Grinning, Angela called a break before walking over to him and slapped him on the shoulder. "Not bad Mr. Highborn. You did better than I expected."

Laughing ruthfully, Daryn gingerly touched the tender spots on his ribs from where she'd kicked him during practice. "Not good enough to avoid a decent number of bruises!"

"Well, what do you expect when all you do is attack? I get the feeling that you won all your fights before just due to your size and strength. You never learned to block or dodge a hit, you just barrel right through them."

Daryn shrugged, "It worked a couple of times today." He said, pointedly looking at where she was rubbing her good arm.

"No man in his right mind runs into a blow! You can hardly blame me for not seeing that one coming!" She laughed, starting to move towards the stream for a drink.

After they'd both drunk their fill, Angela stood up and looked around, "Let's head over to the stump and I'll get you started on knife throwing, then I'll come back down and work with Sacari on my gift for a little while."

"Sounds good to me. Just... try not to pass out this time."

"Ha! Deal. I've never been drunk before, but if that's what it feels like, I have no desire to be!"

Stopping by their campsite, they grabbed Daryn's knives and Angela got him started throwing before heading back to the meadow to find Sacari napping under a pear tree.

Deciding not to bother him, she sat down by the stream and closed her eyes. Now that she knew what it felt like to see with her mind, it didn't take long before she was able to pick out a ladybug crawling along a blade of grass by her feet. Trying to get comfortable, she decided to stick with the bug until it was no longer a strain to do so. But before long, a breeze came through and the ladybug took to the skies. For a brief moment, Angela tried following it but pulled back as she felt a sharp pain pierce behind her eyes.

Drawing back towards herself, she reached out to try and find a new subject to study. Passing over a colony of ants, she landed on a bee that was flying overhead, flitting between flowers on the apple tree shading her. Reaching out, she was able to include two insects in her view. Gradually expanding, she could see an entire section of the tree as it would light up from a dozen different points each time an insect flitted in and out of its leaves and buds. She held on as long as she could, dazzled by the scene she saw in her mind's eye, but ultimately, she had to pull back into herself and open her eyes. Looking up at the tree she'd been studying, she could just make out some of the bees humming through its branches.

Pulling her legs under herself, she got to her feet and stretched, looking up at the sky to judge the time. By her best guess, she'd only been at it for a few hours. Much better than last time! She thought to herself as she headed across the meadow to see how Daryn was doing with his practice.

As she neared the stump she found Daryn sitting down, his head leaning back against the bark, eyes closed. Two knives were sunk inches deep into the log above him. Glaring, Angela contemplated kicking him awake. But deciding that she could use a bit of a rest as well and changed course.

Careful not to make a sound, she made her way closer, watching him for any sign of movement. Stopping where she was partly hidden by a tree to his left, she studied him for a moment. He was so unlike anyone she'd ever met that she had a hard time reconciling it. For the most part, he was light-hearted and care-free, as if he'd never had a single worry in life. But then there were times, like when he'd given her his family's ring, or when they'd been fighting earlier, that made her question how well she really knew him.

How she hated herself for pushing him to complete their bond last night. She hadn't wanted it to come out like that. While she did wonder why he didn't want to share the connection, more than anything she just wanted to know more about him. What had his life been like before they'd met? What could have shaped a man to have character strong enough to stay by her side, despite everything he'd have to go through because of it? They were all things she doubted she'd ever get the answers to now.

Pulling the ring out from under her shirt, she let it fall into the palm of her hand and studied it. Rubbing her finger along the de-signs around the edge of the band she tried to trace the intricate patterns they made.

"I used to spend hours doing that," Daryn said, making her jump in surprise. "The longer I'd look at the thing, the more con-vinced I'd become that the lines were rearranging themselves." He shook his head ruthfully and stood up, walking over to where Angela was before sitting down next to her.

"I've never seen anything like it before," She whispered, look-ing back down at it. "It feels so light when I'm holding it like this. But when it's hanging around my neck it might as well be fifty pounds."

"I know what you mean. It's felt that way since my father gave it to me when I turned eight. All my family's expectations - car-ried inside one little ring. How very heavy that has felt. And how strange to not feel it anymore."

Angela looked over at him, trying to read his expression. His eyebrows were drawn low over his eyes, making them appear almost black instead of green. He had stubble growing along his jawline from days of not shaving that gave him a fierce look. His broad shoulders and strong arms were draped casually across his legs as he fiddled with a twig, a gentle giant.

"I don't want to dredge anything up, but I do want to say that I'm sorry for last night. I shouldn't have pushed you. My mental state at the time is no excuse for my behavior."

Looking over at her, Daryn nodded silently.

"Could you tell me a little bit about your family?"

"Why? It wouldn't complete the bond. . ." his mouth pursed and eyebrows lowered. She shrugged, suddenly self-conscious for asking.

"It's not about the bond, I was just curious."

"Well, in that case, let me see..." His face split into a smile he leaned back, resting his hands behind him. "Let's start with Gabriella. You'd like my youngest sister. You guys are complete opposites but have a similar spirit about you. I imagine you don't take 'no' for an answer very often?" Angela grinned and shook her head, "Well, neither does Gabriella. She's got a backbone to her that drives my parents nuts - but that I've always adored. Actually, now that I think about it, maybe you two shouldn't meet. I have a hard enough time staying out of trouble when I'm with one of you!"

Angela leaned back against the tree behind her and laughed.

"My other two sisters are older and engaged. I suppose I'll most likely miss their weddings since they were scheduled for the fall." He said, before picking up on the guilt she felt at the revelation and moving on, "They won't mind. I doubt they'll even notice. My parents will just be upset that I will have slighted another one of their attempts at matchmaking." He rolled his eyes, looking back down at the ground.

"They mean well, they really do. Both of them are great! I'm just nothing like they expected. Or probably wanted. Everything my siblings love... the society drama, the latest fashions, the balls, and high-end functions... those things just don't matter to me. What do you do when your entire social standing depends on your children marrying well and forming connections; and your son not only doesn't attend the events but avoids any attempts to match him up?"

"At least now I understand why I didn't fit in. If what Sacari said was true, maybe my title has been affecting me long before I had the barrier removed. It would explain my strength and size, even though neither of those run in my family. It also would explain why society and the city seemed so... constricting." Daryn shrugged.

Angela watched as he worked to reconcile who he was with what he had learned about himself. Shaking his head, he moved on.

"I have two older brothers who are set to take over the family business next year. They're married and have been apprenticing under my dad and Archabold for a good ten years now. They love it, and I think they'll do a great job at it. I'm sure my father will stay on as an advisor for as long as his health allows. And my mom will most likely be throwing parties long after that." Daryn laughed. "I have a good family. I just don't fit into it very well."

"What did you tell them when you left?" Angela asked, watching his face closely.

"I gave a note to one of our servants to inform them that I'd found a business opportunity and would be gone for a while pursuing it."

"You left a note?!" Angela laughed in shock.

Daryn shrugged. "It was Gabriella's idea. As she pointed out, I'm a terrible liar. So I couldn't tell them in person. And hopefully, the prospect of their son getting out of the games at the Training Center and chasing a respectable career will buy me a decent amount of time before they start asking questions around town."

"Hmm, so Gabriella is the one I need to watch out for when we get back".

"Oh definitely! I pity the man she marries. He'd better have a good head on his shoulders and a strong backbone, or she's going to walk all over him." He laughed, imagining what she might be like in a couple of years. "I can't even begin to go through all the trouble she's gotten me into. And the problems I've had to get her out of!"

"Ha, I hope I get to meet her someday." Angela grinned, tucking the necklace and ring back under her shirt. It didn't feel quite as heavy as it had before.

"How did practice go?" Daryn asked, cocking an eyebrow at her. Challenging her. He'd answered one of her questions, now it was her turn.

"Well, as you can see," Angela spread her hands out to either side, "I didn't blackout this time!"

"Ha, thank you for that!"

"Any time," She chuckled. "It was really neat today. I wish I could show you what I saw. . . It was so beautiful. But I don't know if I have the words to describe it."

"What do you mean, 'saw'? Every time I've seen you practicing, your eyes are closed."

"Well. . . I'm a far-seer," She said, trying to choose her words carefully. "With enough training, I should be able to see life forms that are hidden from the human eye. So let's say for example we're traveling and someone is hiding in the trees with a bow. I could see them with my sight before we ever got close enough for them to fire."

"Wow, so I might as well give up on my plan to one day sneak up on you," Daryn chuckled. "But. . . I don't understand how that leaves you vulnerable? You said you needed someone who could guard your back. That's why you've been training me, right? But it sounds like you'll be untouchable."

"Not exactly," Angela said, drawing circles on the ground in front of her. "You see, when I use my sight, my mind's eye leaves my body. I can't hear, see, or smell what's around me. When I'm using it, I don't have control of my body."

Silence spread between the two as Daryn pulled back into his own thoughts. It was no surprise she'd been hesitant to share it. She didn't strike him as the type to give away her weaknesses readily. And this? Well, it left her extremely vulnerable. Reaching over, he took one of her hands in his.

"Your secret is safe with me, Ange. If you will do your best to train me, I will do my best to have your back." Angela looked up at him and felt a tug at her heart. Shaking herself and jerking her hand from Daryn's grip, she nodded, trying to push the feelings down before they had time to cross the bond.

"One thing that seems unique to my gift that I haven't mentioned to Sacari," She continued, attempting to distract herself, "is that I don't just see the life forms around me. I can see their intentions as well. I've only been able to see small bugs so far, but I could tell which ones were looking for food, which were caring for the young. . . It was amazing!"

"So as you get stronger with your gift, you might not need the bond to know how I'm feeling?" Daryn asked cautiously.

"I'm not 100% sure, since insects are a far cry from people, but I don't think that's how it works. From what I understand, the link transmits feelings. Emotions. Right?" Daryn nodded, "So things from the heart. My sight seems just to pick up on things from the mind. So let's say you were hunting. I could pick up on that, but not on how you were feeling about it. I couldn't tell if you felt guilty for hunting, just that that's what you had set out to do. Does that make sense?"

"Yes. . . And no." Daryn chuckled. "But enough that I get the idea. It sounds like if we can both master our new abilities, we might be a force to be reckoned with!"

"I suppose you could put it that way. I just don't know how long it's going to be before I'm strong enough with my new talent for it to be useful. For all I know, it's going to take years before I can even see 10 feet away from me."

"I bet you'll get there before you know it," Daryn chuckled and began standing up, stretching out his hand to help Angela to her feet as well. "What do you say we check those traps you set yesterday and get some dinner going?"

"That sounds great," she smiled, grateful for the change of subject. It didn't take them long before they'd checked all her snares and found three rabbits and a squirrel. Pulling them out, Angela reset the traps, letting Daryn try his hand at one of them, before heading back towards the meadow, their dinner slung over her shoulder.

Once they got back, she showed Daryn how to skin their catch and which pieces of meat were best for cooking. After they'd stripped off the flesh from two of the rabbits, which they'd use in their stew, she gathered up the remains and took them into the wood. Hopefully, there'd be an owl out there who'd enjoy the free meal. Coming back into the clearing she saw Daryn cleaning off their knives after having finished chopping up the vegetables for their soup. Walking down the hill towards him, Angela smiled and sat down.

"So, how did knife throwing go today?" She prodded. "Did your nap give you any extra insights into the elusive art?"

"Nope. Turns out, knife throwing is a lot like the bow as far as my gift is concerned. So once I figured it out, it was really easy to hit the target." Daryn shrugged, "I kept with it for about an hour before calling it quits. My arms felt like jello and my throws weren't even making it to the stump." He chuckled, twisting his wrists and feeling the muscles further up his arms scream in protest. "I was sitting there wondering what was taking you so long to get the hang of your new ability."

"Oh, I see how it is! He wins a little and suddenly thinks he's a pro. You want to play another game of hide-and-seek out in the woods? See how well your new-found archery and knife throwing skills help you out when you can't even find your target?" She smirked as his grin turned into a scowl.

"Keep it up Ange and I'll throw you into the stream over there." He growled, nodding his head to the brook in front of them.

Holding up her hands placatingly Angela tried to smother her mirth. "Ok, ok, I give. . . Speaking of which, how is it you knew how to dodge my uppercut today in practice?"

His grin instantly returning, Daryn thought back on their fight earlier. "Well, a highborn in the Center doesn't exactly fit in. As I'm sure you can imagine. And my temper didn't handle the insults so well when I first started." He shrugged, his massive shoulders pulling at his shirt, "I didn't know a thing about fighting when I first got there, but I picked it up quick enough. And as you've mentioned, I'm bigger than most of the boys there. And older. It didn't take long before they stopped picking fights with me."

Angela laughed, "Probably not how I would have gone about making friends."

"No, I bet you didn't talk to a single person while you were training. You just blended into the background and watched everyone else, then showed them all up at the games."

"If I'd been able to compete, that's precisely what I would have done," She muttered, looking down at the fire.

Daryn smiled and leaned back on his hands, looking up at the stars. They were silent, both lost in their thoughts. Once the soup was finished, they dished up their helpings and eagerly scarfed them down before heading to bed.

"Hey, Daryn?" Angela whispered once they'd gotten settled.

"No, I'm not completing the bond Ange," He joked, turning over so he could look at her.

Tossing a clump of grass in his direction she glared, "Not what I was going to say, smart-aleck."

Laughing, Daryn wiped the weeds off his blankets, "Ok, what were you going to ask?"

"I was going to say thank you. For helping me... so that I don't have to do this on my own."

Smiling, Daryn laid back on his bedding and looked up at the stars, "Any time".

DESCENT FROM THE PLATEAU

Their days fell into an easy rhythm on the meadow. They'd wake up and have breakfast together. Then Daryn would work on either knives or archery while Angela practiced with her gift. Coming back to camp for lunch they'd move on to their sparring session before practicing tracking and hunting in the Old Wood and returning to camp where she would grill Daryn on different fighting scenarios and how he should react in each given situation as they ate dinner. Sacari was rarely in the meadow when they were and Angela often wondered what it was he was doing all day.

Walking across the glade one afternoon as she was working on her gift, Daryn hesitated. She had her eyes closed, her head cocked to the side as if she was listening to something. Seeing his opportunity to sneak up on her, he began inching forward, careful not to make a sound. As he got closer and she still hadn't moved, a grin teased at his face. Just a mere few strides away he raised his hands, getting ready to grab her.

"You're going to have to do better than that if you're hoping to sneak up on me," She said, not opening her eyes.

"Oh come on," Daryn groaned, lowering his arms and walking around to stand in front of her. "I almost had you that time."

"No you didn't! I was tracking you since the moment you entered the meadow. You were broadcasting your intentions so loudly it flooded out the other animals I was trying to hone in on." She said, snapping her eyes open and glaring at him.

"Is there a way to block that so you can't pick up on me?"

"You'll have to talk to Sacari about that one. I haven't been able to get a single read on him since I started training. When I reach out to try and find him, it's like he's disappeared."

"Wait, your *sight* can't see Sacari? How's that possible?"

"I don't know!" Angela flung up her hands in frustration. "The only thing I can think is that, because he communicates mentally, maybe he also has a way to block mental communication as well."

"So if there's another dragon down there once we get off the plateau, you probably won't be able to pick it up either?"

"That would be my guess. . . I can't help but wonder why Sacari doesn't want me seeing him." She whispered, more to herself than to Daryn. Shrugging the thought away, she got to her feet. "You ready for practice?"

"Are you?" Daryn grinned, flexing his arms and bouncing in place. Over the last week and a half any excess fat he'd had before he'd met Angela had been worked off, leaving dark, well-toned stretching running across his chest and forearms. Many of his shirts now pulled at his shoulders and he'd taken to either wearing ones without sleeves or skipping the shirt altogether. With his added muscle also came additional speed. And as he'd learned while fighting with Angela, it was speed that won a fight, not brawn.

Jogging over to where they normally sparred they both began stretching as tree sprites started drifting out of their trees to watch. Glancing around, she grinned. It was a large crowd today.

"I think they're anxious to see their Wood Lord live up to his name. And I'm anxious to disappoint them. You ready?"

Without answering, Daryn lunged out of his stretch, pausing as he reached her and spinning with his foot out, hoping to catch her midriff as she moved to dodge his attack. Seeing the move for what it was, Angela ducked into a roll, his heel just missing her head, and came up outside his reach. Circling, they eyed each other.

Knowing that her greatest advantage was her speed and staying out of Daryn's arm span, she stayed just beyond his arm's grasp and kicked at his knee caps instead. But after a week of fighting together, Daryn was prepared for the move, spinning to the side just in time to avoid the strike. Utilizing his full weight, he plowed into her, wrapping his arms around her waist and taking her to the ground.

Keeping her pinned, he drew back to punch, but Angela bucked her hips up, encircling her forearm around his supporting wrist and using his momentum to roll them so she was now on top, him on the bottom. Before she could get away, he wrapped his free arm around her head and drove his other into her side. Knowing she wouldn't last long pinned like that, Angela shoved her palm into his chin, forcing his head back and allowing her to slip out of his hold. Twisting, she got loose and jumped back, holding her side.

Leaping to his feet in one fluid motion, Daryn started circling again, wiping blood from his lip where he'd bit it. As he predicted, Angela moved to her left so as to avoid using her right arm in an attack. As she did, she ducked right, bringing her fist down towards his face. It was a powerful swing, with the full force of her body behind it. And Daryn knew from experience how much it would hurt. Leaning back, he let the blow graze him as he spun and leveled a hit into her shoulder.

The contact put Angela off balance, struggling to get out of Daryn's reach. He had indeed gotten stronger and quicker over the past week and her victory in this match was looking less and less likely. Rather than fighting the blow, she allowed her body to follow the momentum of the punch and rolled to the ground. Knowing Daryn would come after her to try to pin her down, she lifted her leg up just in time to connect solidly with his cheek. The kick sent him reeling backward, giving her time to get back on her feet and out of his reach.

Lowering his hand from his face Daryn watched Angela circle away from him. She was smaller, but every bit of her was honed muscle. However, she'd only trained with one person before he had come along - her dad. And judging by what he'd seen of him, Daryn guessed he must have fought a lot like she did. Lots of quick, fast hits in an attempt to wear his opponent down rather than full-on attacks. She liked to dart in, land a blow and then dash back out. Like a cat playing with a mouse.

Well, he was a whole lot bigger than a mouse, and he planned to use it. Coming in cautiously, he circled, both of them focused on what the other was doing. Making her move, Angela dove in and ducked in under his arm, raising her's for an uppercut.

Turning his head to the side so the blow scarcely nicked his cheek, he tucked one leg around behind hers. As her punch went through, he brought his fist under and shoved backward, tripping her over his shin as he followed her to the ground. Pinning both her legs down with his so she couldn't get her hips up to throw him off, he leaned all his weight on his forearms which were wrapped around her's, forcing her arms back in a painful hold.

A grin stole across his face as he looked down at her. She jerked her head up to try and smash his nose, but it caused her wrists to twist painfully under his grip and the attack came up short. Seething, she tried to pull her hands free, but Daryn was too strong. Bucking her hips she sought to roll him, but couldn't get enough momentum with her legs pinned flat.

"Gotcha, little bunny." Daryn grinned. "Do you concede?"

For a minute, Daryn thought maybe she'd keep fighting. The fire in her eyes was promising him a world of pain, but he didn't care. After a few more seconds of struggle with no progress, Angela ground her teeth and glared up at him.

"Fine! Yes, I yield! Now get off me, you big oaf".

"I don't know, I kind of like this position. . ." Daryn laughed as he felt her aggression boil across their bond. "Then again, maybe another time," He chuckled, his gaze lingering on her face, her lips mere inches from his own. But judging by the look in her eyes, she'd be just as likely to bite his tongue off as to return a kiss if he were to risk it. Preferring to keep his mouth intact, he pulled back and let her stand up.

"Man, you're a big one!" She grimaced, rubbing at her wrists.

Chuckling, Daryn sat back on his heels as he raised a hand to his cheek where she'd hit him earlier. His first win. Looking around, he noticed the tree sprites excited talking between themselves in hushed whispers as they moved back towards their trees.

"You know, it'll be nice when I don't have to worry about what the trees are saying about me," Angela muttered, walking over to give Daryn a hand up.

"Well, what's stopping us, Ange?" Daryn asked, taking her hand and getting to his feet. "Your shoulder is healing up well. Well enough that you're able to use a bow again. I think it's strong enough for us to make it down off the plateau. And we might have another couple weeks of travel after that before we even get to Eurcalp."

"I don't know. . ." Angela said, looking down at her hands. Bird song filled in the silence between them before she finally nodded, "Let's do it. We've been here long enough."

"That's my girl!" He beamed, putting his arm around her shoulders as they turned back for camp.

Elbowing him in the ribs she sent him back a step. "Winning one sparring match does not make me your girl, Daryn" she called over her shoulder.

"You want to go another round? I'll be happy to make it two wins if that's what it takes!" He invited, his hands held out at his sides in an invitation. Looking back, she smirked before continuing on to camp. Daryn lowered his arms and grinned, not having expected her to take him up on the challenge anyway.

He knew he should feel apprehensive about leaving the plateau, but as he'd gotten more comfortable with using his abilities this week, and as Angela's range had grown with her's, he couldn't help but feel that maybe it was those below that should be nervous. After all, they had driven out the gifted. If what Sacari said was true, he and Ange would be the only ones down there with any gift at all. And he certainly wouldn't want to be the man standing between Angela and her brother when it came down to it.

When they got back to camp Sacari was waiting for them and Angela filled him in on their plans to leave the plateau the next morning.

After listening to her explanation, he nodded, "I will travel with you down the mountain. But once we get below, I will need to go my own way. My wings are strong enough to allow me to fly now, and I am anxious to see the affairs of the land. And to see if I can find out what became of the dragon I faced... And his stone."

"I understand," Angela said, turning away. Sacari had more than doubled in height since they'd come to the meadow, his head now a good foot or two above Daryn's. His size combined with his black scales made him a fearsome sight to behold and Daryn had looked forward to having him watching their backs once they got off the plateau.

Leaving the two at camp, Sacari moved off into the Old Wood to make his preparations for their departure. *Whatever that means.* Daryn thought. After all, how much could a dragon possibly have to prepare? It's not like he could take anything with him. But deciding not to question him, Daryn and Angela turned to their own supplies.

Working together, they decided to skip their normal afternoon training to get ready to leave. They'd need to wash their clothes in the stream and hang them up to dry, bedding and tarps to be cleaned, and food to be either caught or found.

Once everything was set, they worked to stow it all away in the saddlebags and packs. The sun was high in the sky when Daryn and Angela headed into the Wood to see what kinds of plants and roots they could find to bolster their meals while traveling.

As they walked, chills ran up Daryn's spine. It was a feeling he now associated with the approach of one of the old races. Turning, he found the same pine sprite that had originally welcomed them to the meadow draw near. Touching Angela's shoulder so she'd stop and turn, they both waited for the man to draw closer before exchanging bows.

"I hear you will be leaving our Woods on the morrow," The man said, coming up out of his bow to his full height.

Daryn translated for Angela and then turned back to the sprite, "Yes. Angela's brother is being held captive somewhere down below. We need to move on before it is too late."

"I understand," the man responded before pausing, a pained look crossing his face. "Please remember what we have done for you here when you leave, my friend. Our fellow sprites and many of the other old races are suffering at the hands of the humans," The sprite glanced at Angela before continuing. "I understand that you have other obligations, but I pray that after you have fulfilled your oath to the young lady, that you will turn a kind eye towards your brothers and sisters of the Folk who also need your help."

Once again, the man bowed low, "There is a path down the side of the mountain which we have kept guarded ever since your first parents arrived here. It is not an easy route, but you should be able to take your mount with you if you are careful. If you would like, I can have the guards stationed there begin clearing the way for you?"

"That would be greatly appreciated," Daryn said before whispering what the man had said to Angela, her eyes going wide. "We will not forget your kindness when we leave your Wood," Daryn said, turning back to the sprite. "I do not yet know what my path will be once we reach the lands below, but I can promise that I will not turn a blind eye to the suffering of the old races."

"That is all that we can ask." the man said, raising his hands to his lips. "My people will bring you supplies from the forest for your journey. There will be no need for you to expend your strength in search of food tonight." He said, drawing back and blending into the woods behind him.

"Looks like they are going to bring us food," Daryn said, turning to Angela.

"Wow. There are definitely some perks to having a Wood Lord as a traveling companion! I'm glad I didn't leave you behind back at the caves."

"I am too," Daryn chuckled before his face turned serious once more. "Why do you think your dad sent your brother down below?"

"I don't know," Angela said softly, leaning back against a tree. "It doesn't make any tactical sense. If he was planning on leaving the plateau, you'd think he'd want his best hunter with him. And that would have been me. The thing that worries me more is that he already knew of a place to send Calle. And men who could take him there. Dad must have been down to the lower lands before that night. And if that's the case, what was he doing down there?"

Daryn knelt opposite her and picked up a rock in his hand, spinning it around in his fingers before standing and throwing it off into the wood. "What do you know of your dad? Of his family?"

"Very little. His parents were killed in a fire, and my mom never spoke of who her family was. It was strange - neither of my parents ever mentioned their life before they got married. I really don't know much at all."

"Hmm, is it possible that neither of your parents are from the plateau?" Daryn asked, chancing a glance at Angela. They hadn't discussed personal matters since their first couple days in the meadow, and he wasn't sure how she'd react.

Thinking about it for a time, Angela shook her head. "How would I have my sight if that was the case? According to Sacari, the only people with the gift should live here on the plateau. And mine can only be passed down by blood - so my parents would have had to have been gifted".

"You're right," Daryn sighed. "I'm stumped."

"It doesn't matter," Angela said, shrugging and wiping the bark off her pants, "None of it matters. We've got plenty of questions, but we know the answer to the most important one. My dad has been to the lower lands before. That means he knows a way off the plateau - and I bet it's safe to assume it's a different one than the one the tree sprites are taking us to tomorrow. Which suggests he's going to be down there waiting for us."

The excitement Daryn had been feeling to leave the plateau

vanished, replaced by foreboding. They really didn't have a clue what they were heading into. And abilities or not, there were just two of them.

"Let's head back to the meadow and work on some dinner," Daryn suggested, standing as well. "It sounds like we're going to need our strength tomorrow."

* * *

Raising early the next morning Angela found woven baskets piled high with nuts, fruits, vegetables, and berries left for them as they slept. Crawling over to shake Daryn awake, they worked together to get the new supplies put away, munching on some of the more perishable gifts as they packed.

By the time they got everything loaded, Sacari had joined them by the fire as they waited for the tree sprite that would lead them to the path down the plateau. The three of them were quiet, all lost in their own thoughts. Angela remembered stories her mother would tell of fields covered in wildflowers as far as your eyes could see with large herds of deer and elk that would travel through them. While she didn't know much about her mother's family, she knew that many of the tales her mom had shared with her were passed down from her great grandmother who was a small child when they'd come to the plateau.

Looking out over the meadow, she let her mind drift. The sun wasn't up, but the sky was starting to turn pink in the pre-morning dawn. Mists embraced the valleys and hills, droplets clinging to their clothes and boots. It felt like the glade was holding its breath. Even the birds seemed subdued. Looking over at Daryn, she smiled weakly and he nodded, understanding how she felt. This might be the last time that they'd be home.

Sensing movement, Angela glanced up to find several pine sprites coming out of the treeline towards them. Touching Daryn's arm to let him know it was time to go, they went over to Charger and walked out to meet them. Once they drew close,

Daryn bowed his head, bringing his hand up to his lips in the same show of gratitude they'd seen the head sprite use the previous day. Their leader returned Daryn's bow and motioned for them to follow him into the woods.

Looking back, they gasped as they watched Sacari take a running start and jump into the air, climbing above the treetops and out of sight. Smiling, Daryn put his arm around her and pulled her into a sideways hug as they both took one final glimpse at the meadow that had been their home.

"You ready, Ange?" he asked, looking down at her.

"As ready as I'll ever be." She said, taking a deep breath and squaring her shoulders before turning to follow the sprites into the forest.

The sun's rays sent long fingers between the trees as they came to the edge of the wood. Up ahead the forest dropped away and clouds drifted in its place, giving the illusion that they could step off the plateau and walk through the skies. The sun hadn't risen above the mists yet, turning the sky a deep orange except in some places where small pillars of sunlight had managed to break through the weak points of the clouds into the sky above.

Turning to Angela, Daryn grinned, "I think that counts as a good omen".

"I don't know about that, but it sure is beautiful. . ." She trailed off, noticing the tree sprites gathered further down the cliff face waiting for them. Elbowing Daryn she nodded her head towards the sprites and they reluctantly moved off to join them.

As they got closer, a narrow winding path appeared between the trees, hugging the side of the cliff and shrouded by small shrubs that clung to the mountain, scattered sporadically along the mountainside so as not to draw attention to the trail.

"This is where we will part ways, young master." The head sprite said, coming up to Daryn. "The land below is treacherous and in great turmoil. We have sent messages to our fellow sprites to watch for you. If you get in trouble, they will do their best to help."

Turning to Angela, his eyes grew sad, "Have his back far-seer.

The kingdoms off this plateau harsh, the hearts of the men even harsher still."

"I will," She promised after Daryn had translated what the sprite had said.

"My guards have worked through the night to clear the way for you to go down. We have redirected the roots that would normally catch and trip, retrained branches that could snag, and cleared the larger stones. But as you get closer to the base of the cliff, our reach will lessen. We are not able to travel off the mountain, and so do not know the state of the trail at that point."

"We will be careful, thank you," Daryn said, bowing once more before taking Charger's reins and heading towards the path, Angela leading the way. They'd agreed that she would stay in front to remove any barriers that they might come across, while Daryn's job was to keep Charger from falling off the side of the cliff. All in all, she felt that she was getting the better end of the deal.

Before they reached the path they felt a rush of wind as Sacari dropped down through the trees to land behind them. "The winds up the side of the mountain are too strong for me to navigate," He growled into their minds as he moved in front of Angela. "I will go first so as to reduce the risk of spooking your beast of burden. And if a part of the path gives out, it would be better if it happened with me, rather than one of you."

Not willing to argue, she motioned him on ahead. Stepping onto the path, she carefully made her way forward. The track was about five feet wide in most points which allowed Charger to navigate it without too much trouble, despite the saddle bag's extra width on his back. The problem came when the trail would narrow, or the edges would crumble underfoot. The further down they went, the winds whipped with greater speed along the side of the cliff, grasping at their clothes as if it meant to pull them off.

Hunching their shoulders, the group pushed on, praying the gusts would ease up the further down they got. Rather than a straight path leading down around the mountain as they'd expected, the way had multiple switchbacks in order to reduce its otherwise steep grade. At each end where the path would change directions, they'd hold their breath as Charger would be forced to contour at an impossible angle to keep all four feet on the trail. After the third such switchback, Daryn suggested tying a rope around each of them, just in case one were to fall. But when faced with the challenge of getting around Charger on the narrow cliff in order to reach the cord, the idea was promptly discarded.

The winds made communication during their journey impossible. Thankfully, both Daryn and Angela had decided to carry their own packs, so they were able to eat as they hiked down the mountain without fear of falling off in an attempt to reach Charger's saddlebags. But even still, by noonday Angela had to call a halt so she could rest. The constant decline combined with the battle against the wind had sapped her strength faster than she had expected.

"How far do you think we have left?" Daryn yelled, his voice being whipped away mere inches from his lips.

"I don't know! But I hope we're over halfway... I don't want to have to try and sleep up here tonight." Angela hollered back.

They were in the middle of the clouds now, making it impossible to see more than a few paces in front of them. Rising to her feet once more she nodded that she was ready to go on and started moving. Sacari, having the lowest center of gravity out of the four of them was handling the trip better than the rest. But she knew that if the winds managed to rip his wings away from his sides, there would be little any of them could do to save him. He walked in front of her with his head down low, his body pressed up against the mountain's wall, his steps slow and deliberate, claws digging into the rock beneath their feet.

After several breaks and a few close calls, they eventually broke through the cloud cover and got their first glimpse of the Shurkan plains. As far as the eye could see were waves of rolling hills covered in deep green summer grasses. Splattered throughout the prairies she could make out small groves of trees and forests, thin lines of blue weaving their way through the plains, connecting them. And spread out between these were clusters of what she assumed to be buildings and homes.

"How am I ever going to find Calle in all of that?" She whispered into the wind, still unable to believe the sheer size of the land below them. It made the plateau look minuscule in comparison. On the mountain, she could walk from one side to the other in a day and a half. But from what she could see, she might be able to travel weeks before ever reaching the edge of the plains. And who knew how large the other two nations were! Shaking her head, Angela hurried to catch up to Sacari who hadn't stopped to appreciate the view as she had.

As they drew closer to the base of the mountain the path changed. More and more trees and vegetation began growing along the mountainside as it fanned out, being supported by other smaller mountainous craigs. The trail veered through these lower mountains at a steep angle, no longer doubling back on itself but weaving through the supporting ridges towards the plains, almost as if the path was as anxious as they were to reach solid land.

As the trail moved away from the plateau, it meant that in many places they were traveling along ledges and between towering rock faces where the path dropped off on either side of them, offering no cliff to lean against and no shelter from the raging winds. It was in such a place that Angela's foot fell on a loose stone, causing the trail beneath her to crumble away. Lunging back towards Daryn she leaped as the section of path tumbled down the mountain, scrambling for a handhold. Diving for her, Daryn managed to grab her arm as she began sliding down with the rocks. Straining, he hauled her up until she could get a solid foothold and scramble back onto the path.

Both breathing heavily, Daryn pulled her in close, wrapping his arms protectively around her before looking back at where she had been standing. The path was all but gone leaving only a gaping hole at least four feet wide. He felt confident that he and

Angela could jump across, but could Charger? Sacari stood on the other side of the gap, hissing and snarling against the wind as he looked around to try and find another way past the crevice.

Pulling back from Daryn, Angela turned to survey the damage and groaned. They were at a point where the path bridged the space between two large mountain faces, meaning the only option was to go all the way down one ridge and up the other or to jump the chasm. The sun was already well past noon and they couldn't afford to waste a lot of time here if they didn't want to be sleeping on the mountain tonight. *How are we going to get Charger across this?* She thought, looking around to see if she could find something to span the gap.

"You get across first!" Daryn yelled against the wind. "Sacari will catch you if more of the path crumbles."

Angela stepped back and looked at him, "Are you sure?"

"Yes! Go! The longer we wait here the worse off we are. We need to get off this open stretch and into the mountains."

Nodding, she took a few steps back and sprinted forward, easily spanning the gap and landing on the other side by Sacari. Turning back, she motioned for him to follow. Signaling for her to wait, he turned back to Charger. "You ready to do this boy?"

The massive beast pawed at the ground and pulled against his lead as Daryn turned him around and led him back the way they'd come until they got to a wider part of the path where they turned back towards the gap. Leaning his head against his horse's mane, Daryn took a deep breath. They'd practiced jumps together before, but never one this wide. And never in conditions like this. If Charger were to spook, he could throw Daryn off the side of the mountain. But what choice did they have?

Climbing into the saddle he bent low, rubbing his hand through his horse's mane before urging him into a sprint. Charging down the path, he had trouble seeing the way as the wind from the mountain whipped around him and pulled tears from his eyes. Reaching the area where the trail had fallen away he yelled, digging his thighs into Charger's sides. Not hesitating, Charger sprung forward, flying across the gap and landing on the other side, struggling to find purchase for his hind legs as the cliff began to give way under them.

"Come on, you can do this!" Daryn called, urging him on. After a breathless moment, Charger found a solid lip with his back hoof and clamored further onto the path and away from danger. Dragging breath into his lungs, Daryn climbed down from Charger's back and patted his side as he tried to slow his raising heart.

"That's my boy," He whispered, leading him forward to where Angela and Sacari were waiting.

"You're insane, you know that?" Angela hissed as he drew near, giving him a fierce hug before turning back to the trail.

As they made their way into the low mountains surrounding the base of the plateau the wind died down and they were able to communicate without yelling once more. Vegetation started growing in earnest in these kinder conditions and they found themselves sometimes struggling to see the path. If it weren't for Angela's experience in tracking, there were several points where Daryn was sure they would have been lost.

Descending closer to the plains the air hung about them like a thick, wet blanket, causing sweat to soak through their clothes. On top of the plateau, they'd never experienced such heat. Even their summers were mild enough that most of the members of their community would still wear shirts that covered their arms. But the group swiftly realized their mistake in assuming seasons in the land below would be the same as they were used to.

As they walked, they began stripping off layers until Daryn was traveling shirtless, and Angela was down to a lightweight sleeveless top. Sweat dripped from their faces and into their eyes as they struggled to conserve water until they could find a stream to refill their containers. Seeing a gap in the trees ahead, they pushed forward, hopeful that it would lead to a brook. But as they ducked out under the branches, Angela's breath caught in her throat.

Before them as far as the eye could see were the Shurkan plains.

The sun had just begun to set and all around them, it looked as if the sky had fallen to the earth as fireflies lit up the night.

ENEMIES OF THE KING

Taking to the skies, it wasn't long before Sacari found a stream winding its way out of the mountains and they were able to set up camp for the night. Waking before dawn the next morning Angela snuck out to find a low hill not far from their campsite. Crossing her legs she waited, watching as the sky gradually turned pink and the first rays of the sun peaked into the horizon. The plains weren't flat as she'd thought they'd be, but looked more like a rolling sea of green, the sun's light skittering across the tops of the hills.

"It's beautiful, isn't it?" Sacari asked, coming up to sit beside her.

"I've never seen anything like it," Angela whispered in awe, not taking her eyes off the sunrise. "On the plateau, we don't see the sun until it's already risen into the sky. I've never seen the sky change colors like this."

"There are many things down here that will be different than on the mountain. I love this land. The creatures, the warmth, the beauty. And it makes my heart ache to think of what it's become."

Pulling her gaze away from the rising sun, Angela glanced at Sacari, "What will you do now that you're back home?"

"I need to find out what's happened to the old races. I also need to find the incarnate stone from the dragon that defeated me. If I can prevent it from hatching, I can save this world from a great evil."

"Would you mind helping us with one last thing before you go?"

"What do you need, young one?" Sacari questioned, craning his head to look at her.

"Would you fly ahead and find the nearest town so we'll know which direction we need to start heading? With no map, we could wander through the plains for weeks without finding anyone." Turning back to watch the horizon Angela added, "Even in my wildest dreams I'd never imagined it being this large."

"I think, considering you could have killed me the day that I hatched and you held your hand, I can spare a few hours of flight to help point you in the right direction." Sacari said, standing to his feet and walking a little ways from Angela. Looking to the sky, he unfurled his large wings and leapt up. A great shadow rising into the pre-dawn light.

After watching until she could no longer see him, she reluctantly rose to her feet and headed back to camp to join Daryn. Eating breakfast, they didn't have to wait long before Sacari returned and informed them that they'd need to head due west where they'd find a town about a week's travel from them.

Once they'd said their goodbyes, Angela and Daryn watched as Sacari flew East, disappearing into the light of the rising sun. Turning back towards camp, they worked to get their supplies packed up and started moving once more, keeping the sun to their backs. The grasses came up to their waist in some places, making travel slow and arduous. Daryn could feel Angela's mood worsen as the hours went by and the reality of the task before them began to sink in. By the time they stopped for lunch, both of them were exhausted.

"At least we don't have to worry about finding food for Charger while we're out here," Daryn chuckled, watching the horse graze contentedly before moving to get their own meal out of the saddlebags and coming back to sit by Angela. "Do you think there are any Old Races that live in the plains? Kind of like the tree sprites that inhabit in the Old Wood?"

"I have no idea," Angela said, looking around them. "But I do know this one wood lord that could probably find out".

"Find me a member of the other races and I'll ask," Daryn laughed, looking around at the obviously deserted plains. "I've got to admit, I kind of expected there to be more... people once we got down here."

"I know what you mean. Do you think they just didn't want to settle by the mountain, or do you think all the cities will be this spread apart?"

"No clue, but I'm hoping they just didn't want to live by Heaven's Rock. Otherwise it might take us months to find Eurcalp." Hastily biting his tongue, Daryn looked down at his food. *I can't seem to say anything right,* he sighed inwardly. Ever since they'd started their trek down the cliff she'd been quiet and withdrawn. The lightness he'd felt from her while they'd been training on the plateau was all but gone.

"Okay, that's it" He said, swallowing his last bite of food and standing up. "Get up, we're sparring."

"Not now Daryn. We've got a long way ahead of us and I'm tired enough as it is just by walking through this grass," she moaned, motioning to the plains around them.

"Coward," He spat out, crossing his arms and glaring at her.

"I'm not being a coward, I'm being practical!"

"You haven't fought me since I won back at the meadow. You're either scared, or weak. Either way, you need the practice."

Raising to her feet, Angela glared at him, some of the fire coming back into her eyes. Grinning, Daryn took a step back as he waited to see if she'd rise to the bait. Turning back to Charger to put away her food, she spun in mid stride, dropping the bread and lunging towards him. Ducking out of the way he landed a weak punch in her ribs before once again getting out of the way.

"How are you going to save your brother fighting like that?" he taunted.

Yelling, Angela whirled out of her charge and swung her leg up high, her heel grazing him in the jaw before he was able to get his head out of the way. Stumbling back, he swiftly brought his hands up.

"That ego of yours is going to get you hurt one of these days," she snarled. Coming in hard, she sent her fist in towards his head. Knocking her arm aside, he stepped back. Bending and blocking the blows he let her come at him, biding his time. Letting her vent. After a good half hour of sparring, Angela called a halt, collapsing on the ground, panting.

"Thank you for that," she said once her breathing slowed, accepting his offered hand and rising to her feet.

"Anytime. You ready to keep going?"

"Just waiting on you," she smiled, moving around him to head westwards once more.

"You know, maybe I should have let you stay mopey and quiet." He joked, coming up to walk next to her.

"Eh, you missed me. Admit it,"

Looking over at her, his face turned serious, "I did. You're all I've got out here, Ange. You can't just withdraw like that, we can't afford it."

"I know, and I'm sorry." She said, looking down at the ground. "I've never had someone to lean on when I'm in a tight spot. I don't have a lot of practice at it".

"Well, it's a good thing we've got plenty of time to work on it then".

The rest of the day went by swiftly as they discussed their upcoming plans, the new lands around them, and stories from their years growing up. By the time they stopped to make camp both of them were feeling better about what lay before them. Sure, they didn't know the land or the people, but they weren't going at it alone.

✻ ✻ ✻

Each morning as they travelled they'd wake up before the sun had risen and pack up their supplies. When they'd stop for lunch, Angela would train with her sight while Daryn either explored or participated as a practice dummy. Once they were rested, they'd hike until it was nearing sunset and set up camp before sparring together and having dinner. By day five, they'd gone through most of the food the sprites had brought them and were having to rely on the small animals she was able to find with her sight and bring down.

It didn't take her long to pass the hunting responsibility to Daryn though, claiming that it was good practice. Once they learned how to work together, Angela would search out the game and then use hand signals to direct Daryn towards them. It took him several tries before he figured out how to hit a moving target, but once he did, the hunt became easy. The challenge was understanding where she wanted him to go in order to find the prey in the first place.

By day six on the plains, they came across a narrow dirt path leading west and were grateful for the break it provided from having to wade through the tall grasses of the prairies. It didn't take long after that for them to start seeing large farms covering the hillsides around them. Wheat, barley, corn, beans. There was almost every type of produce being grown, and it was in quantities Angela had never imagined possible. How big must this town be in order to require estates at this scale to support it?!

As they got closer to their destination, the farms began getting smaller and the crops changed from grains to vegetables and fruits. Daryn's stomach growled as they walked through the aisles of fruit and Angela's rumbled in response. She was just as hungry and would have offered to buy some food from the villagers, but everyone they saw in the fields would duck their heads to avoid her gaze. For a town so clearly prosperous, why were the people so skittish?

Pausing as some of the first buildings came into sight, Angela stretched out her mind. Something just didn't seem right. The village didn't have any walls around it and all the houses looked to be in desperate need of repair. Why? With all the food that their fields were producing, these people should be wealthy and living well.

As her mind touched on the first farmer, his concern for his family washed into her. His inability to put enough food on the table for his four children weighed on him. His anxiety for the safety of his wife and his distrust of the strangers on the road was evident. Spreading her mind out, she picked up similar thoughts in the other farmers within her reach.

Opening her eyes, she looked over at Daryn, her brows drawn low in a scowl.

"What is it? What did you find out?"

"I'm not sure," she said cautiously, looking around. "But something isn't right. These farmers... they are all worried whether or not they'll be able to put food on the table. They fear for their safety, and that of their families. But with what we can see of their fields, that doesn't make any sense."

"Not unless it's because of them," Daryn said, his face drawing into a glare as he watched two men in black, loose fitting uniforms entire a home up ahead. "Can you get a read on them?"

Closing her eyes, Angela reached out in the direction of the home. It was at the edge of her range, so she couldn't pick up on their thoughts, but she could clearly see the women and children in the home cowering away from the men. Snapping her eyes open Angela's hands clenched into fists.

"You were right. I couldn't find out what they were thinking or why they were there, but these people are definitely afraid of them. I just don't know if we can get involved before we get directions and find some more supplies. We have no idea how many of those guys are in this town."

"Best to lay low then. Is there a way for you to hide your knives? I'll do the same with my bow." Nodding, Angela tucked a knife in each boot before hiding the other two in a saddle bag.

"I don't like this Daryn," She whispered as they started making their way into the town once more.

Looking down at her Daryn watched how she moved, scanning the streets around her. Any experienced fighter would know in a second that she was one too. Sighing, Daryn turned his gaze outward and noticed several of the farmers watching them as they passed. It didn't take long before he saw why. Every horse out in the fields looked half starved and about to collapse. Charger, on the other hand was well fed, well rested, and a magnificent specimen of his breed. Nothing like the plow horses these villagers must be used to.

"Angela, could you try and find someone around us that we could leave Charger with? Maybe someone who could use the extra coin we'd pay for the service? He's drawing too much attention."

Closing her eyes, Angela scanned the people around them. Everyone she touched needed the silver, but judging by their fear and distrust of them, she doubted they'd watch over their horse. At last she touched on a man in a field separated from the others who didn't seem afraid of them. Motioning to Daryn she pointed towards the farm she'd found.

Making their way through the narrow dirt streets they turned a corner as the man's home came into view, the farmer himself coming around the side of his barn to watch them approach.

"What brings you to my home?" He asked, his tone anything but friendly.

"We are looking for someone to board our horse for the day while we gather supplies in town," Angela said, moving towards him with her arms raised. "We mean you no harm and are willing to pay you for the service."

Studying Angela and Daryn for a few minutes, the man motioned them into the barn, "Eh, you can leave him here for the afternoon. I'll put him in one of the extra sheep stalls so he can't get into any trouble."

"Thank you," Daryn said, coming forward and handing him a silver piece. Glancing down at the coin the man raised an eyebrow, taking in their dirty clothes and travel worn appearance. "I expect to find him in the same condition and the same stall when we come back, or I will take back that silver. With or without your consent," Daryn growled.

"I catch yer meaning young sir," The man said, unfazed by the thinly veiled threat. "Yer horse will be right here when ye return."

Nodding their thanks, they both turned to leave, feeling the man's gaze on their backs as they left.

"Are you sure he was the best option?" Daryn whispered once they were out of earshot.

"He was the only one I could find that wasn't afraid of us."

"At this point, I'd feel more comfortable if he were afraid. It'd keep him from pawning Charger off to someone else and making a small fortune."

Looking over at Daryn, Angela chuckled, "If we managed to tame the old wood, get down the plateau and are now planning to find my brother in a town we don't even know the location of, I think we can find your horse and get him back."

"Fair point," Daryn grumbled, the scowl still not leaving his face.

Stopping a woman in the street Angela got directions to a tavern where they could get some supplies and a hot meal. Making their way in the direction the woman pointed to, they came to one of the few buildings that didn't look like it was about to fall down. Stepping inside they saw that it was mostly empty with just a couple locals scattered through the main room. Finding a table off to the side, they waited for the owner to finish talking and come over.

"What can I get for you folks?" He asked cheerfully, smiling down at them. He was a portly fellow with bright red cheeks and food stains smeared across the white apron he wore. Taken aback by his friendly demeanor, Angela stumbled over her words, asking for water, soup, and some bread. Daryn echoed her request and the man moved back behind the bar at the front of the room and into the kitchens behind it.

"Was it just me, or was that man actually smiling?" She joked, looking back over her shoulder at where the man had gone. But Daryn wasn't listening, his eyes fastened on four newcomers to the building, all dressed in black. Following his gaze, Angela's hardened and she looked down at the table so they wouldn't see.

Closing her eyes, she reached out towards them, easily picking them out from the locals. Their thoughts were confident and strong, going over their latest accomplishments. Learning what the men had just come from doing, Angela's blood started to boil. Opening her eyes, she glared down at the table, hands balled into fists as she attempted to control her urge to get up and start a fight.

"What'd you see?" Daryn whispered carefully, leaning towards her before pulling back as a barmaid bustled by and deposited their food and drinks on the table between them.

"I found out why the women and children are so afraid of those men," Angela ground out, the muscle in her jaw jumping as she clenched her teeth. "Let's just say the men in uniform enjoy amusing themselves with the local's wives and daughters during their spare time."

Looking around them, Daryn reached across the table and put his hand on her's, "Hey, look, you've got to calm down. People are starting to notice" he whispered.

"Did you hear what I just said?" Angela hissed, but managed to unclench her hand and take a bite of her stew.

"Yea, I did. But like you said, we can't pick any fights until we get supplies and directions. And especially not till we find out who those men are and how many of them are here."

"Fine," she growled, watching the men in uniform out of the corner of her eye as they ate. Once Angela and Daryn had finished their meal, the same man that'd greeted them came back to take their plates.

"Is there anything else I can get for you?" He asked as he stacked their bowls and moved them to another table.

"We've been traveling a long way and have depleted our food supplies. Could we purchase some from you to restock?" Daryn asked, putting a silver piece in the man's hand. Swiftly tucking the coin into his apron the man beamed.

"Of course, of course! Give me just a moment and I'll be back with what you'll be needing." bustling back towards the kitchen the man deposited their dishes with the barmaid before ducking out of view.

Talking quietly amongst themselves they didn't have to wait long before he reappeared with several loaves of bread, cheese, meats and dried fruits.

"I hope this will work for ya," he said, setting the food on the table and wiping his hands on his apron.

"This will be great, thank you," Daryn said, tucking the supplies into his pack.

"You all in town for the matches?" the man asked, eyeing them.

"Matches?" Daryn questioned, looking up from his bag.

"Yea! Been having soldiers such as yourselves flooding into the city to watch 'em. You should check them out while you're here, they're just on the north side of town in one of the farmer's corrals."

Angela and Daryn exchanged a look before Daryn turned back to the man, "Thanks for the advice, maybe we'll swing by there on our way. But I do have one more thing I could use your help with before you go".

"Sure, what can I do for you?"

"Could you give me directions to Eurcalp?" Daryn asked, surprised to see the smile slip from the man's face as if it had never been there. Wiping his hands on his apron nervously, the man looked around to make sure no one had heard.

"Now you know us locals don't know nothing about the location of the king's bases. I don't know what you're trying to pull, but I think you'd best leave now."

Turning before Daryn could say another word, the man hurried back into the kitchen.

"King's bases?" Angela hissed in surprise, watching the men in uniform out of the corner of her eye. "The men over there must be the king's soldiers."

"Yea, and it sounds like there's a lot of them, so let's not go picking any fights." Daryn said, slinging his pack over his shoulder before standing up, waiting for Angela to follow suit before ducking out of the building.

"Ok, no fights," she whispered, coming up beside him. "But I do want to see what these matches are the man mentioned".

"Fine, but then we get out of here. We've got our supplies, and it's safe to say no one in town is going to help us with directions. It would appear that our comparatively nice clothing has made the locals believe we're with the king. We need to be moving on."

"Agreed," Angela said, turning down a street that would take them north. The further they walked, the more soldiers they saw. Most of them carried long blades half the length of their body across their backs. She had never seen weapons like them and couldn't think of a single use for them except in the fighting ring. Thinking back on her lessons with her dad she tried to remember what he had called them.

Keeping their gazes down, they tried their best to avoid the men as they made their way towards the edge of town. Yells and cheers from a group of soldiers gathered in a loose circle around a pen drew their attention. Working their way through the crowd, Angela's breath caught. Inside the fence were two wolvrons, easily large enough for their backs to be even with her shoulders. They were covered in long, blood red scratches and scars, chained together with iron links just long enough to tangle each other up, but not long enough for them to get to opposite sides of the corral. In the pen with them were four men, weapons drawn, taunting them.

As they'd lunge at one of the men, another one would come up behind them and swing at their backs. Unable to split up, the wolvrons couldn't defend themselves. No matter where they turned, there was a man ready to protect his companion and attack them. Putting her hand on Daryn's arm, she felt his muscles tense and flex, his hands clenched at his side. His eyes were riveted on the match, anger etched in every line of his face. Turning back to the fight she saw one of the wolvrons pause in its attack and turned to look straight at Daryn before throwing back its head and howling into the sky.

Grabbing Daryn's arm, Angela drug him back through the crowd before anyone could notice, waiting until they were out of earshot to speak.

"I'm getting them out of there," Daryn growled before she could say a word, never taking his eyes from the pen. "They're just pups, barely a year old Ange." Grinding his teeth, Daryn slammed his fist into his thigh. "How could they do such a thing? And just for the sport of it! They're monsters!"

"Daryn, I hear you, but we can't take on all those men! Did you see how many were watching the fight?! We need to get out of here and find another town that's not crawling with soldiers."

"I'm not leaving them." Daryn said, turning his glare on her. "I saved you when you were hurt with nowhere to go. I won't turn my back on them, either. And if you're willing to, then you're not the woman I thought you were."

Holding his gaze as long as she could, Angela was forced to lower her eyes to the ground. He was right, they couldn't just leave them.

"Fine!" She said, throwing up her hands in defeat. "What's your plan? Just run in there and break their chains with your bare hands and slay the twenty some odd soldiers watching the match right now? Without a weapon?"

Grinning Daryn glanced back at the corral, "Something like that".

"Great, well I'm glad we at least have a well thought out plan. That makes me feel much better." Angela grumbled, following him back towards the pen.

"You see that wheat field over there?" Daryn whispered, nodding his head past the pen to a farm about a mile from where they stood.

"Yea,"

"I'm going to go into the ring next to fight. I'll get their collars off, you find a way to get the slats off a section of the corral. Then we make our way to that field. The wolvrons will help us clear a path, and hopefully we can lose the soldiers once we get to the wheat. We'll at least get them to split up so we can pick them off one at a time instead of all together."

Casually looking around the arena Angela scanned the men in uniform, trying to judge their skill level. Most were young, and many of them looked to be half drunk. But they all carried those long blades. Even if they had never been in a fight in their lives, that blade could do some damage. And Daryn didn't have a weapon.

"Okay, let's say I agree to your crazy plan. What are you going to fight with?"

"Give me one of your knives. I'll use that until we get out of the ring. Once you get one of the poles free from the pen, throw it in. They look a little shorter than I am tall, and small enough around for me to grip. I should be able to hold off their blades with that." Bending over, Angela slipped the knife from her boot and handed it to Daryn.

"There are so many ways for this to go badly," she murmured, moving off to a side of the ring roughly facing the wheat field where there weren't as many people watching. As she got into position, Daryn made his way through the crowd and stopped to talk to a soldier by the gate. Laughing, the man slapped Daryn on the back before whistling to the four men in the pen. Climbing through the bars of the corral, they went around to where Daryn stood, listening as the man no doubt explained Daryn's desire to face the wolvrons on his own.

Joining in the man's laughter, the men nodded and moved back into the crowd as the man started announcing the next contender. Looking down at the pen, Angela studied the panels. The wood poles had been lashed to the larger vertical posts with thick ropes, impossible to untie by hand. Pulling out her last remaining knife, she leaned up against the post and brought her dagger up behind her to start sawing at the cords, leaving a small strand intact so the beam wouldn't fall till they were ready.

Finishing with the lashings on one side, she hurried to move to the other end of the poles and began sawing as Daryn walked into the ring, circling on the edge and eyeing the two wolvrons. Catching his eye, she nodded, letting him know she was ready. Faster than she would have thought possible had she not spent the past week sparing with him, Daryn changed direction and lunged at the wolvrons, coming up under one and slicing through the leather band that held it chained to its companion.

By the time the crowd realized what he had done, he had already freed the second wolvron and gotten to his feet. Angela finished cutting through the lashings and threw a pole into the pen for Daryn before turning as she felt the wind from a blade swinging towards her head. Ducking, she rolled forward and brought her foot up into the man's stomach before spinning out of the way and bringing her knife's hilt into contact with the side of the soldier's head, knocking him out as she turned to face the next contender.

"Here's your chance! Let's show these savages what true strength is," Daryn yelled, turning from the now free wolvrons to the open gate. Men were flooding over the walls of the ring and he knew if they didn't hurry, they'd be trapped. Sprinting to where Angela was defending the opening he picked up the pole she'd thrown in and twirled it overhead, bringing the end in contact with a man who'd gotten too close. As he did, the two pups charged past him to the gate to help Angela who was desperately trying to hold off four attackers.

Tearing through the men, the wolvrons paused, waiting for Daryn to join them before the group took off at a sprint towards the wheat fields up ahead. Daryn blessed their luck as it became obvious that no one in the ring had brought a bow to the matches and they were able to make it to the fields shortly before the king's men managed to catch up. Splitting up, they weaved their way through the stalks, grateful that it was close to harvest and already taller than they were. Kneeling down, Angela put her hand on the ground and closed her eyes, stretching out her mind.

Picking up on the wolvrons, which were staying to either side of Daryn; no doubt hoping to protect him, she moved on. All around them were the king's men. She counted at least a dozen before giving up and opening her eyes, moving in their direction. Keeping low and silent, she slipped through the wheat like a ghost, using her gift to find the soldiers and take them out one by one. She guessed she might have gotten about half of them when she heard a man yell in shock, his call cut off by a snarl. Another man down.

Making her way towards Daryn, she started seeing men scattered through the field, either dead or dying. It looked like Daryn had been busy hunting as well. Hearing fighting up ahead, she found him using his staff as a shield, trading and blocking blows from another man wielding a sword. Moving as a blur, it was hard to tell where the staff ended and Daryn began. He was every bit as large as the man he was facing and looked as if he'd trained for this his entire life, spinning and dodging hits, creating openings to land his own. Watching him, Angela started to understand the value the old races placed on Wood Lords. She'd never seen someone able to move so quick, and the righteous anger behind his attacks meant that even as skilled as his opponent was, he didn't stand a chance.

In less than a minute, the match was over and Angela came up to him and put a hand on his shoulder, "I think we've got them all."

Breathing heavily, he scanned the area around them before turning back to her, "Can you make sure?"

Lowering her head, Angela reached out through the fields as far as she could, but all she was able to find were the wolvrons. Looking back up at Daryn she nodded.

Whistling to the pups, they made their way towards the edge of the field. The sun had begun setting by the time the fighting ended and they decided to find a good spot to wait till true night fell before heading back to town and retrieving Charger. Emerging from the wheat they turned to see the wolvrons exit on either side of them. Keeping to the edge of the fields, they made their way around the outskirts of the village until they came to a small grove of trees bordering a large pond. Ducking under the protection of their branches, they knelt down to wait.

The branches offered a defense from prying eyes, but also allowed them to see anyone approaching them. It was a good spot to hold up until night set in and it allowed them a little more cover before going any closer towards town.

"Thank you, young Wood Lord," One of the wolvrons said, coming up to stand by Daryn. "We know that you risked much to set us free and will make sure your sacrifice is known among our kind."

"Will you be able to make it back to your pack?" Daryn asked, eyeing the many wounds they'd sustained, both during the escape and in the ring.

"We will be fine," the other said proudly as she came to stand beside her brother. "We are stronger than the humans think. And you have granted us the blessed taste of revenge, which will sustain us on our journey back."

"It was an honor to fight at your sides," Daryn said, bowing his head. "You made your pack proud this day. Do you know where they will be?"

"They would not have gone far, we will be able to find them with ease." The male said, looking over at his companion. "Shall we run, little sister?"

Snarling, the female let out a howl before they turned and took off into the night.

"What was that all about?" Angela asked, coming to stand beside Daryn.

"They were brother and sister," he whispered, watching them disappear before turning to look at her. "Thank you for helping me free them".

"I'm glad that we were able to get them out," she responded, her eyes following the direction the wolves had taken. "I just pray that I will have the chance to fight by my brother's side one day and save him as well."

Daryn rested a hand on her arm, "You will,".

It was another hour or so after the wolvrons had left before it was finally dark enough for Daryn and Angela to feel comfortable leaving the wood and making their way towards the farmer boarding their horse. The streets were empty as they made their way through the farms, turning on the lane that would lead to the man's home. The plan was to sneak in and get Charger without anyone being the wiser, but they pulled up short as they came to the barn and saw the farmer leaning against the door, watching for them.

Motioning them inside, he closed the door behind them before lighting up an oil lamp and hanging it by the door, turning back to look at them, "So ye aren't with the king then, eh?"

"No, we're not with the king," Daryn growled, bringing the staff out to his side in case the man decided to attack.

"From what I hear, you took out almost thirty of them. Though they think there may still be more in the fields that they missed. Right mess, there. Too much attention. They'll be hunting you from here to Sheek by the end of the week."

"Unless you have some useful information for us, we'll take the horse and be on our way," Angela retorted, tired of the man's patronizing tone.

Chuckling, he turned to take in Angela for the first time since they'd arrived. "The rumors mentioned a man that fought like a beast. They didn't mention a woman."

"That's because the only men who saw me won't be telling anyone about it," she growled threateningly.

"I don't doubt it," the man said, inclining his head before turning back to Daryn, "I heard you were asking about the location of a king's base? Eurcalp, I think it was?" He waited until Daryn nodded before going on. "You'll want to find the rebel's camp. They're the only ones who will speak of such things, and they are the ones who will have the most up to date information on where the king's men are stationed."

"How do you know this? And why are you telling us?" Daryn asked cautiously.

"Let's just say that I have no love for the king, or the man he's put in charge of this land. You clearly have no regard for the Commander either, so I don't feel I'll be risking the rebel's safety by sharing directions with you. Besides, I owe you. The silver you gave me is a month's wages, much more than an afternoon of boarding is worth."

"The Commander?" Angela questioned, moving towards the man so she could see his face better.

Giving her a strange look, the man ignored her question and turned back to Daryn. "You'll want to ride south until you hit a large wood. Once you see it, follow the border for two days, then turn west into it. The camp's hard to find, but I'm guessing that won't be much of a problem for you."

"Thank you for your help," Daryn said, turning towards Charger's stall.

"Don't thank me yet." The man chuckled. "The rebels don't take too kindly to strangers stumbling into their camp. Just as likely to kill a local as they are a soldier. You'd best be on your toes, or you won't get the chance to die in Eurcalp."

"Well he's a cheery fellow," Angela said dryly as they watched him leave the barn.

"Let's just get out of here and find these rebels." Daryn growled.

After checking Charger over to make sure he hadn't been injured, they transferred their newly acquired food supplies into his saddlebags and moved back out under the stars, heading south towards the rebel's woods.

THE LOST BATTLE
OF SHEEK

After another week of travel Angela and Daryn arrived at the point in the path where the man had said would them lead to the rebel camp. During their travels they'd come across very few people using the roads, and had often ducked off to the sides to avoid being seen by soldiers passing by, neither willing to risk being seen after what had happened in the previous town.

Stepping off the path and into the woods Angela breathed in a sigh of relief as the cool shade offered shelter from the sweltering heat they'd been traveling under. The forest looked much like the ones back home, full of towering oak trees, the ground littered with small brush and fallen leaves. Putting her hand on Charger's side to steady herself, Angela let her mind spread out, but didn't pick up on anyone else in the wood besides themselves. Shrugging her shoulders to Daryn, they started making their way deeper in.

Every mile or so Daryn would have them pause so Angela could scout ahead. But it wasn't until they'd gone about five miles in that she picked up on the first signs of a camp. Motioning to Daryn, she pointed out where three sentries were stationed, high up in the trees just out of sight. Scanning the surrounding forest, they retraced their steps and found a good place to leave Charger before turning back towards the encampment.

Following Angela's lead, Daryn waited until she signaled that a guard was looking the other direction before sprinting ahead to join her. Their weeks of training began paying off as they were able to make their way silently past the guards and towards the rebel's tents. Hiding their weapons except for Daryn's staff, which he used as a walking stick, their plan was to get in without being noticed and split up to find someone who could give them directions.

Splitting off from Daryn before they reached the compound, Angela sneaked between the tents trying to get to a heavily populated area so she could search more of the minds at once. Maybe at least one of them would be talking about the enemy bases and she could pick up directions without having to explain her presence to anyone.

"Hey, woman, what are you doing here?!" A man boomed, coming out from one of the tents ahead of her. Quickly deciding against a fight, Angela cowered back, attempting to act the part of a scared young woman.

"I... I'm sorry. I'm lost. My brother and I, we got separated in the woods. I was just trying to find him." She stuttered, looking around her as if she was searching the tents for her missing sibling.

"What were you doing in these parts to begin with?" The man questioned, crossing his arms over his chest and glaring at her. "And how did you sneak past the sentries?"

"S...sentries? What sentries? You're the first person I've seen." She quivered.

"Hmmm, something doesn't seem right. Come with me," he said, roughly grabbing her arm and leading her deeper into camp.

"Where are you taking me? I didn't do anything!"

"Mitch!" he called to a man ahead of them, ignoring her pleas. "Where's Chief?"

"He's on up that way," the man said, pointing off to their right, watching Angela with open curiosity.

"Thanks," her captor growled, dragging her in the direction the man had pointed until they came upon a group of twelve or so men making their way through camp, a large man walking in the middle of the crowd.

"Chief Duroc!" The man hollered, throwing Angela to the ground in front of the men. "She claims she's lost, looking for her brother."

Keeping her head down, she felt a shadow fall over her as a man came to stand before her, blocking out the light that filtered through the trees. She could feel men gathering around to watch the scene and knew she was in trouble. There'd be no fighting her way out now.

"That.... That's right, sir. My brother and I, we're orphans you see? We were in the woods looking for nuts and berries. We were hungry" She said, careful to keep her head down.

"And how did you come to be out this way? There aren't any towns near these parts." The man Angela assumed was the Chief asked menacingly.

"We were... were supposed to meet some relatives at a town close to Eurcalp. We were on our way there and got lost," She whispered, praying they were at least somewhere close to the base and that she might be able to get a hint towards where they needed to go.

"Hmmm, you're heading to Sheek then?" Duroc asked, softening his tone and bending down in front of her. Not wanting to risk giving something away, Angela kept her eyes down and merely nodded.

"Your brother's not here." The chief said after a brief pause, reaching a decision and standing to his feet. "Sheek is another three days to the southeast from here." Speaking to the man who'd brought her through camp he added, "Blindfold her and take her to the edge of base beyond the sentries. If she is ever seen back here, kill her."

"Yes, sir!" The man said, harshly grabbing her arm and wrapping a cloth that smelled like body odor over her eyes before dragging her back through the tents. Not wanting to risk going limp while scanning for Daryn she just had to hope that her meeting with the Chief had caused enough of a stir that Daryn would realize where she went and come find her.

After what seemed an eternity, the man eventually took the

rag off Angela's face and let go of her arm. Rubbing it where he'd held her, she glared at him. But he just sneered back at her before turning and walking into the woods. Trying to get her bearings, Angela looked around. None of the wood was familiar, though that wasn't much of a surprise.

Closing her eyes, she stretched out her mind, barely picking up the sentries at the edge of her vision. Giving them a wide berth, she started making her way around the camp until she was able to find Charger. Leaning back against the tree, she waited until she saw Daryn quietly weaving his way through the branches towards her.

"Did you have any luck?" He asked, drawing up next to her.

"You didn't hear? I got to meet with the chief. And by meet, I mean thrown to the ground at his feet, the rebels gathered around to watch."

"Hmmm I didn't hear about any fights, how'd you get out of that one?"

"Convinced him I was a poor orphan girl, lost in the woods." Angela laughed. "But I did find out the closest town to Eurcalp is Sheek, which is three days southeast of here."

"Ha, not bad!" Daryn said, untying Charger from his tree and turning him the right direction. "I was able to find out who the Commander is, along with the same directions to Sheek"

"Oh? Do tell!"

"He's the king's appointed head of state for Shurka. Basically the Arachian's idea of their ruler. He's in charge here, and rules with an iron hand. It sounds like the rebel chief has been hunting the man for a long time, but he moves around a lot, so he's never been able to pin him down."

"Hmmm, and how did you find this out?"

"Apparently there are wanted posters up for me in all the towns around the area. One of the guys in camp recognized me right off and brought me over to chat. They were really helpful, though they couldn't tell me much about Eurcalp itself besides that it's guarded by large walls which have never been breached." Ducking below a branch, Daryn glanced over at

Angela. "I'm just glad we can put the camp behind us. Sheek in three days and then Eurcalp from there. I don't want to get our hopes up, but we might actually make it back to the plateau before fall sets in." Lost in her thoughts, she didn't respond. Finding Eurcalp was great, but it didn't do them much good if they couldn't get in it.

* * *

Over the next several days of travel they continued to train while spending most of the walking time exploring different options for getting into Eurcalp undetected. But no matter how many plans they came up with, they always came back to the same thing: they needed more information on the base itself.

By the time they could see the walls of Sheek, they had decided that it was worth the risk to go inside and see what Angela could discover about Eurcalp with her gift. They'd leave Charger outside the city in a sheltered area far from the road where it was unlikely someone would happen upon him. Entering the town at noon day when it'd be the most crowded they'd try to find out as much as they could about the base before leaving once more and setting up camp outside the walls.

Sheek was a lot larger than the first town they'd entered, easily ten times the size from what Angela could see. So hopefully it would be easier to blend into the crowd and get around unnoticed. Once more hiding their weapons, except for Daryn's staff which he refused to leave behind, they fell in with a caravan heading towards the city's gates. Walking through the large opening, Angela looked around in awe.

From the opening, cobbled paths led off in every direction, like streams breaking off from the main tide. Brick and stone buildings crowded the pathways making it impossible to see more than a couple feet ahead of you at any given time. Swiftly moving onto one of the more densely populated streets they followed the crowd as it moved towards a large square in the center of town. The noise in the plaza was deafening as vendors called out their wares and passerbys haggled over prices. Guards lined the edges of the space, lazily watching the proceedings with little interest.

Weaving their way through the throng, Daryn kept his head low and tried to avoid making eye contact with any of the soldiers stationed around them. Finding an area that was mostly vacant he had Angela start probing the crowd to see if she could find the information they needed. Ducking behind a crate, she knelt down and closed her eyes, letting her mind fan outward as Daryn pretended to admire the baubles on the cart beside them.

Keeping his head down, he watched as a couple guards nodded to each other, splitting off from their posts. His heart rate spiking, Daryn glanced down to see Angela still working, eyes closed and oblivious to her surroundings. Cursing under his breath, Daryn noticed two more soldiers leave their stations, making their way through the crowd. It couldn't be coincidence. He'd been spotted. Gripping his staff tighter, he continued to act as if he hadn't noticed their movements.

Seeing a black blur to his right Daryn twirled, bringing his pole up to block an incoming attack. Stepping around Angela, he pressed towards the man, forcing him back on the defensive as he looked for an opening. It didn't take long before the man moved his sword low, trying to cut into Daryn's thigh, and he was able to jump back, using the extended reach of his own weapon to bring his staff down across the man's temple, knocking him to the ground.

But short as it'd been, the fight had drawn the attention of the other guards and Daryn was soon hard-pressed as he tried to hold off three of them. He was faster, but the cramped space of the market area made it difficult to use his staff, giving the soldiers the upper hand.

Raising his pole up to block an overhead blow from two of the guards he felt the wood give way, shattering in two pieces as the blades fell through, slicing into his upper arm before he could get out of the way. Bringing one of the broken halves across, he used it as a club and brought it around to hit one of the guards in the throat, sending him to the ground gasping for air.

It was then that Angela darted from behind the crate, dagger in hand as she took down another one of his attackers.

"There's more coming, we need to get out of here, or we'll be blocked in!" She yelled as she charged towards another guard, ducking his sword thrust and bringing her knife down to cut through the tendons in his wrists, causing the sword to clatter to the ground before sprinting down one of the side streets.

Racing through the pathways they dodged startled women and children in their attempt to outrun the guards. But no matter how fast they ran, for every guard that they managed to lose, another one would appear from a side street to replace them. And with neither Angela nor Daryn knowing the streets or the city layout, they were just as likely to be running towards the town center as away from it!

Coming to a crossroads Angela looked down both directions, unsure which way to go. They could hear the king's men on all sides of them, but with how sound echoed off the buildings, she couldn't be sure which way they were approaching from. Panicked, she looked back at Daryn to see him panting, pulling out his knives.

"Go down that way," He said, nodding his head to a deserted street to their left. "I'll stay here and slow them down. We can't keep running like this."

"No! The entire city guard is probably after us by now. You can't fight them all." Angela whispered harshly, grabbing at his arm to pull him after her.

Shaking her off, his eyes turned hard. "Get out of here Angela. If they take me, your sight can help you get me out. But if we're both taken, we have no hope of allies coming to our aid. We can't risk it." Looking around them, they could hear the guards closing in. "Now go!" He said, pushing her in the direction he'd chosen earlier.

Stumbling, Angela turned to see him charging towards two large guardsmen as two more came out of the side alleys. Ducking behind a crate, she watched as Daryn's elbow took out the first man, his fist coming up to knock the second to the ground. But the two supporting guards had been joined by three more, and they easily overpowered him, pounding into his face and stomach until he fell to the street. Picking him up by the arms, two of the soldiers carried him back the way they'd come, flanked by two more.

She wanted to scream. To race out and save him. But instead, she closed her eyes and reached out with her sight, feeling for the guard's minds. She needed to find out where they were going to take him.

Eurcalp! They're taking him to Eurcalp?! Why aren't they holding him here? Angela thought, her eyes flying open. Sneaking out from behind her crate, she hugged the sides of the buildings as she tried to get closer to the guards and get a better read on them.

The Commander wants to question him. . . What does Daryn have to do with the war? Does he think we're a part of the rebels? Digging deeper, it didn't take long to realize that she wasn't going to get anything more from them and turned to flea, taking one last look at Daryn. As if he could feel her gaze, one of his eyes opened and he gave her a slight nod.

"I'll come back for you, I promise," she mouthed, tears slipping down her cheeks before she ducked behind a building and sprinted as fast as she could in the opposite direction. Leaving the city behind, she found Charger tied up where they'd left him, patiently waiting for them. Ripping the lead off the tree, Angela leaped into his saddle, slapping his hind quarters with the line.

"Ha!" She yelled as Charger's ears flattened and he took off through the fields back the way they'd come. Back towards the rebel's hide-out. The only people she knew that would stand up to the king's men.

"Hold on Daryn" Angela prayed, tears streaming from her eyes as they rode. "I'm going to get you out, just hang on."

162

THE FIGHT FOR REBEL ALLIES

Riding the rest of the day and on through the night, Angela stumbled into the rebels' woods as the sun was high in the sky the following day. Not caring if the sentries alerted the rebels, she leapt from Charger's back and fell to the ground, her legs unable to support her. Grinding her teeth in determination, she pushed herself up and pushed herself the rest of the way into camp, Charger following close behind. Using her sight she easily located the chief and wove through the myriad of tents and men towards him. Anyone who noticed and attempted to stop her got kicked and bit at by Daryn's horse until she was able to slip through the chief's tent door.

"You have to help me," She said, staggering against a post and looking up to find Duroc glaring at her, his advisors standing around a table in the center of his tent with a large map spread across it.

"I do not have to do anything. Get this girl out of here," He dismissed, waving his hand in her direction before turning back to his men.

Bringing her knife up, hilt out, she slammed it into the jaw of the man moving towards her before stepping forward, resting her hands on the table for support. "Please sir," she begged.

Whirling in a rage, he seemed to see her for the first time. The matted dirt and leaves in her hair, the haunted shadows around her eyes, and the several knives that she still had tucked along her cross straps. His eyes moved to his man groaning on the floor behind her and narrowed.

"Everyone out." He barked, returning his gaze to Angela as his men walked around him to leave the tent. Everyone except the man she'd hit, who was still holding his face and moaning. "And someone get this imbecile out of here!" he yelled, motioning towards the man on the ground.

Coming back in, two of the men grabbed their comrad's arms and dragged him through the doorway, leaving Angela and Duroc alone in the tent. It was the first time she'd seen the rebel chief up close. He was taller than she'd expected, probably even taller than Daryn. If she had to guess he was in his late 40's. Maybe early 50's. But the way he held himself spoke of a man used to fighting, and used to getting his way. His frame filled the tent as he walked towards her, dragging a chair behind him.

"I'd rather stand," Angela said, looking over at the offered chair like it might bite her. From what she'd picked up around camp the first time she'd been here, this man was known for his temper. And if the meeting went south, she wanted to be able to get out of his reach fast. A seat would greatly hinder that.

"I intend to find out why a young woman we helped along her way but a few days ago has just attacked one of my men and looks to have ridden straight through the night in order to do so. I'd prefer you not pass out before I get my answers. Now sit."

The tone of his voice broked no discussion and Angela couldn't deny the quiver of fatigue running through her body. Nodding, she lowered herself to the edge of the chair, keeping both feet under her so she could get out fast if need be. Duroc grunted and turned around, pulling out a seat for himself.

"Now, talk. Why are you here? And why do you think I would help you?"

"A friend of mine, Daryn, was captured back in Sheek. He took on the city's guards to allow me to escape, with the plan of me coming back and setting him free." Angela paused, seeing the captain's incredulous look. "It would have worked, had they planned to keep him in the city. But they aren't - they're taking him to Euralp."

"Why take a mere boy to the army's headquarters?" Duroc

asked, leaning back in his chair and rubbing at the stubble along his jaw. "That doesn't make sense."

"Because the Commander is there." Angela whispered.

"How? How do you know his location?" Duroc growled, coming out of his seat and taking a threatening step towards her. Jumping from her own seat, she took several steps back, not wanting to challenge the man if she didn't have to.

"I followed the guards and overheard them talking. The Commander has notified the cities that if anyone was to apprehend Daryn, that he was to be taken directly to him. At Eurcalp. For questioning." Angela hoped that the captain wouldn't question how she'd managed to get close enough to overhear such sensitive information or why the guards had been so loose lipped about it. After all, they hadn't actually *said* anything.

"So he's in Eurcalp," Duroc mumbled, turning back towards the map on his table. "After all these years of trying to track that man down..."

"You could bring your rebels," She offered softly. "Create a diversion at Eurcalp so I can get in unnoticed. Do that, and I can get you the information you want. Troop numbers, plans, all of it." Angela put a hand up to her head. She didn't know how much longer she could manage to stay upright. She needed something to eat. And she needed some sleep.

"Who are you to promise such a thing?" Duroc grumbled, still looking down at his map. "You're an orphan, barely out from under your mother's skirts. Just because you bashed Braiden's face in, doesn't mean you can infiltrate the army's most strongly defended base and get me what I want."

"Fine. Who is your best fighter here?" Angela challenged, worried that she might have rode all the way back to the camp for nothing.

"That would be Kreg." Duroc said guardedly, glancing up from his map to regard her once more.

"If I beat him in a fair match, will you consider my proposal?"

"You're in no condition to fight," Duroc dismissed, turning away.

"We don't have time for this!" Angela growled, her fists clenching as she took a step towards the chief. "The Commander won't stay at Eurcalp long, and Daryn won't survive his questioning very long either. Our time is limited. With the Commander on site, the plans for the army will be too, right?"

"Yes, that would be my assumption" Duroc said, not turning around. "But why do I need you? Why send in an untrained, unoathed child, rather than one of my own men?"

"Because I am better than any man in your camp." She retorted. From what she'd noticed, they'd be lucky if there was a single man in the entire compound that had been trained to fight. Sure, some had learned from the school of hard knocks, but she would assume the Arachians didn't allow the Shurkans to train fighters. Which meant she had a leg up. "And because I am small enough to sneak in unnoticed and get out without getting caught. If I do get captured, I don't have sensitive information about your base or your plans that they could get out of me. Any of your own well trained men would."

Eyeing her for a time, Duroc turned and whistled to his men outside the tent. "Get Kreg, tell him we've got a whelp asking for a beating. And for goodness sake, someone get this blasted girl a piece of bread before she falls over!" Storming towards the door he paused and looked down at Angela. "You beat Kreg in your current condition and I'll consider your proposal. You lose and you die after the match."

Angela nodded and followed him out, accepting the piece of bread a man offered her and feeling a small amount of her strength start to return as she bit into it. An area in the middle of the camp was soon cleared and a large man stepped out into the empty space.

He was shirtless, wearing nothing but a set of loose fitting pants tucked into his boots which served to show off a myriad of scars that covered his torso and back. His head was shaved except for a line of hair down the center that was tied in a braid at the top of his head. He was a good half-hand taller than Angela, with the same dark eyes. But that's where the similarities ended. Even from the other side of the arena, she could tell his entire body was sheeted in solid muscle from his neck down to his calves. His arms looked to be about as big around as her head and she knew if she got caught by them, the fight would be over before it even started.

Stepping into the ring, she watched his eyebrows raise in shock before turning and talking to his buddies on the side. Apparently no one had told him he'd be fighting a girl. The men around their combat circle began laughing and elbowing one another, pointing towards Angela. Laugh it up, she thought as she kneeled down to retie the laces on her boots, covertly watching Kreg. That will just make it easier for me.

To Kreg's credit, he turned back to watch her as she raised herself to her feet. He was probably in his early 30's and didn't look too excited about fighting what he undoubtedly considered an inferior opponent. Normally, Angela would have taunted him to get him over that hesitation. But today she didn't want a fair fight. She wanted a quick one. She couldn't afford to waste time in the ring, not with Daryn's life on the line and her body at only fifty percent. If that.

Stepping further into the arena, she didn't bother to try and hide her stumble or her fatigue. If Kreg was watching her close enough to notice, he'd let his guard down even more, and she didn't want to expend any more energy than she had to by trying to disguise it.

"Come on Kreg, teach her a lesson!" A man yelled off to the side. She couldn't be sure, but she thought it was the man she'd taken down in the chief's tent.

Stepping into the ring, the chief held up his hands, "The rules of engagement are this: No weapons. No kill shots. Everything else is fair game. Opponents ready?"

Angela and Kreg both nodded, and Duroc stepped out of the ring. Kreg wasted no time in charging, sprinting at full speed towards her as soon as the chief cleared the arena. Which was fine by her. The sooner the fight ended, the less chances he'd have to properly gauge her skill level. Ducking his grab, Angela bounced back out of his arm's reach. Staying on the balls of her feet, she allowed him to come back at her.

Coming in slower, she saw him taking stock of her as a fighter for the first time. Each step he took was solid and grounded. There'd be no knocking him off his feet. The way he moved proved he was used to catching a beating and landing his own in return. And Angela didn't want any part of that. So instead, when he came in to throw a punch, she ducked, kicking out her leg so the heel of her foot drove into him just above the knee-cap, causing it to buckle backward. As Kreg's head lowered in response, she brought her knee up and smashed it into his face, laying him out flat. Eyeing him for a second to make sure he wasn't getting back up, she turned and falteringly made her way out of the ring over to where the chief waited.

"Get me into Eurcalp," She hissed under her breath as she passed. His fingers dug into her as he wrapped his large hand around her upper arm, spinning her back to him. Out of instinct, Angela ducked her head to the side to avoid the punch she thought was coming. But Duroc just stared down at her, his eyes hard and unreadable.

"Who are you?" He asked, his voice every bit as tough as his gaze.

"Right now, I'm your best chance at getting to the Commander's plans." She answered, meeting his glare with one of her own. "Now let go of my arm, sir. I need water, and food if I'm going to be of any use to you. Unless you plan on challenging me in the ring as well?" Raising her eyebrow, praying that he didn't accept the challenge. She didn't know if she had another fight in her. But she needed him on her side. She needed all of them. And she'd do whatever she had to to win their loyalty. Or at very least, their support.

"No, you've proved your point, girl. Go to the cook and get some food while I meet with my advisors. Come back to my tent in an hour." Releasing her arm he motioned to the men she'd seen in his tent earlier to follow him.

Falling into the wake he left behind, she tried to put as much distance between herself and the men who'd been watching the fight as possible. She didn't want to be facing a bunch of bandits high on testosterone and feeling the need to defend their beaten comrade. Nearing the edge of their camp she whistled, hearing Charger neigh in response somewhere to her left. Turning towards the noise, she made her way through the trees to find him tied up and contentedly eating at a bowl of grain.

"Well, at least they seem to like you," she muttered, going over to his saddle bags and pulling out her water container, chugging the last of it before pausing at the sound of rustled leaves behind her. Replacing the pouch, she ducked and turned, bringing her daggers up before she saw that it was only Kreg stepping through the trees.

Lowering her arms, but not putting the blades back, Angela raised up to her full height. "Are you here for a rematch?" She asked, trying not to let the exhaustion she was feeling show.

Raising his hands he smiled ruefully and shook his head, "I underestimated you once, I have no desire to try my luck again this soon. Please, eat." He motioned to her pack, leaning his back against a tree a couple feet away from her and crossing his arms over his chest.

"No thanks." Angela said cautiously, putting her knives back in their loops on her cross strap, but not turning her back on him to retrieve the bread from her saddle bags. She didn't know him well enough to trust he wouldn't attack out of spite if he got the chance. "Why are you here if not to get even?"

"I've never been beat by a single opponent. I came out here to find out who I was fighting back there." He pointed back towards the rebel tents. "Because it's not a poor orphan girl like you led us to believe the first time you were in camp."

"How very astute." Angela sighed, rubbing her forehead. "Look, I'm sorry, but it's been a long day. And I'm not in the habit of handing out my personal history to anyone that asks. If you'll excuse me," She trailed off, waiting for him to leave. But he didn't budge, just watched her. His eyes were drawn low, but she couldn't see any malice in them.

"Fine, stand there all day if you want. I'm eating" she said, turning back to Charger's and pulling out the loaf of bread and dried meat she'd stored there. Spinning back around so she could keep an eye on Kreg, she sat down against an oak and began eating.

"Your horse looks pretty spent - you rode him hard to get here." Kreg pointed out after allowing Angela to finish the loaf.

"Your point?"

"Just an observation."

"Look, Kreg right?" He nodded. "I've had a long night and a long day before that. I don't have the energy for idle chit-chat. Every minute I waste here is a minute my friend might not have."

"Oh yeah, the wolvron sympathizer, I remember him. Tough guy, though he didn't strike me as the type to look for trouble. What was he doing mixed up with someone like you?"

"Helping me," she whispered, looking down at her hands as a tear slid down her cheek. "I'm the one that should be in Eurcalp, not him."

"Did you say he's been taken to Eurcalp?" Kreg asked, taking a step towards her and kneeling down so he could look her in the eye. Angela took a deep breath before nodding, pushing her grief down. There would be time for that later.

"And our fight today was to convince the chief to send you in to get him, am I right?" Once again she nodded, studying Kreg with new interest. So he wasn't as dumb as she'd first assumed. It was no surprise Duroc regarded him highly. "If he agrees to your plan, I want in with you."

"No. Absolutely not," she said, coming to her feet and moving away.

"Do you know where the dungeons are?" he asked, following her. "Do you know what they do to their prisoners that they bring in for questioning? How they beat them till they can't think straight, deprive them of food and water for days before starting. . ." But he was forced to stop mid sentence as Angela whirled back on him, death promised in her eyes.

"Get out of my sight." She ground out, hands clenched, tears streaming freely down her face. "I've beat you once today. So help me, I'll do it again. Except this time I'll make sure you don't get back up."

Rather than back away, Kreg matched her glare with one of his own, "I've been there. I know how to get to the dungeons. I also know that your boy won't be simply walking out. You'll need someone to carry him. Someone strong."

"Why? Why do you want to help me?"

"Let's just say there's a couple guards I'd like to pay a visit to." He growled, his eyes hard.

"I'm not risking Daryn's life so you can get revenge for a few scars," Angela said dismissively, turning around to leave. "I don't know you, I don't know your fighting style, and I have no guarantee you won't turn on me while we're in there. It's not worth the risk."

Stepping forward Kreg grabbed her sleeve, pulling it to try and pull her back towards him, tearing the fabric from her shirt. Spinning back and ready for a fight, she watched his eyes go wide as he took in the long jagged scar that made its way up her arm and under what remained of her shirt.

"So you do know something about torture after all," He whispered, lowering his head so their eyes were level with each other. "What if you'd found out you had a chance to get your hands on the man that did that to you?" He motioned to her arm.

"I'd run the other direction," Angela retorted, ripping her sleeve from his hand.

"Funny, you didn't strike me as the cowardly type".

"The man who did that to me is a better fighter than I am. I'm not a coward, but I'm not stupid either. I don't search out fights that I know I'm not able to win."

"Was it your charming personality that made him turn on you?"

"No, I killed the woman he loved." Angela said softly, hiding her face as guilt over her mother's death welled up inside her once more.

"I don't believe you."

"Look, I don't have the strength to argue with you. I only have a short time to rest before I have to go back in to Duroc, and you've used up most of it. Please, just go?"

"Agree to take me with you into Eurcalp and I'll leave. Just taking out the men we come in contact with will be revenge enough for me."

"And if we don't come in contact with anyone?" Angela asked, raising an eyebrow.

"I don't see how that would be possible, but if it is, then I'll settle for stealing a prized prisoner out from under their noses."

Eyeing him, she considered his request for the first time. If Daryn was in as bad of shape as Kreg thought he'd be, she would need help carrying him. And unless Calle had put on a hundred pounds of muscle, he wouldn't be of much assistance.

"I'll bring you with me under one condition." she said, already beginning to regret her decision.

"What's the condition?"

"Once the Chief gives the all clear for us to go, you're my man until Daryn is back at camp. You answer to me. And what we discuss does not get shared with anyone else, including Duroc. That's my price. I won't have a double agent running at my right hand in there. It's too big a risk".

Kreg studied her, no doubt weighing the amount of trouble he'd get into if the Chief found out versus his desire to get into the compound. "Deal," He said after a pause. "I've never met a fighter that's your equal, and I don't believe you have any love for the king or his soldiers. I will be your man until we return to camp with your friend." Kreg held out his hand. After a moment's hesitation, Angela reached out and grasped his forearm, sealing the deal. To her chagrin, her arm shook from fatigue before he released his grip.

"When was the last time you slept?" Kreg asked, stepping back to take in her condition.

"I was in Sheek when Daryn was captured," she said tiredly, leaning against a tree for support.

"That's three days from here! Maybe even four!"

"I left yesterday afternoon when he was taken. No stops. When the horse couldn't carry me I walked. When I couldn't walk any-more, we rode. It took us the rest of the day, through the night and most of today to get here. Then I had to fight my way into your chief's tent, just so I could have the honor of fighting you." Angela motioned up at him in frustration before looking at the sky, realizing she was due back at Duroc's. "And now I've got to get back to Duroc and have lost my chance at a nap," she sighed.

"Eh, you would have missed your meeting with the chief if you'd gotten to sleep." Kreg grinned, no apology furthcoming. Angela grunted in response before turning back towards the rebel tents.

"When you get out," Kreg said, falling into step beside her, "I'd suggest setting up camp on the outskirts tonight. The men don't take kindly to an outsider beating one of their own. Especially if that outsider is a woman".

"I'm not an idiot. I'll be sleeping out here by my horse," she said tiredly, placing her hand against another tree as a wave of dizzi-ness hit her.

Kreg's look of concern as he watched her nagged at her, re-minding her of the first time she'd met Daryn. "I believe our agreement was that if I let you come with me into Eurcalp, you'd leave me in peace," Angela reminded, looking up at him pointedly.

Chuckling, Kreg took a step back, his hands raised in surrender before heading off in the opposite direction. Sighing, she pushed herself from the tree and made her way into camp to hear what Duroc and his men had planned.

* * *

It was late by the time she emerged from the chief's tent and was able to rejoin Charger. Thankfully, most of the men in en-campment were already asleep, so she didn't have any trouble making it out. Turning to where Charger had been when she'd left, a white tent stuck out in the night, nestled between two large cedars. New logs had been cut to build the frame, with the white tarp being secured to both them and the trees it lay between.

Looking around she listened for anyone else in the area, but only heard the regular crickets and insects she'd expect. Hesitatingly she walked over to the tent and noticed her packs and saddlebags had been brought inside and sat in the corner, but looked to be untouched beyond that.

Too tired to question it, Angela ducked under the flap and let it fall shut behind her. Hastily working to get her bedroll spread out she laid back with a sigh. Duroc was going to help. They'd leave for Eurcalp in three days' time, with a four day journey to get there. One week. Hopefully Daryn could hold on that long.

Curling up in a ball, sobs to racked her body. It was the first time she'd stopped since he'd been taken and the despair that'd been threatening her since she'd fled Sheek hit her with full force. *What are they doing to you Daryn?* Was he already dead, discarded somewhere on the side of a road? She didn't care if he told them everything he knew, she just desperately needed him to live long enough for her to get to him.

Seven days. Seven days and the rebels would have gathered all their forces in the area to mount an attack on Eurcalp. Seven days and the Chief, Kreg, and herself would sneak into the base as the rebels laid siege on the front gate. She'd get the Duroc to the captain's quarters and then peel off with Kreg to get Daryn and her brother, though she hadn't mentioned that last addition to Duroc. They'd pick up the chief on their way out of the compound and get outside Eurcalp's walls before anyone knew they were there. Then the rebel forces would retreat, fleeing in every direction so the king's army would have to split their forces to follow them.

Duroc and his advisors seemed pretty certain that the king's men wouldn't bother to give pursuit, preferring to stay safe behind their walls. Most of the rebels would return to the towns they'd been hiding in, with only the core of the force returning to the woods. Angela and Daryn were to be among that force. She still hadn't decided if they'd follow through with that last bit or not. It depended on what condition Daryn was in. The rebel camp had good healers. If he was beyond her skill level to help, they'd have no choice but to come back.

Angela ran the plans through her mind on repeat until sleep reached its long arms out and claimed her.

TRAINING FOR WAR

Yawning, Angela stretched and crawled out of the tent to find the sun already rising above the trees. But with nowhere to be and no one to meet, she didn't mind in the least. The less time she spent with the men in camp, the better off she'd fair. The sound of a stream not far away drew her from her campsite as she went in search of fresh water.

Finding the creek nestled among a group of cedar trees, she sighed as she realized it was little more than a trickling brook. Bending down she lowered her hands in, careful not to disturb the stream's base and scooped up several handfuls of water, grateful for the cooling relief it offered. Even this early, she could tell it was going to be another hot day. Splashing water on her face, she leaned back on her heels and looked around. There was a strange song in the air that reminded her of the Old Wood back home.

Shaking herself, she stood up and turned to head back towards her campsite when a noise behind her caused her to spin back. A young woman, covered in iridescent blue and green scales stepped from the stream as she turned. Hair fell in waves around her face, obscuring eyes that were slitted like a cat's. Angela would have guessed the woman to be a few years younger than herself, but after spending time with the tree sprites she knew better than to try and guess at the girl's age. Walking towards her, the young woman bowed before asking in halting speech if she was the Wood Lord's bonded.

"I am," Angela answered. "But how is it you've come to speak my tongue? I've never been able to communicate with a member of the Old Races before."

"I have spent many years around humans," The girl whispered. "I have learned your language, along with many other things. Other members of my race do not understand or agree with my choice. I am an. . . Oddity as your kind would say. Much like yourself." Pausing, she looked to be trying to find the right words. "Is it true the Wood Lord has been taken prisoner?"

"It is," Angela said, lowering her head as a fresh round of pain gripped her. "He was captured while giving me a chance to escape."

"And do you intend to try and save him?" The nymph asked, hastily taking a step back as rage lit Angela's face. "Please, I meant no disrespect." She amended, holding her hands up, "I want only to learn of your plans."

"Of course I will go back and save him. It's why I'm here, surrounded by men just as likely to kill me as help me." Angela said, gesturing back towards the rebel's camp.

Nodding her understanding the nymph continued, "The elders of our races sent me. We would like to aid in rescuing the Wood Lord. We will gather our forces and those of us that can, will meet you here in two days' time to see how best we can be of service." With this, the woman slipped back into the stream, disappearing from sight as quickly as she'd come.

"What's a Wood Lord?" Kreg asked, stepping out from behind a tree to Angela's right.

Spinning around with a start, Angela stared at him in surprise, "How long have you been standing there?"

"Long enough. Now, what's a Wood Lord? And why were you talking to one of the lower races?"

"Those 'lower races' as you like to call them live twice, if not three times, as long as we do and yet still they manage not to have a single war amongst themselves." Angela crossed her arms over her chest and glared at him. "You'd think we'd be taking some notes from them rather than degrading them".

Not rising to the bait, Kreg remained silent and waited for an answer.

Sighing, she turned back towards her camp, "A Wood Lord

177

is someone born with a connection to the Old Races. He can understand them, and has gained strength and agility from them. It's made him into an even better fighter than I am. And it makes him the only link between our two worlds. The other races see him as their chance to stop the fighting between our race and their's."

"So what, a bunch of nymphs are going to help us take on the king's men?" He scoffed, coming up beside her.

"No, the wolvrons will. The tree sprites will. The nymphs can spoil their water and turn it toxic. With the Old Races willing to support us, we might actually stand a chance of succeeding with your chief's plan."

"And what is that plan?" Kreg asked, stepping in front of her so she'd have to stop in mid stride to avoid running into him.

Taking a step back, Angela studied him with fresh eyes. It didn't look as if he'd gotten much sleep the night before and he was still in the pants she'd seen him in yesterday. Something was off. What had kept him up?

"We leave in three days, with a four day march to Eurcalp. The rebels will attack, creating a diversion so you, I, and the chief can slip in unnoticed. I will take us to the captain's arena where Duroc will split ways with us. You and I will then continue on to the dungeons to get Daryn... And my brother." she added in a whisper. Here was the test. Would he tell the chief, or would he keep her secret and stay true to their agreement?

"Your kin is in there too?" He asked in shock, taking a step back.

Angela nodded, "It's why Daryn and I were in Sheek. It's why we are in this God forsaken land at all. And it's why Daryn was captured. I won't leave Eurcalp without both of them."

"Why? Why was your brother and your travel companion taken to the most heavily armed base in Shurka? Who are you to have earned such high regard from the king?"

"I don't know," Angela rubbed a hand across her eyes to try and hide the pain she was sure was plainly written there. "I don't know what my family ever did to the king. All I know is that he's taken everything and everyone that I've ever loved. And I'm going to get them back. At least those that I can."

"Okay," Kreg said, lowering himself to his heels in front of Angela's tent and looking up at her. "Then how do you plan on finding the captain's quarters once we get inside? I was never privileged enough to visit that area of the compound, so I don't know the way."

"I'll know the way," Angela said, ducking under the flap to grab some food before returning to sit across from Kreg, holding a piece out to him as she sat. Waving it away he watched her intently.

"How, woman? I am not a patient man, and you're walking circles with your words."

Looking down at her breakfast, Angela weighed the potential harm in telling Kreg about her sight versus the benefit of having him understand how it worked. Making up her mind she whispered, "I am a seer,".

She said it casually, trying to read his reaction. But instead of the surprise she'd expected he sat silent, his face betraying nothing. "I can see any life form within a hundred yards of me. Every bug, animal, and person. Even many of the Old Races. Not only that, but I can understand their thoughts on a limited level. I see their intentions. See their thought patterns. I should be able to recognize the captain's minds versus those of the common soldiers once we are inside the compound and lead is to them."

"And does the chief know any of this?"

"No." Angela said, taking a bite from her loaf and swallowing it.

"Prove to me that you can do as you say. I've never heard of someone with such an ability."

"Okay," she said, setting down her bread and closing her eyes. Reaching out with her mind she easily found Kreg. His thoughts were hard and driven, his thought patterns calculating. He was definitely not a man she wanted to cross.

Stretching deeper, she tried to find out what had stolen his sleep. He wanted answers, and he desperately wanted revenge.

But it wasn't for himself as she'd assumed the night before. The memories were so vivid Angela wondered that she hadn't seen them when she first touched him with her sight. Opening her eyes, she found Kreg sitting in the same position she'd left him in.

"The king's men killed your wife," She whispered. "Hung her up in your doorway for you to find when you came home. . . That's why you wanted to come with me. To avenge her death, not your own torture".

Kreg's cool facade dropped, fear evident in his eyes before being replaced with rage, "How could you know that?" he bit out, coming to his feet "Are you from the king? Even my own men don't know how she died."

Trying to pacify him, Angela raised her hands while otherwise staying perfectly still. "I'm not with the Arachians. Look, I'll prove it." Closing her eyes for a brief moment she reached out and found a rabbit's burrow not far from where they sat. Snapping her eyes open before Kreg could change his mind and charge her, she pointed, "Over there under the maple tree you'll find a den. The mother rabbit is out, but there are three young ones hiding under the leaves."

Walking over to the tree that she'd indicated, with several backwards glances to make sure she wasn't trying to escape, he knelt down and began moving leaves aside. After a few moments, he returned and nodded before sitting back down across from her. "Ok, let's say I believe you. Is that how you bested me in our fight? Did you read me before I moved?"

"No, my *sight* doesn't work like that. Though I wish it did." Taking a deep breath, Angela looked down at the ground, every muscle in her body tense. Every part of her screamed not to tell him. Not to reveal her weakness to a rebel soldier. But if she was to make it through the king's compound, she needed him to know when to watch her back and when he could count on her to have his.

"When I am using my gift I am unaware of my own body. I cannot so much as tell my leg to move, much less fight. I can't hear what is going on around me... I am all but helpless. Vulnerable to any attack. If you had lunged at me while I searched out that burrow, I could have done nothing to stop you until I returned to my body."

Looking at her in silence, Kreg seemed to weigh the information she'd given him. "So that's why you agreed to have me come along. Not to lead you to the dungeons, but to have your back as you scouted the way?"

Angela nodded, waiting for him to finish working through the implications.

"And it's also how you plan to get us there without running into any, or at least few, of the soldiers?" Once again, she nodded.

"And it means that while you're using your gift, I won't have any back up in there. You'll be worse than useless to me, because you won't even be able to run to save yourself if a soldier were to come at you." This last bit he said without question, but she nodded anyway.

"It's also why I couldn't afford to keep my secret from you." She murmured. "Daryn is the only other person who knows what my ability means. It's why he agreed to travel with me. He's my guard. He had my back whenever my *sight* was necessary, like when we first came into your camp."

"You used it to avoid our senteries. . ." Kreg said, putting the pieces together. "And if the Commander were to capture you, with your ability the rebels would no longer have any places to hide." Standing up, he reached for his blades. "For all our safety, I should kill you now."

Jumping to her feet and pulling out her own knives before Kreg could react, Angela took up a defensive stance, "You could try. But I'm well rested and well fed. You couldn't beat me when I was half starved and about to pass out. What makes you think you could take me now?"

"Because now there'd be nothing stopping me from a kill strike. And now I know what I'm dealing with." He growled, starting to circle her.

Turning to keep him in front of her, Angela spoke fast. She

didn't want to fight him, she wanted him on her side. "You're missing the point, Kreg. With my help, the army has nowhere to hide. All their secrets, all their plans, are an open book to me. I am your greatest chance at ending this war. Kill me, and your opportunity to avenge your wife's death ends with me."

"Gah!" Kreg yelled, throwing his knife into the tree behind Angela's head, barely missing her cheek. "Blast it woman! I don't know whether you're a snake or an answer to prayer."

Not sure if she should be insulted or just grateful that his blade hadn't been thrown a little more to the left, she reached up behind her to pull it from the tree and with a flick of her wrist sent it into the ground between his feet.

After a few tense moments he bent to retrieve his knife from the dirt and returned it to his belt, "So long as you don't betray us, I will have your back in the compound. I'll stick to our agreement and be your man until we get Daryn back here. But turn on us, and I'll make sure you become enemy number one. I'll be your worst nightmare until you are either captured or killed."

"Deal," Angela said, breathing a sigh of relief as she returned her knives to their places. "Speaking of which, would you mind if we practice together over the next couple days while we wait for your chief's troops to arrive? Is there anyone you know in the camp that would be willing to pair up against us? I don't have any experience fighting with a partner, and I would rather not learn while we're in Eurcalp"

A grin crept across Kreg's face, "I could think of quite a few men who'd jump at the chance to pummel you. Men willing to face me," he paused and shrugged. "Well, that narrows it down a bit."

Rolling her eyes Angela chuckled, "Someone's not lacking in ego. Just see what you can find, okay? I'd like to start with at least three if we can. I don't want the fight to end too soon. We need to get a feel for each other's fighting style. Especially since I didn't get to see much of your style yesterday," She said, winking at him.

"Ha! Well ain't that the pot calling the kettle black." Kreg laughed "Okay, meet me on the other side of camp in half an hour. There's a roughly cleared practice ring there that we can use. Best the men don't know where you're staying for now."

"Agreed," she said, starting to move off towards the side before pausing and turning back to Kreg. "Was it you that set up my tent last night?"

Shrugging, he glared defensively, "I needed something to do while I waited to find out what the chief's decision was."

"Well, I appreciated it." Nodding uncomfortably, Kreg turned and moved off to the camp as Angela began making her way around it in the direction of the practice ring they'd be using.

It wasn't long after she found it before he and his men arrived. Though rather than the three she'd anticipated, he'd come with almost a dozen. Grinning, she studied the men he'd brought. Some of them were large like himself while others were smaller, though still well built. She guessed they fought with speed instead of brawn, much like she did. By the looks of it, he'd chosen their opponents well.

Stepping out of the trees and onto the field, Angela paused as she took in the men's shocked expressions. Apparently Kreg hadn't told them who they'd be fighting.

"What is this girl doing here, Kreg?" One of the men asked, eyeing Angela distastefully.

"I'm here because I've been assigned as Kreg's partner by the chief." she retorted, stepping towards the man, "And we need to practice. You're welcome to take it up with Duroc if you don't agree with his assignment." The man glared at Angela, but didn't say anything else. "What, you worried I'm going to tip the scales in Kreg's favor today? Or are you just scared to lose to me as he did last night?"

Seeing the men around her tense up she grinned, bouncing on the balls of her feet and shaking out her arms. This was something she was good at. Looking over, she saw Kreg studying her and she felt certain he was questioning his decision not to put the knife through her head earlier, but she didn't care. She needed to blow off some steam, and she wanted these men mad enough to come at her hard. Make her forget about what Daryn was going through, even if it was just for a few minutes.

It didn't take long befor three men volunteered to take on Kreg and herself. The rules were set and the match began. The first couple matches they'd have no weapons and no kill shots. After Angela and Kreg were more accustomed to fighting together, that would change.

The first round didn't last long, with both Kreg and Angela taking out their opponents shortly after the match started. It was the first time she'd seen him fight and was relieved to see that he could hold his own. The next match was four against two. This round took longer, as they each had two men on them. By the time the fight came to an end Angela was dripping in sweat and had a new set of bruises along her arms and side. But looking over, she saw Kreg grinning back at her, his opponents laying on the ground moaning. It was easy to see that he was having as much fun as she was.

Taking a break they got some water and rest, before coming back together for the next round. This time, the first three guys volunteered plus two new ones. The first three had learned from their original match and approached Angela with every bit as much caution as they did Kreg. But she and Kreg made sure they were far enough away from each other that their opponents were forced to split up. In the end, they assigned two men to herself and three to Kreg.

No longer holding back to draw out the match, she dove in under the first man's swing and thrust her arm up towards his chin. The blow missed, but she brought her foot down on his ankle at the same time, sending his leg back at a bad angle. As he fell forward, she rose her knee up into his gut before taking her left fist across in a punch to his face. The man was on the ground and out of the fight before his comrade had been able to come to his defense.

Spinning low, Angela swept her leg out at her other opponent. But he was one of the smaller, quicker men that Kreg had brought and effortlessly jumped her kick. Using her momentum she finished the spin and came to her feet, jumping out of the way of the man's return attack. Circling each other they traded blows with neither coming out ahead. The damaging hits were dodged, the non-damaging ones absorbed so they could get their own hits off.

Growing tired of the game, Angela switched up her tactic and charged him full on, taking him by surprise and knocking him to the ground. Bringing her hands around she slammed her fists into his sides. As his arms lowered to block her, she brought her right arm up and slammed her forearm into the joint between his shoulder and neck.

Jumping to her feet she left him on the ground as she charged in to help Kreg, who still had two guys on him. Raising her arm to block a blow aimed at his head, Angela swung her other hand into the man's jaw, knocking him down. Turning back to the fight, she saw Kreg take out the other opponent. Chuckling, he came over and clapped her on the shoulder, forcing her to stagger forward. The man was strong!

With every match they fought, they began feeling more and more like team mates rather than strangers. Both of them thrived on the challenge of the fight, refusing to back down even when the match looked hopeless. Maybe this partnership could work. Despite how swiftly she'd taken him down when they had first fought, Angela wasn't all that certain what her chances would be like a second time. The man was fast, and he was tough. What he lacked in training he made up for in brawn and bullheaded stubbornness, plowing into his opponents with little regard for his own safety.

It wasn't until they were faced with eight foes that it looked like they might lose. Not knowing how to work together in tight quarters they started tripping each other up as their opponents closed in on them. Their lack of experience ended with Angela on her hands and knees from a blow to the head and Kreg on his back from a kick to the stomach, another man on top of him, pounding into him.

Growling, Angela lunged from where she was on the ground and into the man straddling Kreg, knocking him off and allowing Kreg the chance to get back on his feet. The man she'd tackled was more than twice her size and easily turned the tables, driving his fists into her. It was all she could do to hold off his shots to the head, leaving her sides unprotected from his large fists. Breaking through her defenses, he sent her head flying back, busting her lip open and causing her vision to blur over.

Trying to get her eyes to refocus she turned her head to check on Kreg, only to see him doubled over clutching at his side. The fight was over. Turning her gaze back up, she saw the man on top of her had gotten to his feet and was extending his hand to help her up. Taking it, Angela got to her feet and gingerly felt her face. She was going to feel that one in the morning.

Walking over, Kreg was holding his side and laughing with the guys who'd managed to bring him down. "Thanks for the save! You haven't done too bad out here today,"

"I would have faired better if I weren't constantly having to save your neck," she mumbled, touching her bruised ribs, but unable to hold back the grin pulling at her lips.

The men around her guffawed and pounded on Kreg who took it in all stride, smiling and laughing with the rest of them. She was grateful he didn't seem to be the type to get his hackles raised easily. Shaking her head, she turned and started making her way back to her tent, leaving the men to their fun. But before she'd gone a dozen yards, Kreg's large arm draped over her shoulders, turning her around.

"Come back to camp and get a bite to eat with us. You've earned a hot meal." he said, a grin pulling at his own busted lip. Was it the fourth round that he'd gotten that? She couldn't remember.

Looking back in trepidation at the guys still in the arena laughing together she tried to shove him off, "No thanks, I'd just spoil the fun."

But his grip tightened and he leaned in closer, "Look, you've earned the respect of these guys. They'll have your back while we eat, just like you had mine in the ring. And you need the rest of the camp to see that. If we're going to be storming Eurcalp in a few days, you don't have a lot of time to win the other rebels over. And the last thing you want is to have to be watching your back while you've got enemies to your front."

Unable to deny his point Angela reluctantly nodded and turned back to join the rest of the men. But not before elbowing Kreg in the ribs and slipping under his arm. Laughing, he followed her back to the group.

High fiving her as she joined them, the men formed a loose circle around her and Kreg before making their way to the camp's makeshift kitchen, just as he had predicted they would. Eyeing them all, the cook passed out bowls of hot soup to them each in turn. Finding a long table that was mostly empty, the group crowded in.

Between bites, they teased one another over their weak points during the fights and pointed out possible improvements. Angela listened quietly to the men talk, content to enjoy her first warm meal in almost a week. Once she finished she pushed her bowl aside and looked up at the man across from her, "So, how do you guys know each other so well?".

The man smiled, looking at the men around him, "We were thrown together on a mission to find out troop numbers from an enemy brigade that had just come into the area. We were all green and anxious to get a shot at the king's men." He chuckled and Angela tried to remember what his name was. Was it Jaime? She was pretty sure he was the fast one that she'd ended up tackling in the third match.

"We were so cocky that we got caught and had to fight our way out. Been fighting together ever since." He shrugged and grinned around the table. "There's no one else I'd trust to have my back like I do these guys."

"What about you?" A man yelled from the other side of the table. "Where'd you learn to fight like that?"

Several of the men seconded his question and Angela looked around the table, trying to find a way to appease their curiosity without giving away too much. "I've been training for this since the lot of you were still excited about getting your first kiss."

She bragged and the men whooped, elbowing each other as they fell into comparing the women they'd been with. All except for Kreg whose face had turned solemn, studying her. That man certainly doesn't miss much, Angela groaned inwardly.

"Now if you'll excuse me, I'm going to go take a look at the rainbow of bruises you bunch saddled me with today." She grinned as she stood up from the table and took her dishes back to the cook. Heading out towards the woods she listened to the men taunting each other behind her.

"I wouldn't mind having that one keep my bed warm!" One of the men bragged, before grunting in response to getting hit.

"That girl beat you three to one today, what makes you think she'd show any more mercy when your pants are caught around your ankles?" Kreg retorted.

"Awe you just want her for yourself," another man moaned.

"I prefer to not worry about my women killing me in my sleep. And so should all of you." Angela moved out of range before she heard the group's response. Smiling to herself, she didn't notice an assortment of men coming up on her before they were just a few yards away.

Pulling up short she eyed the group. They looked younger than Kreg's gang and much less experienced.

"Look fellas, the chicala came to join us," one of the men jeered.

"Chicala. . ." Angela said cautiously, taking a step back. "I don't know that one."

"It's a wolvron's whelp." One of the men spat off to the side, stalking towards her. "A female whelp." He added, his eyes moving over her.

"It's been a long time since we've had a girl around, eh man," one of the other guys said, a gleam coming into his eyes as he elbowed the man next to him.

"It has," The other answered, his lip curling in a snarl. "It's going to be nippy tonight, I wouldn't mind having a warm body in my tent. Even if she is a little prickly. What do you boys think? We could split the night up five ways".

Scanning the men in front of her, Angela's pulse quickened as she tried to find a way to respond that would avoid a fight in the middle of camp.

"How about a wager gentlemen?" She asked, pushing out a hip as she took on a sultry look. "I'm going to be training in the arena outside the compound tomorrow morning. Whichever of you beats me in a fair match will win me all to himself. No sharing necessary."

Looking at each other, the men whistled and elbowed one another in agreement as they moved back towards their tents. Letting out a sigh Angela turned to find Kreg standing off to the side, arms folded across his chest watching her.

"Thanks for the help," she grumbled, making her way past him.

"You had it covered," he gave a slight shrug. "It was clever of you to divert the fight to the ring. It kept you from setting a precedence that you'd engage in fights in camp." He paused, stepping out to walk beside her. "Though I'm not sure it was entirely fair of you to give them the false hope of a woman joining them in bed tomorrow night."

Snarling, Angela turned and glared at him, "No less fair than them coming to me five-to-one to try and force me there." She shivered, her skin still crawling from the way the men had looked at her. What kind of culture raised men like that?

"Fair enough," Kreg conceded. "I suppose they have what's coming to them."

"Of course they do. Speaking of which, shouldn't you be back with your guys?"

"I came to make sure you got out of camp okay. You took quite the beating in that last round and I wasn't sure if you'd be up for any more fights tonight." He paused to look down at her, "Glad to see you know how to get out of a fight without throwing punches."

Walking the rest of the way to her tent in silence, Angela turned and gave him a nod, "Thanks for escorting me back. And for practicing with me today. I needed that. I'll see you in the morning,". Smiling hesitantly, she waited for him to leave. But instead of leaving, he folded his arms over his chest and studied her as if she was a riddle he was trying to decode.

"You have an annoying habit of not knowing when you've out-lived your welcome." Angela mumbled, crossing her own arms and scowling back at him. But rather than send him packing, her tone only only served to bring a grin to his face. Unable to help herself, she returned his grin and sat down, the smile fading. After her encounter with the men back in camp, she felt a bit nervous having a man alone with her this close to her tent. Par-ticularly one that very well might be able to beat her into sub-mission if he wanted to.

No doubt guessing where her thoughts had turned, his grin faded as well and he knelt down in front of her, making sure to keep his distance., "I just need some answers," he said cautiously, "First off, who are you?"

"What do you mean?"

"At dinner you mentioned you were trained. By who? Are you Angorian and fled? Your skin's too dark to be Blackoff and the Shurkans wouldn't teach a woman to fight, even if there were anyone left in this land who knew the art. So, who are you?" His eyes bored into hers, trying to pull a response out of them.

"I guess you're just going to have to sit there all night," Angela sighed, starting to stand up. "I don't have the answers you want."

"You at least know where you come from!" Kreg exclaimed, moving to intercept her.

Glaring at him until he backed up a step she retorted, "If I were to tell you where I'm from it would just bring more questions. What you really want to know is why I've been trained. And who trained me." Sighing, her shoulders slumped. "Well, I do too. But the only man who can answer that gave me this," She motioned to her shoulder. "And I'm not in a position to force those answers from him. Now if you'll excuse me, it sounds like I'm going to have quite a few challengers tomorrow and I don't want to risk losing just because I wasn't well rested." Turning her back on Kreg, she ducked into her tent.

"You'll want this," he called, tossing a small jar into the shelter after her. "It'll help with the soreness." He finished before she heard his footsteps heading away from the tent.

Letting out a sigh, she laid back on her bedding and closed her eyes. "Hang on Daryn," she whispered. "I'll be there soon. I promise"

Gingerly taking off her outer layer of clothing, she sat up and began rubbing the salve Kreg had left onto her bruises. Once she'd taken care of the worst spots she laid back down and shut her eyes, replaying the events of the day before sleep blanketed her mind.

SECRETS IN EURCALP'S TORTURE CHAMBERS

Daryn woke with a start as two hands grabbed his arms, pulling him to his feet. Trying to get his eyes to focus in the dark, he saw someone step forward and unlock the chain that secured his wrists and legs to the wall of his cell. Not having the energy to fight them, and knowing it was useless to do so even if he did, he allowed the men to drag him across the hall and into a larger room.

This room had torches notched into the side of the walls so he could see a large chain hanging from the ceiling which the guards secured the cuffs around his wrists to. The cable hung just low enough to allow him to dangle from it with the tips of his boots scarcely touching the ground.

After being transported here from Sheek he'd lost track of time. There was no light other than the torches the guards carried. Time was tracked by how often the guards visited the cells. By Daryn's best guess, they brought food and water, if it could be called such, about once a day. Meaning he would have been in the dungeon for two days now. Up until this moment, those days had been spent in his cell where the guards would routinely come in to 'remind him' of their authority. Very little sleep was ever obtained and the food did little more than make him sick.

So far, no one had been taken to this room since he'd arrived and he wasn't overly excited to find out what it was for.

"You've got a special visitor today," One of the guards said, circling him before suddenly turning and bringing his fist into

Daryn's ribs, causing him to swing from his wrists until he was able to get his toes back on the ground. Snarling, Daryn raised his head up and spat in the guard's face.

"How dare you!" the second guard growled, swinging a batton into his back as the first guard finished wiping his face off and brought his own club into Daryn's side.

"That's enough," The words cracked through the space and the guards quickly backed away from Daryn.

"We were just getting him ready for you, sir. Sorry, Commander" They mumbled, continuing to move away from Daryn.

Unable to find the strength to lift his head enough to look the new man in the face, Daryn stared at his boots instead. They were made from a deep grey leather, though Daryn couldn't think of what animal they could have been made from. They were small, smaller than his feet. But he had a feeling that wouldn't keep them from hurting whoever they happened to land on.

"Leave us," the man growled, and the guards slinked to the exit, closing the large wooden door in their wake. "Do you like my boots?" The Commander said, walking towards Daryn. "Made from wolvron skin. Appropriate don't you think, considering that's how I found you."

Studying him, the man paused before continuing to walk around him. "They call me the Commander. Do you know why, Daryn? Yes, that's right. I know your name. But I'd like to be able to see your face while I talk to you, so how about I let that chain down a bit, what do you say?"

The man moved to the side of the room where a crank was set into the stone and Daryn felt himself gradually lowered until he could stand, his arms only slightly raised above his head. Turning his head imperceptibly, Daryn watched the man's feet as he stepped away from the device and returned to the torch light.

Raising his gaze, Daryn took in his jet black pants, his loose fitting shirt that fell down just below his waist, a general's ring hanging about his neck, and. . . "No," Daryn whispered in horror, looking up into the man's face, seeing the all too familiar scar etched across his jaw.

"You have caused me quite a bit of trouble young man, almost as much trouble as my daughter," he said, moving closer to Daryn.

"You're trying to kill Angela... why? Why hunt your own child?" Daryn snarled, never letting his eyes leave the man in front of him. The man he'd previously known as Ben Argon.

"Tsk, Tsk, I'm afraid no one explained the rules of this room. In here, I ask the questions." He whispered, taking a step closer. "Let's try this again, where is my daughter?"

"Filing for adoption," Daryn sneered back.

Faster than Daryn could follow, Ben swung around, his heel coming to land on Daryn's side where the guard had hit him, and he heard one of his ribs crack as he gasped, trying to double over but being held up by the chain attached to his wrists.

"That was not the correct attitude," Ben said, moving off to the side of the room and picking up a spiked baton, swinging it at his side as he came back up to Daryn.

"Let's start with something a little easier, shall we? How did you two survive the Old Wood?"

"Pixie dust" Daryn spat out, coming back to a standing position and kicking his heel out towards Ben's stomach. Dodging the kick, he brought the spiked club down on Daryn's thigh. Crying out in pain, Daryn let his leg fall back down, unable to put weight on it.

"Where is my daughter?" Ben growled, walking around to the edge of the room. Only the sounds of Daryn's heavy breathing filled the room in response to Ben's question. "Where is she hiding?!" he snarled, trading out the club for a short barbed whip and bringing it down on Daryn's back. Moving around Daryn he knelt down, his face inches from his. "Why are you protecting her?"

Weakly raising his head to look at him, Daryn drove his face forward, feeling the satisfied crunch as it connected with Ben's nose.

Staggering backwards, Ben cursed. Bringing his hands up to his nose he twisted, popping the cartilage back in place. "You'll regret that boy," He snarled, his eyes blazing as he walked back towards where Daryn hung.

By the time the guards came to take him back to his cell, he couldn't even groan in protest as they dropped him from the chain and drug him into his cell, kicking him into the space before stepping around him to lock up his arms and legs.

"Did you hear? He actually broke the Commander's nose!" one of the men whispered, turning the key on the manacles holding his hands.

"I bet he regrets that now," The other one said, locking Daryn's ankles up to the wall and strolling back to the door with the other guards. "I don't know what he wants with this guy, but I certainly wouldn't want to be in his place!"

Daryn listened as their voices faded down the hall before closing his eyes in defeat. Warm blood ran in small streams down his back and chest. His legs were too damaged to hold his weight and his left eye was swelling shut where Ben had punched him. Even if Angela could get to him, there'd be no way for her to carry him out.

Giving in to the darkness tugging at the edge of his mind he slipped into his only sanctuary. The only place he could go where the pain stopped. Where all was mercifully black.

❊ ❊ ❊

Daryn couldn't tell how long it was before the Commander returned to his cell and had him moved over to the room with the chain. The scabs that had started forming on his chest and back cracked as the guards lifted his wrists onto the hook, fresh blood leaking over what remained of his shirt before they left the room.

"I won't. . . tell you." Daryn growled out, trying to raise his head. "You've lost, you'll never get your hands on her."

"You see, I don't think I have." Ben said, studying him. "We've barely scratched the surface of what I can do with you. I can keep you on the cusp of death for weeks if I so choose. Or you can end it now and tell me where she is."

Letting his chin fall back to his chest Daryn clamped his mouth shut, refusing to give Ben the satisfaction of hearing him call out.

"Ok, if that's the way you want to play it," he said, stepping over to the table and picking up a thin wooden switch. "You know, you're really quite lucky." he noted, coming back around and taking stock of Daryn's condition. "Most of the men who come into this room are not my only option for information. So if they refuse to talk, I can make sure they suffer for it, but they are ultimately killed rather than have me waste my time on them."

Pulling a knife out he spun and drove it onto Daryn's thigh, "Where is Angela?" he growled twisting the blade. Moaning, Daryn's vision went dark before his eyes flew wide as Ben yanked the blade from his leg and the switch was laid across the now open wound.

"Now, now, no blacking out. I want to talk to you first." Ben said, walking back around to stand in front of him. "As I was saying. Others I can let die after a day or two. You, my dear boy, can't. You see, you are the only one who can help me find the little whelp that has the potential to mess up all my plans."

"She's. . . taking a vacation." Daryn ground out, raising his face to glare across the room at Ben.

"I don't know why you're defending her when she was the one who abandoned you in Sheek. She sacrificed you to save herself. You see, my daughter is just like me. I've raised her since birth. Shaped her into a weapon. She doesn't care about you".

"Then why... hunt her?" Daryn could feel the blood loss starting to take effect and fought to keep his eyes open.

"To tell you would be to secure your death warrant. Then again, you already did that with your little stunt the first time we were here, so I'll let you in on the secret." Ben knelt down in front of Daryn so their eyes were level with one another. "When her mother was dying from the poison I'd been giving her, she begged me to take care of her daughter. Her daughter. Not mine! You see, turns out she'd been pregnant the day we met, carrying the rightful heir to the Shurkan throne inside her. Allowing me to raise her up as my own. Train her, coach her." Ben spat to the side before standing back to his full height, his eyes glazed in black from the torchlight.

"Why... kill your wife?"

Hanging his head, Ben's facade fell for a moment. Grief and pain etched across his features before he turned away, "The king found out I'd married. In order to retain my appointment as Commander of Shurka, I had to dispose of her. Prove my loyalty remained with him. Otherwise, he'd give the post to someone else and have Caplana destroyed, my family along with it." Whirling back on Daryn, his hands were clenched at his sides.

"I lost the woman I loved trying to save Angela and Calle. But once Angela found out who she was, she turned on me. Attacked me. Followed me here. All so she could take the throne. Don't you see? She was using you from the very beginning. And if she were to take control of Shurka, what do you think would happen? Do you think the king would sit back idly and do nothing?! No. If I fall, there's nothing standing between him and the annihilation of this people. Just like the Blackoffs." Bringing out his knife once more, Ben circled Daryn, dragging its tip against Daryn's skin, watching as the blood peeled in small waves across his abs and back before dripping to the floor.

"So you see, I will not let my wife's sacrifice go to waste. I will find Angela. And if I do so without your help, I will make you watch me as I kill her. Slowly. Painfully. I will not lose all that I have worked so hard to preserve to a bastard, ungrateful orphan! Now where is she?!" Putting the knife away he pounded into Daryn's sides, kidneys, and damaged legs, fighting against Daryn's continued silence. Struggling to stay awake, Daryn held his head up to stare into Ben's eyes until the darkness at the edge of his vision wrapped around his mind and took him away from the Commander's reach.

Waking up in his cell Daryn painfully moved his head to see a dirty bandage tied around his leg where Ben had stabbed him. *I guess I won't be dying from blood loss.* He thought distractedly. He tried to remember what Angela's face looked like before she'd turned to run in Sheek. Could it be true what Ben had said? Could she have just been using him... But no. The bond couldn't lie. He knew Angela, and he knew she had no idea that she was heir. All she wanted was Calle. How he longed to have just one more moment with her. The chance to feel her in his arms. Hanging his head, sobs racked his body.

"I'm sorry Ange," he moaned. "I promised I wouldn't leave you, but I don't know if I'm going to make it. I just wish. . ." his voice cracked and he laid his head down against the wall where his hands were chained. Drifting in and out of fever dreams, wakefulness and sleep mingled together in a complicated weave.

* * *

The only times that he was sure were real were when the Commander would come down to question him. At these moments he tried to remember his time back in the meadow with Angela, training together. He stopped trying to answer the man's questions and instead focused on keeping his mouth shut. He could feel his mind slipping and he wasn't sure what would come out if he attempted to respond to the Commander's demands.

Pain was his constant companion and he forgot what it was like to be free of it. How it felt to walk or use his arms. All he could hope for was that the Commander would break one of his bones and give him a chance at death. But even this seemed unlikely as he learned how talented Angela's father was at torture. He could hit an area of the body just hard enough to cause maximum pain, without truly breaking anything so that he'd be able to come back and beat that point again and again in the following sessions without fear of killing his subject from internal infection. He could break down tendons and muscles, without ever touching bone.

But knowing what had happened to Angela's mother, and who she was stole his ability to dream of the day when Ben would go too far. Now his only hope was that Angela would find a way to come for him. A way to get him out so he could tell her the truth. He hated to think of her in this place, so close to her father, but she had to know. Somehow, he'd have to hold on.

"Please hurry, Ange," he whispered into the darkness of his cell, tears rolling over the cuts on his cheeks and dripping off his chin. "Please..."

WINNING ALLIES & ENEMIES

Rising early the next morning Angela grabbed the bar of soap from her pack and went down to the stream to wash off. Stripping, she splashed water over herself before scrubbing and rinsing off. The cold water sent goosebumps across her as she hurriedly slipped her clothes back on and walked to her tent, pulling up short when she saw Jaime waiting for her.

"Jaime?? What are you doing here?" She asked, cocking her head to the side and trying to get a read on him.

He chuckled nervously, rubbing the back of his neck as he looked at the ground, "Kreg sent me over. He was worried you might have trouble getting to the arena this morning and gave me directions to your camp. Promised to do some... unpleasant things to me if I went in too."

"Ok, just give me a second," she said, ducking into her tent to retrieve her straps, knives, and her last piece of bread. Coming back through the flap she dropped her cross straps through each arm and over her head, making sure both were secure before slipping her knives into them.

Sticking the piece of bread into her mouth she reached back and tied her hair into two tight braids. Kneeling down she laced up her boots before standing and taking the food out of her mouth with her free hand.

"Ok, I'm ready," she said, eating a bite and moving up to where Jaime was waiting.

"I hope you know what you've gotten yourself into," he said, falling in step beside her as they made their way towards the practice area.

"What do you mean?"

"Well, there's a pretty big crowd at the arena today. It seems the challenge you issued last night made its way around camp. I don't know how many guys are planning on fighting and how many are just spectators, but..." he paused, shrugging his shoulders.

"Great," Angela groaned, "The five last night were bad enough. I don't want to have to face a whole group of them!"

"Can I make a suggestion?"

"Go for it".

"Well, perhaps if you're tougher with the first ones. Beat them down fast and hard, maybe the rest will change their minds about fighting you and leave."

Angela nodded. She'd had the same thought. "Who are the men in this camp, Jamie? Why are they here?"

"Well, most of them were picked by the chief. Either they were too volatile to be trusted hiding out in the towns, or he needed them to defend the base in case we were discovered. There's also his advisors, of course, and the different faction leaders that come and go."

"Great. I'm stuck in a camp full of a bunch of hotheads." Angela grumbled, more to herself than to Jaime.

"On the upside, many of the hotheads are that way because they haven't been in any real fights yet." Jaime shrugged, "They are angry about what's happened to them and their families. Once they see you as an ally in our cause, some of their vehemence should fade."

"So how do I show them I'm on their side?"

"By letting them see you fight beside Kreg." He said without hesitation. "Take on a few challengers to get warmed up, then welcome everyone else to wait till after you've finished training. Let them see you take a beating for him the way we did yesterday and they'll come around. You'll see."

Angela eyed Jaime as they continued walking towards the practice ring, "And how do I know you're not just hoping for a chance to pummel me again?"

Throwing back his head he laughed, "Kreg's right, you're a quick one!" But his face soon turned serious, "Even if I was, I still think your best shot at winning the camp over is to see you protecting one of their own."

"Yea, I know," she sighed, a rock settling in her stomach. Suddenly the day ahead didn't seem too bright.

As the practice ring came into sight Angela pulled up short. The circle they'd used to fight in the night before was completely surrounded. It looked like the majority of the camp was there!

"You see why Kreg sent me now?" Jaime asked, grinning at her.

"Yeah. Yeah, I do." Angela whispered, trudging forward. "I'm going to have to watch my mouth around here. You boys clearly have too much time on your hands."

Laughing, Jaime stepped in front of her as they neared the crowd and whistled. It wasn't long afterward that Kreg and his guys pushed through the mob to make a path for them.

"This is a disaster!" She whispered as she drew up next to Kreg. All around her she could hear the catcalls and perverse insults of the men waiting to fight her.

Putting his arm around her, Kreg tried to shield her from some of the jeers. His face was hard, but his eyes danced as he leaned in close, "Scared?"

"Maybe a little," Angela attempted a grin, but it came up short.

"Eh, this'll be easy. You get to take on just one at a time. And we'll make sure you don't get overwhelmed" He jostled her as they stepped into the ring, smiling at the guys around him before leaning his head closer to whisper, "Every man that you beat here today, is one more helping you get to Daryn rather than trying to find a way to take you out before you get the chance."

As his words sunk in, Angela let her gaze sweep the men around the ring. Looking at them individually, there wasn't a single man she'd be concerned about fighting outside of Kreg's party. Most were hardly better than untrained boys hyped up on adrenaline. There were only a few in the crowd that looked to have experience with combat, and she doubted those would be challenging her in the ring as they weren't taking part in the jeers and insults. *Whatever happens to me today, it can't be worse than what Daryn's going through right now. I'll win him the allies he needs, no matter how many I have to fight.* She thought, rolling her shoulders in preparation and nodding to Kreg.

Lifting his arm from her shoulder he quieted the crowd with a raised hand. "Who's first in line?" He called, looking around the circle.

One of the men Angela recognized from the night before stepped into the ring, high-fiving his buddies before turning to regard her. The way he looked at her told her he wasn't judging her fighting powers but was envisioning her in a much different setting. Angela's lip curled in disgust as Kreg yelled out the rules of engagement. No kill shots and no weapons.

As soon as Kreg stepped out of the ring, the man charged. Deciding to let him come in close, she feinted a dodge and let him grab the front of her shirt. Hoots and hollers resounded from the sides as the spectators thought he'd gained the upper hand. Grinning, he pulled her closer, "You're mine now" he sneered.

Her distaste spilling over, she spat in his face before turning her head to the side to dodge his fist. Grabbing the small finger of the hand holding her shirt she ripped it and his arm off to the side with her right hand, using her left to come down hard on the joint between the man's neck and shoulder blade, dropping him to the ground.

Sneering at his back, she walked over him and moved to stand by Kreg as they waited for one of the guy's friends to help him off the field. As she'd predicted, one of his buddies soon volunteered to take his place. There was no lust in this guy's eyes, only rage over his fallen comrade. She preferred that.

Stepping forward, she waited for him to come at her. Apparently thinking he'd learned a lesson from his friend, he charged in. But instead of grabbing hold of her, he came in fists swinging. Staying in place, hands clasped behind her back, she dodged the blows. Growing bored, she stepped forward, ducking a right hook, and brought her left arm around to slam it into the man's kidneys before drawing her other first up into his jaw. The match was over in under ten minutes.

After all five of the young men who'd stopped her in camp had a chance to fight, Kreg called a halt. The matches had taken less than an hour and Angela was warmed up and anxious to start training instead of wasting time. Jaime had filled Kreg in on their plan, so he made the announcement that anyone who would like to challenge her could do so after they were done practice. All were welcome to stay and watch.

To her surprise, only a couple of men pulled back and headed to camp. Most of them choosing to linger instead. Angela desperately hoped that wasn't because they all wanted a chance to challenge her afterward. Pushing the thought aside, she walked over to where Kreg was talking with his men.

"What do you say we invite a few of these guys watching to help us out with training today?" He asked, turning to her. "It'd add a little more variety. And many of the groups we'll be facing in Eurcalp probably won't have fought together like me and the boys have, so it'll make it a bit more realistic."

"Sure," Angela shrugged. "If it makes for a few less guys waiting to challenge me after practice, why not?"

"Great!" Kreg turned back towards the arena before calling out, "Are there four men here willing to join us in our first practice round? We need a couple of extra guys to even out the odds".

After a tense pause, four of the men Angela had picked out as not being challengers stepped from around the ring and into the center of the arena. They were all large, though not quite as big as Kreg. They also looked like they'd seen their fair share of fights. She guessed they were some of the ones the chief kept here to protect the base in case it was ever threatened.

Kreg nodded to them and picked out three of his guys to join in. When his men walked over to stand alongside the four, and Angela and Kreg stepped out to face them, the crowd began to murmur. After all, seven to two couldn't be a fair fight. Especially with some of the camp's best fighters being members of the seven!

"Even out the odds, Kreg?" one of the new guys asked, looking around at the six other men on his side. "I knew you had a big ego, but this takes the cake man."

"Eh, you haven't seen my partner fight yet. She just got done warming up." Kreg grinned as he started stretching out his arms. Jaime rattled off the terms before stepping back and allowing the match to begin. Once again, Angela and Kreg made sure to keep a decent amount of space between them so that their opponents would have to split their forces. Predictably, three of the seven charged Angela while the other four went for Kreg.

Ducking the first couple blows, Angela took a hit to the side before she was able to get a kick off at one of her opponent's shins, slamming her knee into his face as he doubled over. One down. Dipping, she came up inside another man's reach. As he moved to wrap his arms around her she slammed the top of her head into his nose, sending him back several steps, cursing. Sensing the third man coming up behind her, Angela sidestepped and whirled, bringing her shin into the man's side. As he bent over, she brought both hands down on his back, dropping him out of the match.

Before she could turn, a set of arms wrapped around her shoulders like a vice, and she struggled to grab the man's hands, working to pull her wrists wide while at the same time thrusting back her hips. It didn't give her much room, but it was enough for her to duck out of the hold and send her elbow into the man's ribs as she spun away. Kicking the back of his legs, she dropped him to the ground.

Glancing over to find Kreg backed to the edge of the arena with two men still on him, Angela left the man she was fighting and sprinted over to where Kreg was. Bringing her elbow into a man's back, she drove her knee into his side, forcing him out of the match before he could attack Kreg from behind. Ducking in under Kreg's arms, she kicked her foot out into the other man's stomach, distracting him enough for Kreg to finish him off with a right hook.

"Not bad," Angela grinned before the wind was knocked out of her. Falling to the ground, she raised her heel up into her opponent's shin. "You guys just don't quit, do you?" She groaned, turning to find the same man she'd taken down two times before bent over his injured leg. Extending her hand to help him up she noticed the scars running along his arms, mottled flesh creeping up to his elbows from where a fire had left its mark on him.

"No," He groaned, taking her outstretched hand and pulling himself to his feet before letting her go. "We don't quit. Because to quit would be to die. To lose our homes and our families. It would be to accept that this bleak life the Commander has left us with is all we'll ever have." Nodding to Angela, he limped out of the ring to join his companions. Watching him go she began seeing the men around the arena in a different light.

But before she could think on it too long, Kreg had lined up another eight men to come at them. This time, rather than splitting up, Kreg charged into the oncoming group, using his bulk to split the tides and injure as many as he could. Angela came up behind him, taking out the ones that got around him until there were only four men left.

Seeing that he was outmatched, she ran into the fray, receiving several blows to the ribs and thighs before she was able to get off some punches of her own. She was so focused on the two men she'd managed to distract, that she didn't notice when one of the guys that had been fighting Kreg turned and threw a kick at her side, sending her onto her hands and knees in the dirt. The man she'd been trading blows with instantly took the opportunity and jump on her, turning her onto her back and bringing his arm back for a strike.

Wrapping her leg around one of his and her arm around the hand he still had on the ground, she thrust up her hips and rolled him, getting on top and slamming her forearm down on his neck before he could raise a defense. Staggering off of him, struggling to pull air in her lungs from the kick that had taken her down, she looked over and saw Kreg take the last guy down. They'd done it. Eight against two and they'd won. Collapsing on her back and holding her side she smiled.

Looking up at the sky her face fell as she found the chief staring back at her. The practice arena had fallen deathly silent, nothing but the groans from the men who'd competed in the last match to break the stillness. The look on Duroc's face clearly explained why. "My tent, NOW!" He barked, whirling around on his heel and storming from the ring.

Groaning, Angela rolled over onto all fours and pushed herself to her knees. Seeing Jaime's extended hand, she gratefully took it and let him help her to her feet. "I've got her Kreg!" He hollered over his shoulder before turning back to finish helping her up.

Taking a step towards the chief's tent she stumbled forward, her leg giving out from a kick she'd received during the last match. Catching her before she could hit the ground, Jaime brought her arm over his shoulders and wrapped one of his around her waist.

"Let's get you to Duroc," He said, glancing down at her. "He didn't look to be in a patient mood". Not wanting to risk speaking she nodded in response, grateful for his help. As they hobbled through the camp, instead of the catcalls and insults she was used to hearing, all she heard was hushed whispers.

Reaching the chief's tent, Jaime helped her in before quickly ducking back out. Finding a chair, Angela slowly lowered herself into it as she waited to hear what the chief had to say.

"I let you into my camp," He boomed, turning on her, "And what's the first thing you do?! You pick a fight with almost every man on my compound!"

"Hey, I didn't pick any fights!" She retorted, holding her side where she'd gotten punched. "Five of your men stopped me as I was heading to my tent last night - ready to pass me around between them all night." Closing her eyes she swallowed, remembering the looks they'd given her. "I tried to avoid a fight in camp and convinced them to challenge me in the ring instead. I did my best to keep the peace."

Glowering down at Angela the Chief studied her for a moment before his face softened slightly, "I knew having a woman here was going to cause a problem," he grumbled, leaning back against the table.

"To be fair, Kreg and his men have been keeping a pretty good eye on me. And I think the matches today might have quieted most of the troublemakers." She added, trying to ease his mind. The last thing she wanted was for him to think she was too much trouble and send her packing.

Waving her away in dismissal, he turned his back and crossed his arms, staring into the side of the tent. Not wanting to push her luck, Angela noiselessly got to her feet before remembering that she hadn't told him of her meeting with the nymph. Cautiously turning back around she whispered, "Ummm chief?"

"What?!" He barked, spinning back, annoyance written plainly across his face.

"One of the low races, as you call them, came to me the other day. They would like to help in the siege. I won't know how many they have until tomorrow morning when I meet with them again, but I was planning on having them attack Eurcalp's opposite wall to split the Commander's forces and avoid having them come in contact with your troops. That is," She hastily amended, "If you think that is the best plan of attack. I will defer to your judgment of course."

Sighing, Duroc rubbed his hand across his face and sat down. "They could be a great help to us if we could work together, but I think you are right. It is best to keep them away from the men, for now, otherwise, they are just as likely to fight each other as they are the Commander's men. Go ahead and have them attack the south-facing wall to split the king's troops as you proposed."

"Thank you," Angela bowed, ducking out of the tent before he could think of anything else. As she stumbled through the flap she pulled up short, finding Kreg and his men waiting outside.

"What are you all doing here?" she asked in surprise, looking around.

"Well. . ." One of them said hesitantly, looking down and shuffling his feet. "We thought you might need some back up in there. The chief can be pretty tough sometimes, and has a bit of a temper to go with it."

The other men nodded their heads in agreement. Looking to Kreg in shock he just shrugged, a smile tugging at his features. Astonished that they'd come to her defense after only knowing her a day, she smiled. "Well, after the pounding you guys gave me during practice today, I suppose you owed me one."

"The pounding we gave you?" One of the men questioned, rubbing the side of his face. "What about the pounding you guys gave us?! I'mma be sore for a week because of you two!"

Laughing, the group began comparing bruises as they moved back through the rebel tents towards the cook's station. Lining up for their bowls, they all gathered around their table from the night before. Slurping down their soup they started reviewing their fights and what they could have done better.

As they talked, someone from the camp came up and slapped her on the shoulder, "Good job out there today!" he said before moving on. Looking over at Jaime with eyebrows raised, he smiled and mouthed 'I told you' before turning back to talking with the guy next to him. By the time they'd finished their meal, Angela guessed that nearly two dozen men had come by to congratulate her on the matches she'd won. The sun had begun setting behind the trees by the time the group got up and started heading back to their tents.

Looking around and seeing no one watching her, she ducked away from the men and slipped down a path that would take her out of camp. Sneaking one last look behind her to make sure she wasn't followed, she turned into the woods and slipped into the shadows. The moons were up and the stars were bright, affording her plenty of light to find her way by. Letting out a sigh she relaxed for the first time that day. Running her hands along the bark of a tree next to her she started walking, not caring where she was going. It was soothing to be back in the woods, even if they were different than the ones she was used to back home.

Thinking back on the day's events she struggled to put the pieces together. The longer she spent with the rebels, the more she felt drawn to their cause. What if her own home had been taken over by the king? What if Caplana was turned into a town like Sheek? What would she do? She hoped she'd have the courage to stand up and try to change things like these men were. How could she go home now and abandon them?

The plan had been to rescue her brother and return home. It's what Calle and Daryn wanted, she was sure of it. But how could she sleep at night knowing she could have done something to help and hadn't? How long until the king turned his sights on Caplana? Who would come to their aid then? And then there were Kreg's guys. . . She'd never had older brothers, but she imagined that this might be what it would have felt like if she had.

The moons were high in the sky and the last rays of light had long since faded from the woods before she came to a decision and returned to her campsite. Stepping through the trees she paused as she made out the shape of Kreg's large form pacing in front of her tent.

"The men are going to start talking if you plan on spending this much time at my camp," she teased, strolling out of the forest towards him.

"Where were you?" he asked, eyes narrow as he scanned her for damage.

"Even if I had gotten carried off and beat up, you wouldn't be able to tell the difference," She laughed ruefully, holding her hands out to her side. "I'm already covered in scrapes and bruises from your own guys."

Crossing his arms Kreg glared at her in silence.

Sighing, she walked over to check on Charger before sitting down by her tent. "I needed a walk. Time to think without people around."

"In the middle of the night?" He asked, raising an eyebrow doubtfully.

"Well, it's the only time I don't have someone watching me. Jaime almost caught me bathing this morning!" She said, flinging her hand back towards the stream. Kreg's glare intensified, pulling a chuckle from her, despite how much it hurt her ribs to do so. "I'm fine Kreg. I just had a lot on my mind tonight. . ." She trailed off, looking down at her hands. "Could I ask you a question?"

Nodding, he lowered himself to the ground across from her.

"Do you think Daryn's still alive?" She whispered, kneeling down as well.

"I'm not going to lie and say the torture chambers at Eurcalp are a place I'd ever willingly return to. Not as a prisoner anyway." He paused and looked up at the moons high overhead. "But from what I saw of him, Daryn seemed like a man that didn't give up easily. And he knows you're coming. That hope will get him through more than I did."

"Did the Commander do that to you?" Angela whispered, motioning to his scars.

"No, I don't think I would have made it a day with the Commander in charge of my torture! No one survives his questioning." He answered before noticing how Angela's face fell at his response. Burying her face in her hands she tried to control her breathing and hold back her sobs threatening her.

Moving forward Kreg put a hand on her arm, "The Commander is in Eurcalp? He's the one after you?" he asked softly.

Angela nodded, raising her face from her hands. "And despite everything I've done, I'm going to be too late to save the only man. . . I should have just gone on my own, found a way, instead of coming back here for help". She stood and turned her back to Kreg, wrapping her arms around herself. Taking deep breaths she tried to push down the pain.

"Don't grieve for him yet." Kreg came up to stand beside her and placed a hand on her shoulder. "I know what it's like to lose one you love. Don't put yourself through that till you know for certain. It will steal your strength right when you need it the most." Looking over at her, he gave a weak smile before his gaze dropped to the chain around her neck. "I noticed the ring you carry." He said softly, "Are you betrothed to him?"

Reaching up, Angela traced the outline of the band through her shirt. "No," She whispered, "The ring was his promise not to leave my side until we rescued my brother." Hanging her head she turned back towards her tent. "Even my own father couldn't bring himself to love me, no man will ever want to marry the woman I've become," she finished, looking back at Kreg before ducked into her tent, leaving him standing in the shadows outside.

Lowering herself to her bed, Angela closed her eyes against the memories. The pain of her father's rejection and Daryn's absence threatened to consume her. Tortured by thoughts of what Daryn was going through, and what she could have done differently to stop it, she ground her teeth in anger. But the rage eventually ebbed, leaving nothing but regret. Sobs ripping through her, she clutched Daryn's pack in her lap and buried her face into it to try and muffle her grief. Exhaustion finally winning out against the pain, Angela laid down and drifted into a fitful sleep.

MEETING OF
THE RACES

Yawning, Angela stretched her hands above her head, immediately regretting not putting salve on the night before as her muscles pulled from the strain. Reaching over for the bottle of ointment, she rubbed it on the worst spots before changing into fresh clothes.

Stepping outside her tent she hesitated as she looked up to find both Kreg and Jaime waiting for her, huddled around a small fire. They glanced over as she stepped out and Jaime gave her a smile before turning back to the flames. Kreg just nodded, his eyes sunken as if he hadn't slept any better than she had.

"Morning guys," She said, trying to find a smile for them as she walked over to them. She felt hollow from the night before and had looked forward to some time to herself before she had to meet with the old races.

As she sat down, Jaime grinned at her, oblivious to her mood. "Morning! Chief asked me to be here when you met with the. . . umm, other races, this morning. I'm to catch him up on the strategies you plan to employ with them. I found Kreg here," he said, kicking him with his boot, "Sleeping on the ground when I arrived."

Turning her gaze towards Kreg she tried to find some answers in his face, but he kept his eyes glued to the fire, giving nothing away. Why hadn't he returned to his tent last night? Blushing, she looked down at her hands. If he'd been outside her camp all night, what all had he heard?

"Well, I guess you can both come along since you're here," Angela said, pulling her mind back to the upcoming meeting. She could question Kreg later. Standing up and wiping the dirt off her pants she turned and started towards the woods in the direction of where she'd first met the nymph.

Pausing before making it out of camp she turned back to Kreg and Jaime, "You should probably leave your weapons here. They aren't expecting anyone to be with me, and I don't want to scare them off. Or to have them think that this meeting is an ambush." Kreg and Jaime exchanged a look before pulling their knives from their belts and leaning them against the side of her tent. Though Kreg managed to slip a small one into his boot cuff without Jaime noticing before on towards the stream. Shaking her head, Angela couldn't hold back a small grin. She and Kreg were cut from the same cloth, there was no question about that.

"Ok. Now no matter what insults they might throw your way, no matter what happens, I don't want you to make any aggressive moves unless I do." She said, looking over her shoulder towards the stream. If any of them messed this meeting up, she could lose the Old Race's support, and Daryn's chances at being rescued would drop. If he were even still alive.

"We won't interfere, you have my word," Kreg said, stepping forward and speaking for the first time that morning.

"Thank you," Angela smiled, trying to read him. But his face remained as stoic as ever. Sighing, she turned back towards the stream. Once they reached the meeting point she took a deep breath before dipping her hand in the water. She hoped the nymph she'd spoken with earlier would recognize her presence and let the others know she was there.

The water's soft caress flowed around her and she let out a breath, closing her eyes for a brief moment before turning back to find a clear spot on the bank to wait. It wasn't long before the nymph she'd met before stepped gracefully from the water. Eyeing the two men behind Angela, she tentatively approached and bowed.

"My lady," She said, sending furtive glances at Kreg and Jaime. Kreg stood to Angela's right, his arms folded, watching the nymph as if he thought she might try to slit Angela's throat. Looking over at Jaime to her other side, she saw he was much more relaxed and looked for all the world like a young boy seeing a butterfly for the first time in his life.

"It's ok," Angela said, putting her hand on the nymph's shoulder and smiling, trying to set her at ease. "These men are friends. They are simply here to witness the proceedings this morning. They have both given their word to not initiate any fights."

Nodding, the nymph sent a coy glance towards Jaime before turning and sending up a soft, shrill whistle that sounded more like a swift breeze cutting through a patch of tall reeds than any whistle Angela had ever heard. Not long afterward, three tree sprites stepped out from behind the oaks on the other side of the stream. They were followed by two large wolvrons, their hackles raised and lips curled towards Jaime and Kreg. To their credit, neither man rose to the implied threat but remained silent and watchful.

The water nymph motioned for everyone to be seated, but it wasn't until Angela and her men sat that the tree sprites folded their legs and knelt, followed by the wolvrons. Smiling tightly, the nymph walked over and perched down between the two groups next to her stream so she'd have a quick escape if need be.

"Thank you for coming," Angela said, allowing the water nymph to translate before continuing. "I deeply appreciate your willingness to help in retrieving the Wood Lord from Eurcalp."

The taller of the wood sprites bowed his head in response, "It has been many ages since a Wood Lord has been born to this land. The Old Races will do all that we can to ensure he has a long life."

"Are those of us here the only ones that will be able to join the siege?" Angela asked. She'd expected more and felt her hopes fall as her eyes scanned the five creatures on the opposite bank.

"No, we are merely here to represent our individual factions." The man said, inclining his head at the other representatives. "I speak for fifty tree sprites from my forest."

"And I speak for seventy from mine." another sprite spoke up, bowing to Angela.

"I represent thirty-five from mine," the last sprite said apologetically. "Our wood is further from Eurcalp, and not many of us are able to travel such a great distance from our trees."

"I will bring thirty-seven wolvrons from my pack," The wolf on the left growled.

"And I will lead forty-two from mine. We may not be large in number, but we are anxious to repay our debt and taste the blood of the Wood Lord's enemies." The last wolf snarled.

"The nymphs will not be joining in the fighting, we are not violent creatures after all, but we will do what we can to pollute their water sources so that many of the men will be ill on the day you attack."

"Thank you," Angela said, inclining her head to each of them in turn. Two hundred and thirty-four of the old races to fight by their side, not counting the nymphs. That was nearly a third the number of rebels Duroc was hoping to have gathered for the invasion. And she would wager that a wolvron was worth at least five of his soldiers. If not more.

Not wasting time on pleasantries, the group began discussing strategies for the day of the battle. Everything had to be planned down to the smallest detail since the nymph could not be relied upon to translate once they reached Eurcalp. It was decided that a couple of the tree sprites would break a hole on the east wall of the camp large enough for Kreg, Angela, and the chief to sneak through while the rest of the force would focus on the south.

Once they were able to enlarge the opening enough for the wolvrons to get through, the wolves would flood the city, causing as much mayhem as possible to further distract the army from Angela's party. The water nymphs would not only taint the city's water but would be present behind the tree sprite lines to put out any fires the enemy troops might send into their midst. Once Angela's group emerged from the city with Daryn, the old races would retreat.

As the meeting came to an end, the wood sprites handed a

whistle across the stream to Angela. They said it was too high pitched for human ears, but would give a clear signal to the Old Races when it was time to flee.

When she blew the whistle once, the wolvrons still in the streets would gather to her position and help safely escort her group outside the walls where they would meet up with six wolves who would have stayed behind with a cart, one which the tree sprites agreed to construct, to transport Daryn beyond the army's reach as fast as possible.

If necessary, they would leave Angela and the rest of her party behind in order to ensure he made it back to the rebel camp where the healers could tend to him. Once they were outside the city walls and had Daryn loaded onto the sled, Angela would blow on the whistle three times to signal the old races to retreat.

The plan was for the siege on the base would take no more than a couple of hours with minimal losses for the old races. Hopefully. It was never mentioned what the races hoped to gain in return for their help in the battle, but Angela was sure it would be brought up with Daryn in a tactful manner after he had sufficiently recovered. If they managed to succeed.

As the representatives melted back into the forest once more, Angela approached the water nymph, stopping her before she returned to her stream. "Is there any way for one of your kind to get into the keep to see if Daryn is still alive?" She whispered.

The nymph's eyes were sad as she reached out to touch Angela's cheek. "He will not die before you get to him, my lady. My people have been doing what we can to cleanse the water they are giving to him. It's helping his wounds to heal a little faster. But I received word early this morning that they have stopped bringing him water. We are trying to get a trickle into his cell so that he might keep up his strength, but there is no guarantee that we will be able to make it through the rocks in time to be of much help."

The nymph's face reflected the pain Angela was feeling and the girl tried to offer her some comfort, "One of my sisters heard the guards mention this morning the Commander's frustration with not getting information from him. Do not lose faith, he is stronger than any normal man thanks to his connection to us. He is strong."

He's alive! Angela thought, unable to believe it. *He was still alive, and still tough enough to deny the Commander what he was asking for!*

Leaning in closer to Angela so that only she would hear, the nymph added, "And you are welcome to bring that handsome young man back to my stream any time." Giggling, she glanced over Angela's shoulder at Jaime before slipping into the water and disappearing from sight.

"Well that was fun," Jaime said after a pause. Standing up, he stretched his arms above his head. "I've never actually seen a wolvron up close! Those things are massive!"

"Yes, they are," Angela chuckled, her thoughts elsewhere. "Would you mind informing the chief of our plans, Jaime?"

"Sure thing!" He said, taking one more look at the stream where the nymph had disappeared before heading back through the woods towards the main camp.

"Will you walk with me?" Angela asked, catching Kreg's eye. He'd been silent throughout the proceedings and she wanted to get his thoughts. And to find out what he'd been doing at her tent all night.

Kreg fell into step beside her as she made her way through the woods, not walking in any particular direction. "So, what do you think?"

"Well, I'm grateful to have their help," He said slowly, taking his time to put his thoughts together. "Though it does concern me that we're putting so much in the hands of the wolvrons. What if they turn on us as we come out of the compound? Or take Daryn somewhere else instead of back here for healing?"

"I hear you," Angela said, ducking under a branch and taking a sidelong look at Kreg. "But there's a piece of the story that you don't know. Shortly after Daryn and I. . . entered the Shurkan lands we crossed through a village where the king's men were using two wolvrons as living target practice for their new recruits. Daryn refused to leave without helping them. It wasn't until after that, that we found out his name was on wanted posters in the towns throughout Shurka. The wolves know that if he hadn't helped those two captives, he wouldn't be in a holding cell at Eurcalp right now. They are trying to repay their debt to him. I think they see him as part of their pack now. That's why they wanted to enter the city, and why they are willing to carry him leagues back here to get help."

Kreg's eyes narrowed, "I still don't trust them."

"Neither do I," Angela said with a sigh. "But we need them. I talked to the chief during that first meeting and he doesn't have any horses or carts he could spare to get Daryn back to camp. And I don't think even you want to carry him the whole way back on your own."

Walking on in silence, they both were lost in their thoughts, reviewing the plans that had just been made.

"Kreg?" Angela asked after they'd been hiking for a while.

"Um-hm" he grunted, looking over at her.

"Why did you stay in my camp last night?"

Pulling up short, he looked down at her, his eyes guarded. "After our conversation, I thought you might try and do something stupid."

"Such as. . .?" Angela prodded.

Rolling his eyes, Kreg sighed, "I thought you might try and leave. Get ahead of the army and get to Daryn and your brother a few days sooner." Folding his arms across his chest, he glared down at her, "And by my estimation, you're pig-headed enough to think you could pull it off too."

"What would it matter if I did go?" She pushed. "The chief would still go forward with his plan to attack Eurcalp now that he knows the Commander is there. You'd still get your chance to bash some heads. Why do you care that I stick around?"

"Because you're more valuable to us alive than dead. And if you were to go into Eurcalp on your own, seer or not, you wouldn't make it to Daryn before getting caught." He growled, holding her gaze.

Not able to stay strong, Angela had to drop her eyes to the ground. "People with my skill sets tend to have short lifespans anyway, Kreg," she whispered, turning back towards her campsite.

"Maybe," he said, keeping pace beside her. "But you owe it to Daryn to make sure it's long enough to at least get him out of enemy hands instead of throwing it away on a suicide mission."

"You don't even know if I was considering going. This could all be in your head."

"Could be. . ." Kreg said slowly and shrugged, "Then again, you're defending the idea pretty strongly for someone who hadn't been thinking about it."

"You sure you don't want to practice today? I would really enjoy sparring against you right about now," Angela grumbled.

Throwing back his head Kreg laughed, causing Angela to look up in surprise. "What?" she asked, a small smile tugging at her lips.

"You're what? In your mid-twenties? No one knows your real name or where you're from." He started ticking off his fingers as he went, "It's obvious you were trained by a good fighter, but no one knows who that was either. You've got no past, and no plans for the future that I know of. Yet despite that, you've managed to get the rebels and the Old Races behind you in a suicide mission. And convinced me to lie to my chief and follow you into battle. You talk and fight like one of the guys, but will wet your pillow at night for a man who isn't even your betrothed."

Angela turned her face away from him. So he had heard her last night. Trying to change the subject, she forced a smile, "I can take one thing off that list. My name's Angela".

"No last name, huh? Just Angela?"

"Hey, don't push your luck." she laughed. "Okay, serious question for you. What do you know about the Commander? Where is he from? Does he have any family?"

Kreg's face dropped as he shook his head. "No one knows very much about him. He was handpicked by the king and was head of the Arachian army before being placed as Chief of Shurka, second only to the king. No one knows if he still commands the army, but he rules all of Shurka now." He shrugged, "We haven't been able to find any intelligence on whether or not he has family or where he's from, though I would assume that he's Arachian. He disappeared about twenty, maybe twenty-five years ago and just recently reappeared."

"No one can tell us where he was during that time?" Angela prodded.

"Nope. Captain thinks he was called to handle an uprising with the Blackoffs, but he can't be sure. I'm guessing that's why he's so keen on this mission. He's been trying to track the man down for as long as I've known him."

"Hmm... Do you know what he looks like?"

"That's the kicker, no one outside the Arachian army has seen him, knowing who he was, and lived to tell about it. We've got next to nothing on the man even though he's the one in charge of our country."

"I wish I knew why he's after us," Angela whispered, more to herself than to Kreg. "It can't just be because Daryn freed those wolvrons. That could have been handled by the city guard... But it does explain why the chief is letting me get Daryn out, he should be able to tell us what the man looks like."

Studying her for a while in silence, Kreg bit back what he was going to say and shrugged, turning back towards base. "Let's hope. But speaking of the attack, you might want to stay on the outskirts of camp today. Jaime was telling me that we had a lot of men arrive last night in response to the chief's call. And from what I hear, even more are supposed to be coming in this afternoon. You might have won over most of the guys yesterday that are normally stationed here, but better to keep a low profile till we get on the road and the new men have something to distract themselves with other than the new girl in camp." Kreg looked over at her meaningfully and Angela had no trouble figuring out what he meant.

She instantly agreed, not interested in drawing any more attention than necessary and grateful to have a day to rest and work on her sight. She hadn't had the chance to practice with it since she'd left Daryn back in Sheek and she needed to be at the top of her game once they got to Eurcalp. Besides, she could use the time to herself. She wasn't used to being around so many people and missed having an opportunity to think. Making it back to her camp and scanning the area to make sure there wasn't anyone else around, Angela looked over to find Kreg doing the same thing.

"I'll come back and walk with you to dinner tonight," he said, turning back to look at her. "It'll help make sure there's less trouble. We'll be leaving at first light in the morning."

"You sure you don't want to move your tent out here?" Angela teased. "It'll be more comfortable if you plan on making sure I don't make any more escape attempts."

Chuckling, Kreg shook his head, "I don't think you'll be going anywhere tonight. I heard what that nymph said, he's still alive and holding out against the Commander. You'll stick with us now that you know the amount of support the other races will be able to give you if you do."

Unable to hold back a smile, Angela agreed, "I plan to take the remainder of the day to just rest up for the trip. I'll see you this evening".

Giving her a sidelong glance, Kreg grunted, "I've never seen you sit still for more than ten minutes while the sun's out. How are you going to make it a whole day?"

"Well, by the time you stop badgering me, it'll only be half a day," She said, pointedly looking at where the sun had already started cresting the sky above them before crossing her arms over her chest, trying to look put out.

"Ha! Point taken. See ya tonight."

Watching him walk out of camp Angela let out a breath. *Finally!* She thought as she turned and moved back into the trees. Walking through the wood, she ran her hands over the leaves she came in contact with. Birds flitted through the branches above her as she made her way back to the stream, filling the forest with their song and raising her spirits. Kneeling down next to the water, she closed her eyes and listened as it trickled over the rocks and pebbles before letting her mind stretch out around her.

Starting out easy, she reached out her mental senses and touched the birds and other small animals in the area before expanding her reach. Pushing herself, she managed to pick up on some men milling around the edge of the rebels' camp. As she watched, a couple more joined them with heavy packs on their backs. These must be some of the newcomers. Angela thought, forcing herself further to try and read some of their thought patterns.

The two new additions were older, probably a good five to ten years beyond Kreg's group of guys. They didn't seem pumped with adrenaline like many of the younger men. Their thoughts were slow and deliberate rather than bouncing from one thing to another like the two men she'd first touched. If all the newcomers were like these, maybe they stood a better chance at Eurcalp than she'd thought.

Pulling back in towards herself, she worked on trying to hold as many lifeforms in her mind's eye at one time as she could manage. It was an exhausting exercise, and it wasn't long before she had to open her eyes and lay back on the grass. *How am I going to be able to scan the entire compound of Eurcalp if I can't even keep a handful of birds in my vision at one time?* Laying her hand across her face to block out the sun filtering through the trees, Angela let the familiar sounds and smells of the wood soothe her.

Tomorrow they'd begin their march to Eurcalp. It'd been months since she'd first heard her father mention the place, and in just four days she'd be standing outside its walls. She prayed Calle was still there. That he hadn't been moved somewhere else. And that Daryn would still be alive. Growling, she got to her feet and paced, wishing that there was something more she could be doing to help them.

Too full of anxious energy to return to practicing with her gift she walked back to her tent and changed into her leather moccasins. Taking one last look at her campsite, she took off through the woods behind it. Longing for the peace running usually brought her, Angela pushed herself faster. Desperate to forget what lay ahead, to forget all that had to go right in order for her to succeed, to forget the look on Daryn's face as she'd left him behind.

But after racing for over an hour and still not feeling any better about what was to come, Angela was forced to turn around and make her way back to camp. Sweat dripped down her face and she was breathing heavily as she stumbled into the clearing and ducked inside her tent to grab an old shirt to wipe herself off with. Coming back out she noticed Kreg walking through the trees towards her and waved to him before moving off to the stream to get a drink.

"Just a second!" she called over her shoulder, dipping her water pouch into the current and chugging half of it before returning to camp.

"Told you you couldn't relax," Kreg grinned, taking in her wet shirt and red face. "What'd you do, run halfway to Sheek and back?"

"I'm not good at waiting," Angela grumbled, coming up beside him.

"It'll be easier once we're on the road and moving".

"I know, I know," she sighed. Turning to look at him, she took in his own battered appearance, "So how did you pass the day?"

"Well you know, with all these new guys in camp the pecking order needed to be straightened out a bit," he grinned, flexing his arms.

Angela rolled her eyes and laughed, "You're not any better at resting than I am, you big hypocrite!"

"Maybe not, but I never claimed to be," he said, before a mischievous grin stole across his features.

"Whatever you're thinking, stop it," she said, backing up a step.

"You want to test out your seer abilities?" he asked. "How about you use it to try and find Jaime in there," He nodded in the direction of the rebel tents. "Crowded camp, lots of noise," he shrugged. "This might be your best chance at simulating what it's going to be like in Eurcalp."

Angela looked around them self consciously. "Won't it look a little weird to have me randomly standing still with my eyes closed as we walk through camp?"

"Can't you do it without closing your eyes?"

"I don't know, I've never tried. . ." She said, looking down at the ground. Attempting to keep her eyes open, she forced her mind out. At first, she didn't think anything would happen, but after a few minutes of struggle, her vision stumbled forwards as if she'd pushed through a wall and her vision blurred, being replaced with her mind's view of the camp. Not wanting to tire herself out, she hastily scanned the area until she found Jaime about halfway through the compound ducking into a tent.

Pulling back into herself she looked over at Kreg, "Were my eyes open?"

"Yap, looked like you were trying to find something in the dirt."

"Perfect!" She grinned. "I accept your challenge, let's go".

Making their way through camp Angela tried to remember the general area where she'd last picked up on Jaime. Pausing, she looked down and spread her mind out. He should be close by. . . But she couldn't find him. Stretching out further, she spotted him high fiving another one of the guys on the other side of camp.

Coming back to herself she felt the weight of Kreg's arm around her shoulders, his forehead pressed against hers and his breath tickling her cheek. Jumping back, she pushed him away in surprise.

"What on earth were you doing?!" She hissed, looking around to see if anyone had noticed.

Kreg laughed, studying her face a little longer than normal before responding. "Well, you looked a little ridiculous just standing there staring at the ground, and some of the guys in the area were starting to notice. So I did the first thing that came to my mind," He shrugged. "Besides, I wanted to make sure what you told me was accurate, that you really couldn't tell what was going on around you."

Groaning, Angela gave him a half-hearted punch before moving off in the direction she'd seen Jaime. This time instead of waiting till she got there, she'd pause every couple minutes to keep track of his movements, adjusting their route accordingly. It allowed her to spend less time searching and thus less time unaware of what Kreg was up to.

Using her new strategy, they were able to find Jaime just as he entered the eating area. Thumping Angela on the back, Kreg waved and made his way over to him. Following in his wake, Angela smiled as a couple of the other guys called her over to their side of the table. Turning away from Kreg, she walked over to the cook and got a bowl of stew before coming back to sit with them. Easily falling into a conversation about the fights they'd had that day, Angela found herself enjoying the company for a change.

By the time people started heading back for their tents, Angela could understand why Jamie had said he'd trust these men with his life. They were a little rough around the edges, but they were loyal to a fault. And she felt grateful knowing they'd have her back in the days ahead.

Waving goodnight she turned towards her camp, not at all surprised when Kreg came up to walk beside her. As they passed the other tables she could hear the half-whispered oaths from some of the new recruits, but no one made a move to intercept them. Most of the men would take one look at Kreg and turn back to their conversations.

But as they left the dining area and got closer to the edge of the camp, that began to change. This was where many of the newcomers were setting up tents for the night and none of them seemed too pleased to be sharing space with a woman. And those that were, didn't mean it in a kind way.

Angela's eyes gleamed as she scanned the area around them, making sure none of the men came within arm's reach. Glancing over her shoulder, she saw Kreg following close behind her, his face set in a scowl, challenging the men they passed to make a move. After what felt like an eternity, Angela let out a sigh of relief as they stepped into the woods surrounding the camp and out of earshot of the new recruits.

"I hope it'll be better once we're on the road," she whispered, shaking out her arms to try and release some of the tension. A muscle in Kreg's jaw ticked as he ground his teeth, looking back over his shoulder towards camp. His scars gave him an even fiercer appearance in the dim light and Angela renewed her gratitude that he was on her side.

"Can you see if any of them are planning on following us?" he growled.

"I can try," she said, lowering her head and letting her mind spread out. It was getting easier to do without shutting her eyes. Touching on the minds they'd passed she found plenty of them decidedly against having her back if she were ever in trouble and several that thought she belonged at home with her mother. But she didn't find anyone planning on following them.

Opening her eyes she shook her head, "I'm still learning, but I don't think any of them are coming after us. Most think that you'll be, umm," she stuttered to a stop, looking away from Kreg. "With me the majority of the night."

Barking out a laugh, his features softened. But he didn't take his hands off his weapons, "How about I walk you to your tent, then head back to mine by a different route so they aren't any wiser then?"

Nodding, Angela followed him back to her camp and told him goodnight before ducking inside. No matter what her sight had found, her gut said that she might have unwelcome visitors later on and she had no intention of letting them surprise her.

Grabbing her hunting twine she waited until she heard Kreg leave before slipping out of the tent and setting trip lines up around the clearing. If anyone tried sneaking up on her, hoping she'd hear them stumble and it'd wake her up before they got too close. Stepping back, she looked around the camp to make sure none of the trip lines were too visible before ducking back inside her tent. Taking her cross straps off, but tucking one of the knives from them under her blankets, she laid down to a fitful night's rest.

* * *

Waking up to the sound of someone stumbling into her clearing, Angela groaned and grabbed her knife before charging through the tent flap and scanning the area around her. It was the fourth intruder she'd had that night and she was well beyond frustrated. It was early enough that the moon had set but the sun hadn't come up yet, leaving the area dark and difficult to see in. Turning off to the side, she headed to where she thought she'd heard the noise but pulled up short when she recognized the voice grumbling over the twine.

"Jaime?" She asked in surprise, jogging over to help him up.

Rubbing at his shins he gratefully accepted her hand and got to his feet, "The chief is having everyone pack up. We'll be leaving within the hour. Kreg wanted me to come and tell you. Something about him not being seen," He trailed off, noticing the blade in her hand. "He didn't mention anything about the tripwires though. Everything ok?"

"Yea, just a stressful night" Angela responded, rubbing her eyes and yawning. "I had a couple of unwanted visitors last night."

Looking back at the wires, Jaime nodded his understanding. "I take it you made sure none of them would be coming back?"

Grinning, Angela flipped her knife up in the air and caught it by the handle despite the dim light. "Yap. I just wish they would have all come at the same time so I could have gotten some more sleep. But it makes me feel better that I made sure they got even less rest than I did".

Jaime laughed, shaking his head as he looked around her campsite, "How about I help you get packed up and you can come back with me to camp and return the favor?"

Accepting his offer it wasn't long before they had all her supplies loaded onto Charger's back. Walking through the base was a much different experience than the night before. The men seemed to barely notice them, as everyone rushed around to get tents down, gear stowed, and breakfast cooked.

Reaching the center of camp, Angela tied up Charger and helped Jaime get his supplies packed up. Horses were hard to come by, so most of the men would be carrying their supplies on their backs. It was just one more thing that would set her apart from the rest of the troops and she began second-guessing her decision to stay behind with the rebels.

Working together it didn't take long before all of Kreg's men had their tents down and stowed away in their packs. Moving off as a group they made their way towards the edge of the wood where the chief was waiting with several of his advisors. Duroc nodded to them as they came up before turning back to talking with the men beside him.

"How did Duroc become chief?" Angela whispered to Jaime as they walked by to take their place behind the other men that had beaten them out.

Giving her a look, Jaime hesitated before answering, "Shurkans choose their leaders by blood. He is the closest thing we have to a rightful heir. He's not a direct descendant, as the queen's line ended when the Arachian's took over. But he's descended from her youngest cousin."

"I didn't realize," she stuttered, looking over at Duroc with fresh eyes. "I thought..."

"You thought we were just a bunch of guys trying to overthrow the king's appointed Chief?" He asked, his expression serious.

"Well, yeah. I didn't know you had someone with a legitimate right to rule."

Shaking his head, Jaime turned to look at Duroc, "The rebels were originally just a small group sworn to protect the royal line. But over time, it's grown into something more than that. Only his advisors know exactly what he has planned, but we all hope that maybe he'll pull a trick out of his sleeve and be able to challenge the king's forces and win back our lands."

"Well, why doesn't he?"

"The problem is, since he's not a direct descendent, many of our people won't risk their lives to support his claim to the throne. To even attempt to overthrow the Arachians and get our nation back we'd need all our people banded together. And that just doesn't seem possible without an indisputable heir from the last queen. Which doesn't exist."

"Well, if anyone could pull it off, it would be him," Angela whispered, turning away and joining the conversation the guys were having behind her. The sun had just started cresting the horizon when the chief gave the signal to start moving out. There were still at least half the troops trying to pack up their supplies, but he wasn't going to wait for them. Making a mental note to never sleep in while they were traveling, Angela followed the group as they made their way towards Eurcalp.

* * *

The excitement of finally being on the move began to fade after the second day. Rather than risk being spotted by any of the king's soldiers, Duroc steered his troops through the edge of the forests, giving the main roads and towns a wide berth. This made for slow going and a lot of short tempers. It chafed knowing that she could jump on Charger's back and make it to Eurcalp in half the time, while instead, she was trudging through tick-infested woods at a snail's pace.

She had to be careful to stay close to Kreg and his men during their march, as many of the other guys in the troop were just as frustrated with the slow progress as she was and she looked like an easy target to vent their vexation on.

As they drew nearer to Eurcalp, even the normal banter and teasing Angela was used to from Kreg's men began to ebb as the men withdrew into themselves, mentally preparing for the fight ahead. Listening in, she learned that this would be the first large-scale battle any of them had taken part in, and tensions ramped up the closer they got to Eurcalp. Fights broke out on a regular basis amongst the recruits and Angela did her best to stay out of sight.

As the sun fell on their third day the rebels arrived at the woods bordering Eurcalp and hurriedly worked to set up camp. Sneaking out on her own, Angela stayed low and crept up the hill that was keeping Duroc's men hidden from the guards stationed on Eurcalp's walls. It was the first time she'd laid eyes on the city that had brought her down off the plateau, and she hated it.

The barricades were taller than any of the buildings inside the encampment, making them the only things she could see. The setting sun made them appear inky black, the craigs in the stones casting eerie shadows along the wall and giving the illusion of spikes or blood running down them. Sentries patrolled the top, constantly vigilant for an attack. Large poles had been sharpened to points and dug into the ground around the city, meant to impale a charging horse or army before they could attempt climbing.

Duroc's plan was to strike before dawn, sending men to take out the sentries on the walls and allowing the rebels to use a large battering ram to bring down the front gate without being shot at from above. Once that was down, the men would fan out inside the city and keep the walls clear of archers so that the rest of his forces could get through the opening and take out as many soldiers as possible. The main thing was making sure the army didn't get around behind them and cut off their escape back through the broken down gate. If that happened, all those inside the city would perish.

Creeping back down the hill Angela laid her head on the grass and looked up at the stars. Seeing the city in person she couldn't help but question whether they'd be able to get in at all. She'd never seen a town so fortified. Sighing, she pulled herself to her feet and crept through the shadows back towards Kreg and his men.

Pulling him off to the side she whispered, "What would you

say to setting up camp along the East wall where the tree sprites will be getting us in. I don't want to miss our opening in the morning."

Looking back at his men for a minute, Kreg nodded, "I don't like leaving the night before their first battle, but you're right. Without being able to communicate with the tree sprites at the Eastern wall, we want to be the first ones there tomorrow".

Returning to camp they explained to the guys that they were moving out early and loaded their supplies onto Charger. Clasping hands with each of them Angela offered what encouragement she could, wondering if she'd ever see them again. When she got to Jaime she stood on her toes she wrapped her arms around his neck. "Don't you dare die out there tomorrow," she whispered fiercely.

"I wouldn't dream of it," he said, hugging her back before letting go and stepping away. "Keep an eye on Kreg, he has a tendency to charge into a fight without calculating the odds. I've always had his back..." faltering, he looked over at his friend.

"You stay alive and I'll do my best to keep him in the same condition," Angel said, forcing a lightness to her voice.

"You've got a deal." he grinned, some of the usual spark coming back to his eyes.

Once they'd finished their goodbyes, Kreg and Angela led Charger towards the edge of camp and along the base of the hill, keeping out of sight of the city's walls. Neither of them felt much like talking, both lost in the goodbye's they'd made and what the morning might bring.

Reaching a secluded spot where they could see the East wall, they stopped and unloaded Charger before making camp. There'd be no fire tonight and they'd be sleeping under the stars to avoid having to pack up tents in the morning. Kreg and Angela would need to get into the city before the rebels attacked, meaning they'd be going through the walls before dawn.

Spreading out her bedroll, Angela laid down and rested her head on her arms so she could watch the stars. "My mother used to tell me stories about this place," she whispered. "About beautiful springs when the meadows would be covered in flowers as far as the eye could see. And terrible winter storms that would blanket the same fields in snow that'd come up to your knees. I'd go to bed dreaming of what it might be like to see it, and here I am."

Turning his head, Kreg regarded her for a time before speaking. "Where did you live to have grown up hearing of the Shurkan plains?"

"High above the clouds," she said wistfully, watching a shooting star streak across the sky. "Up where there are no kings, no wars. . . just a quiet people living in a quiet town where the worst thing you have to worry about is the man you fancy marrying someone else."

"If only such a place existed".

"It does," she murmured. "Up on Heaven's Rock".

Leaning on his elbow, Kreg's eyes bore into hers, "You came down from the mountain? That's why you do not know our customs? That's where you learned to fight?"

Angela nodded, sitting up and hugging her knees. "I had a good life there. Until my mother died and my brother was taken away. Taken here. All my life I've been trained for war, but I never knew why. Maybe it was for this moment."

"Do you plan on going back after tomorrow?"

"That had been the idea, yea. Get my family and go home. But. . . now I don't think I can." Looking over at him her eyes turned hard, her anger boiling just below the surface. "The Commander did not know what he was doing when he made me his enemy. I can't just abandon these people and go home, waiting for him to turn his eyes towards the mountain. And I can't leave you and your men to fight for your homes and families while I take mine and return to safety. If we can get to them, I'll send my brother back home, maybe Daryn too, but I'll stay and fight for Shurka."

Kreg searched her face for a long time before speaking, "I'll be proud to stand by your side tomorrow," he said, laying back down and turning his eyes to the stars. "We'll get your guys out ofthere tomorrow. I'll do my best to make sure ofit."

Lost in their own thoughts they watched as the sky danced above them until sleep reached down and touched each in turn.

THE SIEGE ON EURCALP

Angela woke to Kreg's hand on her arm, gently shaking her. Raising a hand to his lips he motioned her up before moving over to pack up his bedroll. Rubbing at her eyes she looked around. Night was still heavy in the sky, thick clouds blocking out the moons and stars. It was probably still a good hour or two before sunrise. Sunrise. Eurcalp. Sleep fell away with the realization that the attack on the city was imminent. Jumping to her feet she slipped her cross straps on, securing her knives in place. Stepping into her boots, she rolled up her bedding and fastened it to the back of Charger's saddle.

After getting everything strapped down she found Kreg waiting for her up ahead, his pack across his shoulders. He was wearing a dark leather vest that she'd never seen him in before, his thick muscles pulling at the ties. Drawing up next to him they carefully made their way to the forest bordering the Eastern wall and discovered the chief there waiting for them. After exchanging greetings, Angela drew back into the woods to secure Charger's lead to a large tree, making sure he had plenty of grass around him to graze on as he waited for them to come back. She tried not to think about what would happen to him if they didn't return.

Feeling like she was being watched, Angela ducked deeper into the woods before drawing up short as she came face to face with six wolvrons. It was so dark in the wood that all she could see was their eyes glowing an ominous orange. Stepping forward, one of the wolves made his way towards her before bowing his head to the ground.

Standing back up to his full height, he turned back to the woods, looking expectantly over his shoulder. Moving up to keep pace with him, the other wolves filed in around her as they led her to a small clearing where the clouds parted and allowed to moons' glow to illuminate an ornately carved cart.

The body was long and narrow, only wide enough to fit two people sitting very close together, but long enough for a tall man to lie down with room to spare. The entire frame seemed to be crafted out of a single piece cedar, almost as if it had grown that way. And for all Angela knew, it had.

There were four large wheels that held the body up a mere few inches above the ground, bringing the top of the cart level with the tips of the wolvrons shoulders. Strong thick vines stretched out from the front of the cart and between them hung six slots, waiting for their hosts.

Brushing past Angela, the wolvrons stepped forward and into their places in the loops left by the vines, waiting for her. Walking up to them she tentatively reached over and tied the straps around each of the wolves' necks and waists. Their fur was soft and thick and she had a hard time resisting the urge to run her fingers through it. Securing the last wolf, she walked around and knelt in front of the lead wolvron. Reaching up with her right hand she touched her lips in the same manner the pine sprite had back on the plateau.

"Thank you," she whispered.

Seeming to understand her meaning, the massive beast lowered his head before motioning back towards where Kreg and Duroc waited.

Slipping through the trees Angela found two tree sprites standing at the edge of the wood, just beyond the two men. Drawing up next to Kreg he bent over and whispered, "Where did you go?"

"I had to get the wolvrons hitched up to the cart," she responded, not taking her eyes off the sprites. "What are they doing?"

Pointing over at the wall, Kreg guided her eyes to a point where two large roots were pushing through the stones. "It looks like they've been working on this for several days. They're using the roots to pull out some of the largest boulders, working to make the gap big enough for us to sneak through. I'm assuming they'll wait until the rebels break down the gate before pushing it wider and allowing the wolvrons through".

Nodding her understanding she nervously started checking to make sure all her weapons were in place.

Watching her, Kreg grinned, "Is this your first time in battle?"

"It's my first time going into a fight not knowing if I have any chance of winning, yea," she answered, glaring over at the wall, fear tugging at her.

"Just remember why you're doing this," Kreg said, following her gaze as they watched the hole in Eurcalp's wall grow. "It'll give you the courage you need, even when the odds are stacked against you."

Reaching up, Angela pulled Daryn's ring from under her shirt and ran her fingers over the runes before tucking it away again. The clouds had started to clear by the time the sprites were able to pull the last two large stones back from the base of the wall and create an alleyway just wide enough to fit two people through at a time. Coming up to them, one of the tree sprites pointed towards the hole, supposedly asking if it was big enough.

Nodding that it would work, she thanked him before turning back to Kreg and Duroc. Carefully they began making their way over to the edge of the wood, waiting for the sentries along the wall to move away from their location. Motioning that she'd go first, Angela darted forward across the open grass, trying to stay as low as she could in case the sentry looked back.

Reaching the wall, she slunk through the misplaced stones and inside before kneeling to catch her breath. Looking around and seeing no one nearby she closed her eyes and let her sight spread out through the camp. She was too far away from where Kreg said the officers quarters and dungeons would be, but she could see a path through the buildings ahead that was devoid of active life other than some rodents.

As the nymphs had promised, she could sense that many of the men in the barracks closest to her were in fever dreams, either tossing and turning or hanging their heads over buckets on the floor.

Pulling back into herself she opened her eyes to find that both of the men had made it through and were waiting for her. Nodding her head in the direction they needed to go, they waited for another sentry to pass along the wall before sprinting across the open space that marked the gap between the buildings and the outer barricade. As they flattened themselves against the first building they saw one of the sentries fall from the wall, another promptly following him. The rebels were here!

Claws skittering across stone brought her gaze around to see a wolvron diving through the hole they'd just left and take off after a soldier down another street. Seeing three more coming through the gap Angela turned her mind outward. Their path was still clear. Motioning Kreg and Duroc forward, they sprinted between the buildings towards the inner center of the keep. There were panicked men moving through the streets all around them as soldiers were woken from their beds by the screams of their comrades.

Coming up on two guards in their path, the men ran up ahead of Angela, dispatching them as she paused to reach out with her mind. Everywhere she looked there were men flooding the streets. The time for secrecy was passed. Jogging up beside Kreg she told him what she'd been able to see and a grin spread across his face.

Rolling her eyes, Angela pulled two knives out of her straps and nodded over to Duroc. They'd need to fight the rest of their way through. Charging ahead, they each split off as enemy soldiers came into sight, taking them out before they'd have time to raise an alarm. No one was expecting enemies inside the keep, so most of the men went down without too much trouble.

Thankfully, the streets were narrow, crowded with hastily

built wood shacks that Angela assumed were the barracks. It would be a long time before someone found the downed men and got word around that someone was in the keep. If everything went according to plan, they'd be on their way out by then.

As they ran, Kreg took out a man to Angela's left and Duroc sprinted ahead to take on two more. Running on his heels, Angela threw one of her knives, dropping a man to the ground clutching at his leg. His companion hesitated, looking over at his downed comrad which gave Duroc time to bring his sword down across the man's side before slitting his throat. Grabbing her blade from the first man as the chief took him out, Angela turned to see Kreg jogging down the street towards them.

Noticing a massive structure up ahead that could only be the headquarters, they ducked behind a building and waited for a large group of men to pass them by before ducking across the alley and up against the main structure. Finding a side door a hundred yards down, they crouched in the shadows as they made their way towards the opening, slipping inside before anyone could see them.

Breathing a sigh of relief, Angela sent her mind out, searching the interior of the compound. Sensing a large cluster of calmer minds to their left about halfway through, she came back to herself and motioned which way they needed to go. The challenging part now was that her sight only showed life-forms and what they were touching, not the rooms and hallways where no one was currently traveling. This meant that they had to double back several times before making it to the right area.

They'd only had to dodge a few close calls as men moved through the halls. It seemed most of the officers that would normally be in this building were out on the walls and streets defending the city. But Angela wasn't about to complain. The goal was for Duroc to get the information he needed without the Commander's men ever knowing he was in this area of the keep, otherwise they might change their plans. The fewer men in this section, the more likely that was to succeed.

As they drew closer to where Angela felt the captains' minds, avoiding troops became more difficult as runners were being sent from the room where the captains were out to the soldiers on the walls.

Motioning for the group to stop, she bent her head and whispered to Duroc, "The room you want is just up ahead, but the commanders are still in there. Should we wait here until they leave to join the fight? Or would you prefer Kreg and I go on? I get the sense that the captains will be leaving soon."

Giving her a look that said she was going to have some explaining to do once they got back to camp, he shook his head. "You two go on ahead. You have a longer way to travel, whereas my destination is here. I'll stay hidden and wait for them to leave before going in and seeing what I can find. You get a head start to the dungeons."

Choosing not to argue, Angela nodded and she and Kreg started moving again. Going around a turn into a deserted area of the keep, she paused. Turning back towards the captain's quarters she cast her sight out to see if she could discover some of their objectives just in case Duroc failed.

Scanning the men, she came to a mind unlike any she'd encountered before. Most minds she'd touched reminded her of a forest, thoughts and plans running between pillars of belief systems and morals. This man's mind was like a finely honed blade. His observations were sharp and precise, with little to no moral columns to bounce off of. Only the Commander could have a mind like that. But as she latched on, the man moved from the room and away from them towards the battlements, out of her reach.

Growling in frustration, Angela turned to the other captains. At first all she found was how they planned to counteract the attack on their walls. But digging deeper, she located a man that was still considering an earlier discussion. One that involved Heaven's Rock. Mentally rearing back in shock, Angela pulled into herself and opened her eyes to find Kreg standing over her, frantically trying to hold off several soldiers.

Jumping to her feet, Angela dove into one of them, forcing him to the ground and slamming the hilt of her knife into the side of his head. Her sudden movement allowed Kreg to slip in a hit to the other man, killing him as Angela took out the third.

"Thanks," she whispered, her heart racing from the unexpected attack.

Kreg glanced over at her, his eyes drawn low with concern, "What took you so long that time?"

"I was scanning the officers and found out some of their plans. And I found the Commander. He's leaving the compound in the opposite direction of where we are."

"Good, then it was worth it." Kreg said, pulling swords off the soldiers they'd taken out and adding them to his collection of weapons. "Which way now?"

Closing her eyes once more, it wasn't difficult for Angela to find the dungeons. They were directly below them, deep underground. But where were the stairs? Stretching to the edge of her limits she picked up on a young boy, pacing in what looked to be a courtyard at the end of her mental reach.

Her eyes going wide, she turned to Kreg and motioned that they needed to change direction. Haltingly, they made their way towards the courtyard, ducking into rooms and around corners to avoid guards before making it to their destination.

"What are we doing here?" Kreg hissed.

"I think my brother is in there," Angela whispered, slinking around the pillar they were hiding behind to try and get a better view of the courtyard.

"You think? Can't you tell?"

"I discovered my talents after he was taken, I've never actually touched his mind before," She mumbled, searching the area for the boy she'd seen. "I'd just assumed he'd be in the dungeons with Daryn and that I'd recognize him by sight."

After scanning the space for a few more minutes and only seeing soldiers pass through she was about to give up, when a young man stepped into view. He was taller than she remembered Calle being, and dressed in an Arachian uniform, but she knew it was him.

Reaching out her mind to make sure there weren't any guards around she opened her eyes before whistling softly. Spinning around to discover the source of the sound, Calle spotted her and his eyes widened. Looking to either side, he darted towards them and barreled into her.

"I thought you didn't want to come," he whispered, fiercely squeezing her neck.

"Didn't want to come?" She choked out, hugging him back before letting go. "We've got a lot to catch up on. But right now, we need to get out of here."

"But what about dad?" Calle said, pulling back from the hug and seeing Kreg kneeling in the shadows for the first time. Stumbling backwards, his eyes widened in fear.

"It's okay Calle, he's with me," Angela whispered, putting a hand on Kreg's arm before turning back to her brother. "Dad isn't coming with us this time, bro. I don't have time to explain everything right now, but I promise I will. And if you still want to stay with dad after I tell you, I won't stop you from coming back."

Looking back and forth between Angela and Kreg, Calle nodded. "Okay, I trust you," he said slowly, stepping forward to stand by her.

Handing him one of her spare knives, she clapped him on the shoulder. "Do you know how to get to the dungeons from here?"

"I've never been down there, but I know where the stairs are..."

"Good. Can you lead me there?"

Calle nodded, taking her hand and leading her around the edge of the courtyard and down a narrow hallway. Every so often Angela would have him pause as she checked to make sure the way was clear before letting him continue. There were a few times when they had to duck into an empty room to avoid being spotted, but they eventually made it to the large wooden door that Calle said would lead down to the dungeons.

Spreading out her mind one more time, Angela found their area of the compound close to deserted. She picked up on a few guards down in the prisons and a few stragglers throughout the building, but everyone else seemed to have been called to the walls to fight.

As they slipped through the door and closed it behind them they pulled up short as a narrow stairwell stretched ominously before them, lit only by a single torch set into the wall. Picking it up, she moved ahead to light their way down into the dungeons.

Reaching the bottom she paused to feel for Daryn. When she found him, his mind was so weak and garbled, she hardly recognized it. Fear driving her forward, she charged through the caverns towards his cell. Coming up on a guard she didn't bother slowing, bringing her leg up into his side and spinning around him as he doubled over, leaving him for Kreg to handle. Spotting two more guards up ahead, she was grateful to see Kreg run by her and charge into them.

Leaving him to his revenge, Angela searched the area around them and saw a set of keys hanging on the wall up ahead. Dodging around the fight, she grabbed the ring from the hook, glancing into a large room beside where they hung, the door left partially open. There was a thick chain hanging from the center of the ceiling with weapons the likes of which she'd never seen before lining the room. Blood splattered the dirt floor beneath the chain and Angela shuddered to think of what might take place there. Reaching out, she scanned the area for Daryn and found him in the cell across the hall from where she stood.

Sprinting to the door, she pulled herself up to look through the slotted bars at the top of the door, but the room was so dark she couldn't see anything. Frantically glancing back down the hall, she saw Kreg finish off the last guard and jog over to her, Calle following close behind him. Handing Kreg the torch she was holding, she pulled out the ring of keys she'd found. Working quickly, she tried to locate the key that would open the door and allow her to get inside. As she was about to give up and search the guards, she heard the click of the lock and yanked the door out, rushing in before pulling back in horror.

Kreg ducked in behind her and the torch lit up the small cell so she could better see a man curled up against the wall, his hands and feet chained to the stone. All that remained of his shirt was tatters, held to his skin by crusted scabs covering his back. Fresh blood still flowed from some of them, weaving its way between the wounds and onto the floor.

The cell reeked of death and decay and at first she feared they were too late. Hesitantly, Angela stepped close enough to see the weak rise and fall of Daryn's chest and hurried to insert the key into the manacles that held him to the wall. As she released his arms from their bindings, blood ran down his wrists from where his bindings had dug deep gashes into them. Slowly reaching out, she touched his brow, moving the hair out of his eyes.

A sob escaped her as she saw his face for the first time, and she bit her lip. One of his eyes was swollen shut and his nose hung at an odd angle. His face was covered in purple and blue blotches, obscuring his features almost beyond recognition. Looking down she saw the same horrible stripes that had laced across his back also covering his chest. An old bandage was wrapped around his upper thigh and was soaked through, still seeping blood.

"What have they done to you?" she choked out in horror, reaching out and touching his cheek.

"Ange?" he asked weakly, opening one of his eyes to look at her.

"It's me," she gulped, wrapping her arms around his neck and burying her face in his hair. Leaning into her, he reached his hands around her, pulling her closer as tears streamed down his cheeks. Weaving his fingers through her hair, he breathed her in, feeling her relief and pain wash into him through their bond.

Leaning back, he met her eyes before cupping her cheeks and bringing her lips to his as he kissed her with all the fierce desperation a week in Eurcalp had built up in him, "Get me out of here, Ange." He whispered, reluctantly pulling away and holding her gaze for as long as he could, part of him still afraid that it was all another fever dream.

"I promise," she said, squeezing his hand before pulling away and turning back to Kreg. "Can you carry him?"

Nodding, Kreg handed the torch back to Calle before stepping forward to lift Daryn off the floor, pulling one of his arms over his shoulders. Standing up, Angela put Daryn's other arm over her and helped Kreg lift him through the cell and back towards the stairs they'd come down on. Calle's eyes widened as they stepped through the doorway and into the light of the torch.

"What happened to him?" He gasped.

"He was trying to protect me," Angela bit out, glaring at the space around them with new eyes.

"Ange, there's something you need to know," Daryn whispered, struggling to stand.

"You can tell me after we get you out".

"No, you need to know this now, in case..." he groaned as his feet caught against a lip on the floor and he stumbled forward.

"Ok, what is it?" She asked, trying to hold him higher so that he wouldn't fall.

"Your dad. . . he's here," He whispered. "He's the Commander."

Pulling up short, she turned to look at him. "What did you say?"

"Your dad, he was the one in charge of my. . . questioning. He's the Commander we kept hearing about. And there's something else..." He struggled to stay awake and tell her the rest, but failed to fight back the darkness crowding in, his last sentence falling away unfinished as his head dropped to his chest.

Angela and Kreg exchanged concerned looks before picking up their pace as they made their way towards the stairwell, Calle several paces ahead leading the way. Had he heard what Daryn said? Once they made it up the stairs, Calle set the torch down and Angela had him take her place so that she'd be free to fight should they come across anyone. Scanning the building she found it was still mostly deserted and easily picked up on the chief heading into one of the rooms not too far ahead.

The keep was eerily silent as they made their way through the passageways back towards Duroc. It seemed too easy. Getting Daryn, finding Calle, the abandoned keep... She knew she'd bragged to Kreg that she'd get them in and out without hardly any fighting, but she hadn't expected it to actually happen. Rounding a bend, they almost ran Duroc over as he came out of a side room and into their path. Looking over their party and noticing the boy in army clothes he turned and glared at Angela.

"Why is one of the king's soldiers with you?" he snarled.

"He's not a fighter, he's my brother. I can explain later, but we need to get out of here."

The scowl not leaving his face he nodded, walking back to relieve Kreg so that he could join Angela in the front.

"The keep is pretty much deserted," she whispered, "But outside of it is swarming with men." Glancing back, she lowered her voice so only Kreg would hear her. "It looks like getting in might be the easy part. It'll be finding a way back out again that'll test us. I'm not sure how we're going to get everyone through the fighting out there with Daryn in such bad shape."

"We'll make it out. We have to," Kreg said, pulling out a pair of swords he'd picked up from some of the soldiers. "Are you ready to fight with me?"

Looking up at him, the fire in his eyes ignited her own. The pain and shock over what they'd done to Daryn turned to rage and she nodded, tightening her grip on her knives.

Together they jogged ahead, watching the side passages to make sure no one was coming up on them. Every now and then, Kreg paused, trying to remember the way they'd used to get into the building before choosing which path to take. Reaching the outside door, they waited for Calle and Duroc to catch up before Angela raised the whistle the tree sprites had given her and blowing on it. No sound came out, but she had to hope that it'd worked.

Looking over to Kreg to make sure he was ready, she pushed open the door and dove out into the street. All around them men were running in every direction, but seeing them, a group of six soldiers changed course and charged them. Motioning for Duroc and Calle to stay next to the building with Daryn, Kreg and Angela jumped ahead to meet the assault.

Quick and lethal, she used any part of her body she could to get the upper hand. But these men were better trained than the men back in camp and she found herself having trouble holding her own against three of them.

As she'd block one blow, two more would come in from another side. Managing a lethal shot to one of the men, she turned on the other two. With one less man to pay attention to, she was able to take out the next man much faster than the first, and the last didn't stand a chance. As he fell, she saw Kreg take a cut to the arm as he tried to hold off four men. Another one must have joined the fray as Angela was fighting her three.

Barreling into one from behind she knocked him to the ground and drove the heel of her knife into the side of his head, knocking him out before pivoting to the side to avoid a kick. Coming to her feet she ducked a swing to her head and brought her foot up, driving it into the man's stomach. Grabbing it, he twisted so that she was forced to spin and land on her hands in the street.

Rolling, she felt a blade tear through her side before she was able to get her feet under her again. Bringing her knife up she sent it flying into a man that was charging towards Kreg's back before diving forward, tangling her attacker's legs and sending him to the ground. Once there, she brought her elbow down on his groin before leaping to her feet as Kreg swung his blade around in a killing blow to his final opponent.

All in counting, they'd taken down nine men and were both injured. It wasn't a good start. Motioning for Duroc and Calle to bring Daryn, Angela bent to retrieve one of her knives before running back to help them cross the street and to the relative safety of the barracks. Pausing to catch their breaths once they'd made it, snarls and screams filled the alleys to either side of them. The wolvrons had made it.

"It's ok, they're with us." Angela reassured Calle. "Hang with me, we're almost out."

Deciding to stay close to the others, Kreg and Angela took care of any men that found their way around the wolvrons and into their path. It was slow going, but they eventually made it to the last shack before they had to cross the large expanse separating the buildings from the outer wall.

Once they arrived at the last building, Angela was grateful to see that the senteries which had been patrolling the walls had been replaced by rebel soldiers. Motioning everyone forward they jogged towards the exit, scanning the area around them as they went.

Halfway across the expanse, yells filled the air behind them and Angela turned to find at least a dozen men charging them, weapons raised. Gesturing for Duroc and Calle to continue on with Daryn, Angela turned back. But as she and Kreg sprinted to cut off the approaching men, they pulled up short as a handful of wolvrons streamed from between the buildings, ferociously tearing into the soldiers.

Not taking the time to watch, they raced back to catch up with the others, diving through the opening in the wall as the first arrows were shot at them from somewhere in the compound. Running across the plain that bordered the Eurcalp walls, screams of men and beast surrounded them, the sickening stench of death carried to them by a change in the wind.

Ducking in under the trees, Angela glanced over at Calle in time to see him stumble and fall, an arrow slicing through his arm. Ripping off a piece of her tunic, she tied it around the gash, hoping that it would be enough to slow the loss of blood until they could get somewhere safe to tend to him.

Helping Calle hobble deeper into the woods she looked up to find the wolvrons that would be taking them to safety emerge from the trees. Ducking under his arm, Angela guided Calle over to the cart as Kreg and the chief worked on getting Daryn loaded up.

"Did you get what you needed from the captain's quarters, chief?" She asked, turning to Duroc.

"Yes, and it's worse than I'd thought. I need to get to the North gate and tell our commanders to pull back. We can't afford to lose any more men than we already have."

"He's not mine to give away," Angela said, walking over to where Charger was tethered and pulled her supplies off his back. "But considering it was thanks to you we got Daryn out, I don't think he'd mind if you borrowed his horse to make it back to your men. We can pick him back up from you when we get back to the base."

"Thank you," Duroc said, walking over to her and putting a hand on her shoulder. "It was an honor to fight with you today. I'm glad you're on our side."

"And there I'll stay," Angela murmured, clapping her hand on his before backing away.

"Kreg!" Duroc called, jumping into Charger's saddle.

"Yes, sir?"

"Bring them back to camp in one piece. This girl still has some explaining to do." Duroc said, yanking Charger's head around and charging towards the rebel troops.

Raising the whistle to her lips Angela blew three times, letting the other races know it was time to retreat before turning to Kreg, "Let's get out of here."

Stowing his pack and new swords on the cart he motioned her ahead, "After you".

Shaking her head, Angela threw her supplies from Charger next to Calle. His eyes were closed and was leaning against the side of the cart, his face drawn.

"Ok, let's go," she said, jogging up to the wolvrons and motioning to let them know they were ready to leave. Raising their heads to the sky the team let out a long, mournful howl before taking off at a sprint through the edge of the woods and towards the rebel's camp. Angela and Kreg filed in behind them, sprinting at full speed after them. But she didn't mind, she wanted to put as much distance between them and the walls of Eurcalp as possible.

❋ ❋ ❋

The sun had just finished cresting the horizon, sending its fingers across the wide open plains when the wolvrons slowed to a walk for Kreg and Angela to catch up. They had chosen to stop by a slow moving stream and she hurried to get the rags out of her pack. Throwing them to Kreg, he dipped them in the water and brought them back over as she pulled aside the piece of shirt she'd used for Calle's arm.

Thankfully, the cut didn't look as deep as she'd first thought and the bleeding had begun to slow. Wiping the area clean, Angela wrapped it in fresh bandages before climbing around him to check on Daryn, trusting Kreg to keep a lookout.

Bending down next to Daryn, she brought her water pouch up to his lips and he greedily took several sips before curling up and retching. Wiping the hair from his face, she knelt next to him, allowing him to lay his head on her lap as she leaned her back against the edge of the cart, trying to catch her breath from their run.

"I'm so sorry Daryn," she choked out as her breathing slowed, her eyes roving across the many cuts and bruises covering his body. How he was still alive she didn't know. No normal man could have survived what he'd gone through.

"Ange. There's something. . . Something you need to know," He whispered, holding his side and grimacing. "Your dad was sent to the plateau as a spy." He paused, struggling to form the words around his swollen jaw. "When the king found out he'd married, he made him. . . prove he was still loyal. He. . . had to kill his wife. According to him, as she was dying she told him a secret. That their oldest child wasn't his. That she'd been conceived before they'd met. . . That her firstborn was the rightful heir to the Shurkan throne. A direct descendant of the last queen." Daryn held her eyes before his body convulsed, his eyes falling shut as his body went limp. Angela glanced up at Kreg in horror. Had he heard any of that?

Turning back to Daryn, she pulled away the bandage on his leg and cleaned the wound as best she could before rewrapping it with a fresh cloth and quietly crawling down from the cart.

Wrapping her arms around herself, she stumbled past the wolvrons and into the plains beyond. Walking until she crested a hill and could no longer see their small rescue party, Angela knelt down in the grass, lowering her head to stare blankly into the field at her feet, tears streaming down her cheeks. *How could he have?? MY mother! My mother died for him to keep his position with the king.* Burying her face in her hands, Angela's frame shook as sobs tore through her.

"So, the Commander is the one that trained you? And your mother is the woman you thought you'd killed?" Kreg asked, coming up behind her and putting a hand on her shoulder.

Nodding, Angela let her hands fall from her face and onto her lap. "Though I guess he's not really my father," she whispered, looking down at her hands. They were covered in dried blood. Some of it Calle's, some of it Daryn's, some from the men she'd fought that day.

Kneeling down beside her, Kreg put his hand on hers, covering them so she couldn't see the stains.

"Are you here to make sure I don't run? To take me back to Duroc so he can raise me up as a beacon and gather the rest of the troops he needs to wage war on the Arachians?" Angela asked, closing her eyes and lowering her head in defeat, all the fight going out of her.

"No. I am your man out here, as agreed." he paused, looking out at the plains. "I was proud to stand beside you today. And I will continue to fight at your side, even after we return." Standing to his feet he glanced down at her for a moment, "But we need to keep moving. It's still not safe, and we need to find a healer for Daryn. He's in bad shape."

"I know, I know. Just. . . give me a minute, ok?" She whispered, balling her hands into fists. Nodding, Kreg moved out of sight back towards the cart.

Clenching the grass at her feet, she closed her eyes, fighting the despair that threatened to overwhelm her. Unable to contain it any longer, she threw back her head and allowed all the pain, all the anger and betrayal, to spill over as she screamed into the sky. And far in the distance, she heard her grief echoed by a dragon's call.

* * *

FROM THE AUTHOR

If you've enjoyed this book, please consider leaving it a review on Amazon! It helps get it in front of others who will love it as well.

* * *

Look for book two, *Seer of Caplana: Rebel's Uprising* coming to Amazon soon!

ABOUT THE AUTHOR

A.e. Dawson

A.E. Dawson has spent many years traveling around the world hiking, backpacking, and exploring before settling down on a forty-three acre farm in the midwest with her husband and three daughters.

She began her career as an author out of a desperate desire for a new book, one that would set her pulse racing and her mind churning. After months of fruitlessly searching Amazon and book stores, she sat down to write her own. As the story evolved she discovered friends and family were drawn to the characters and story, asking when they could read more of Angela and Daryn. It was then that Seer of Caplana: Darkness Falls started its journey towards being published.

"Fantasy books taught me about the value of standing strong in the face of opposition. When my parents went through an unforeseen divorce, it was the characters in my favorite books that inspired me to keep pushing through. Then later in life when I came across my own real life antagonists, it was those same characters that taught me to see them for who they were and forge my own path. I believe, today more than ever, we need heroes. We need friends caught between the pages of literature to inspire us to create our own worlds filled with magic, wonder, and a little bit of mystery."

Made in the USA
Columbia, SC
23 April 2021